MERRIN TAYLOR

For Love and Bylines

For HS and LB. Without one of you this would just be an idea in my head, and without the other, I'd still be wondering what love is.

Contents

Preface

As a romantic comedy connoisseur, I can't help but spend my days making connections between fictional characters and universes. *Never Been Kissed* (*1999*) has long been one of my favorite movies, and I've often thought about how to bring the premise into a more modern day setting. *For Love and Bylines* is my homage to *Never Been Kissed* and the rom-coms I grew up with that taught me the frustration of miscommunication and the importance of true love.

Playlist

Beautiful Words - Oscar Scheller
Long Shot - Transviolet
I Found - Amber Run
I Can't Stay Away - The Veronicas
Fallingforyou- The 1975
Red - Pale Waves
Muscle Memory (Acoustic) - Lights
Like Real People Do - Hozier
So Contagious - Acceptance
Hold of Me - Dean Lewis
Laurel Wreath - Bear's Den
You Are In Love - Taylor Swift
Heartbeats - José González
Kiss Me Slowly - Parachute

I

No Sooner Met

"No sooner met but they looked,"
- William Shakespeare, As You Like It

One

December 29, 2017 - January 3, 2018

"You don't have to do this, Ava," Chris says, his voice low, as he walks up to her cubicle. "Wells has it out for both of us, and this is his underhanded way of showing it." He shakes his head as he takes his place next to her chair, leaning lightly against the standard-issue particle board desk.

Ava looks up from her computer to her work superior and closest friend, Chris Price, unable to hide the grin that's taken up residence since the staff meeting not twenty minutes ago. "You always see the glass half full, Chris. This could be the big break I've been waiting for!"

Despite graduating from Fordham University with a major in Journalism magna cum laude nearly two years ago, Ava Thompson is still "proving herself" to editor-in-chief Cillian Wells. He insists it's because he is a perfectionist, and wants to make sure Ava herself meets those standards. But Chris won't budge from his theory that it all stems from the fact that Ava didn't respond to Wells' advances when she first started at the paper.

"He's consistently given you nothing but fluff pieces and all of the sudden he throws this behemoth at you? I don't trust the..." Chris pauses, taking a quick scan of the thirty-fourth floor office, making sure there aren't any sensitive ears within hearing distance before he continues. "Prick."

Shutting her laptop, Ava's shoulders shrug nonchalantly. Not that she disagrees with him. Just this morning in the break room, she overheard two senior journalists whispering about Wells with similar distaste. Heck, Ava has even taken part in similar conversations.

What Chris seems to be forgetting is how he's easily climbed the corporate ladder. It's no secret Wells favors men like it's the twentieth century.

She pushes her chair back on the linoleum floor and stands up, her hand brushing gently along Chris' forearm in a comfortably affectionate way. "I know you're only looking out for me, but I can do this. I'm tired of wasting my degree on obits and the local news no one else wants to write."

In her short black pumps, Ava is level with Chris, and she meets his dark eyes with intensity.

A small groan sounds from the back of Chris' throat, and he bears the meaningful eye contact a few beats longer before giving a barely discernible nod. "Have it your way. But you have to let me help somehow. Both of our jobs are on the line."

Victory! Ava's grin dances upon her lips once more. "I won't let you down, boss."

"Alright, alright. Get out of here." Chris glances down at her office-appropriate outfit of a tan silk blouse tucked into a pair of navy trousers. "The first thing you need to do is get shopping, bub. No one's going to believe you're a high school student when you're dressed like a Golden Girl."

***

Ava braces herself for the cold as she steps out of the Zara on Fifth Avenue. Her arms are full of the bags of clothes she'd let the shop girl pick out. Even with the after-holiday sales, she's spent a small fortune. With a sigh, she tucks the ridiculously long receipt into her coat's inner pocket for safekeeping.

If Wells doesn't approve my reimbursement request, I'm in serious trouble.

Fashion has never held much of an interest to Ava. Undoubtedly this is because she'd often had last pick over clothing donated to the foster homes she spent 10 years cycling through. Ava never burrowed her way to the front of the line like some of her foster siblings did. This led to a lot of strange outfit combinations while she'd been in school, but that didn't bother her.

Pulling the hood of her coat further down until it nearly covers her eyes, Ava starts toward the 51st Street subway station. It isn't a long walk, just under half a mile, but with dirty slush seeping into her shoes and wind biting against any exposed skin, she feels every step. Her hands push deep into her pockets and she clutches her MetroCard as she walks.

The screeching of subway cars and hundreds of interrupting voices soon replaces the ruckus of outdoor traffic. Ava attempts to make herself smaller as she squeezes through the turnstile with her bags pressed in front of her. She walks down the steps mechanically and speeds up as she sees the subway car slowing down.

Working her way in amongst the other passengers, Ava heads straight for the corner of the car. She finds a seat next to a man with headphones on. Arranging the brown shopping bags on her lap, Ava closes her eyes and thinks about the assignment that awaits her on Wednesday.

Wells used his connections as editor-in-chief of *The New York Times* to enroll her at Eleanor Roosevelt High, a prestigious private school on the Upper East Side of Manhattan. Someone has been embezzling tens of thousands of dollars from the school's account, and the board of trustees views everyone as a potential suspect.

Certainly, a journalist poking around would put the guilty party on red alert. But who would suspect a student of investigating? If Ava does her job correctly, this has the potential to be a front-page article.

Maybe he just chose me because I'm one of the few employees who could pass as a teenager.

But it could bring me closer to my goal. That's all that matters.

Editorial by Ava Thompson.

Just the thought of seeing her name on a serious piece of journalism has Ava smiling wistfully.

The students will be coming back from their winter break, which should make the transfer of a new classmate far from eventful. Hopefully, they'll all be too focused on regaling their friends with tales of their holidays to bat an eye at her.

Ava's body is used to the swaying and abrupt stops of the subway, so when the train makes its sixth stop, she automatically stands up and wiggles her way past crowded bodies and out the door. It's a short walk to the flat she shares in East Harlem with her old foster brother, Nate Torres.

They spent some of their high school years together, staying with the Krowe family. And while there was no love lost among the children and their foster parents, Ava and Nate formed a true familial bond.

Ava can't feel her nose by the time she walks into the apartment building's shared entrance. It isn't heated, but thankfully it keeps out the bitter winter wind. Adjusting the straps of the paper shopping bags into the crook of her arms, Ava quickly jogs up the stairs to the second floor. She pulls her keys out and opens the door to the small two-bedroom flat.

The residence is empty, with Nate at the mechanic's shop where he works until at least dinner time. She walks down the hall past the galley kitchen overlooking the tiny living room crammed with an old, slightly ripped up brown leather couch and the giant flat-screen television Nate had insisted was necessary for gaming.

The framed photo on the coffee table catches Ava's eye as she passes it. Taken over the summer at the Hansborough Rec Center's outdoor pool, both Ava and Nate sport tans. Although on Ava's pale and freckled skin, it was more akin to a faded sunburn. The tan looked much more natural on Nate's already golden skin. In the photo, Nate's arm is slung comfortably over Ava's shoulders while her arm wraps around his waist. Their contented smiles reflect on Ava's face as she remembers the day and continues down the hall.

Her bedroom, in style with the rest of the place, is tiny by most standards. There's just enough room for a twin bed and a desk pressed right next to the closet. But it's all hers. She'd always shared a room in foster care with at least one other girl, sometimes boys mixed in if it were a particularly bad home. Now Ava happily basks in the solace of her own space.

Nate's bedroom is situated across the hall, slightly larger, but that was only fair since he'd secured the apartment for them. A year older than Ava, Nate had defaulted out of the foster program first and immediately begun training as a mechanic's assistant. He'd always had a great mind and picked up whatever caught his attention for the week, but insisted he did not have the patience for college. "I already suffered through the school system once, Ace," was always his response.

It didn't take long for Nate to out-master his mentor, and since he had a knack for burrowing money away, after two years he could buy into 50% of the shop. Theirs is a simple life. But Ava wouldn't have it any other way.

Ava sighs with relief as she slides the shopping bags onto her bed and shimmies out of her coat. She slips the over-sized garment onto the back of her desk chair before absentmindedly rubbing her forearms, red from the weight and irritation of carrying her new wardrobe across Manhattan.

She retrieves a pair of scissors from her desk's top drawer and gets to work, removing the tags and stickers to submit later, piling up the clothes in neat stacks next to her on the bed. Then, after cracking her knuckles, Ava pulls her laptop close and opens a web browser. Fingers fly across the keyboard and soon the homepage of Instagram has loaded.

Ava has never had much use for social media. Everyone she cares about lives here in the city. If she has any family back in the UK, they hadn't come forward 16 years ago when she needed them the most. Nevertheless, Ava knows she's likely to be treated as a pariah without an online presence in a modern-day high school.

This isn't personal, it's part of the job.

She just needs a name to befit her undercover persona. "Ava... Jones? No, too ordinary." She presses her lips together tightly in thought. "Ava... Torres?" Nate would get a kick out of that. Their relationship has always been familial, so it wouldn't be too far from the truth. Still, it isn't quite right.

Her eyes run across the small collection of books stacked next to the laptop on her desk. An avid visitor of libraries, Ava only makes a habit of purchasing books she considers her favorites. The left side of her mouth curls into a smile as her gaze lands on *The Waste Land* by T.S. Eliot.

One of Mum's favorites.

A warm, *right* feeling settles over her as she murmurs, "Ava Eliot. Perfect."

7

***

The rest of the long weekend goes by in a blur, being spent alternating between adding to her online persona and reading up on where the rest of her senior class will be this semester.

ElRo, as the high school is affectionately referred to, gives its seniors elective choices for their core classes. With A and B day scheduling, Ava will have 9 classes in all, but double up and take English 12, AP Government, Economics and Pre-Calc every day. Her other courses of AP Biology, French 2, Fitness, Drama, and Visual Art will alternate.

The school is close enough to her apartment that in the summer, heaven forbid she's still on assignment then, Ava most likely walk. But the first week in January is always unforgivingly frigid, so she opts for the bus to protect her from the elements.

While dressing that morning, Ava does her best to recreate an outfit put together for her by the shop girl. Standing in front of the bathroom mirror, she smooths down the soft fabric of her sweater and studies her reflection.

I actually feel kind of cute. Cheers, Zara.

Her fingers automatically reach for the glass bottle containing her favorite perfume. The sweet jasmine and tonka scent reminds her of childhood picnics in St. James' Park. Ava sprays it once and spins in the mist, soaking in as much as she can.

After a final glace in the mirror, Ava strides out of the bathroom and down the hallway. She slings her new leather satchel, a gift of confidence from Chris, over her shoulder, and grabs a granola bar from the kitchen.

Here goes nothing.

It isn't long before she finds herself seated on the bus. Ava fingers the fringe of her mustard-colored scarf and watches the buildings of the city speed by, nibbling on her breakfast. When the bus comes to a stop a block from Eleanor Roosevelt High, her stomach churns and the light brown hairs on her arms stand at attention. "This is it," she mutters under her breath.

Ava slides out of her seat and follows what must be a few of her classmates out of the bus and onto the crowded downtown sidewalk. She spent more time than she'd ever admit to on the school's website this past weekend, and

8

can now easily call to mind a mental map of the school as the establishment comes into view.

First period is English 12, which is... On the second floor of the building, in the eastern hall.

Students and teachers alike fill the courtyard in front of the school with a chorus of voices. Small groups chat in circles, while others have their heads down, preoccupied with their cellphones. Bundled bodies start to sort into a line as they enter the building. Taking her place in the queue, Ava notices the thick metal detectors arming the entrance.

Glad to see schools finally offering better security.

Ava and her satchel pass through unhindered and she carries on inside. Frantic teenagers are shoving books into small lockers. A couple are locked in an affectionate embrace against one such locker. Others bump into Ava as they speed-walking past her. Pulling up the sleeve of her left arm, Ava checks the time on her simple analog watch. *8:15.*

Five minutes until the first bell.

She walks up the flight of stairs to the second floor, practically on autopilot. Her skin feels clammy and, spotting a water fountain, Ava makes a beeline and guzzles the cool liquid greedily.

Maybe I'm having one of those out-of-body experiences I've always read about because this is starting to feel preposterous.

Chris was right. They're going to see straight through me.

Wiping her mouth on the sleeve of her jacket, Ava straightens and takes a fortifying breath. The door to English 12 is open, and she scans the room with alert hazel brown eyes. Only about half the seats are filled, most of those being in the middle and back half of the room. Her gaze pauses on the smile of a fresh-faced girl sitting in the front row.

"Hello! Are you a new student?" The girl chirps as Ava approaches her desk.

After all the mental buildup, Ava finds the lie comes to her quite easily. "Yes, I'm a transfer student. My family just moved to Manhattan for my dad's job."

"Awesome, welcome to ElRo!" Her smile spreads as she extends a small,

9

well manicured hand. Tiny pink lotus blossoms bejewel her nails. "I'm Chloe."

"It's nice to meet you, Chloe, I'm Ava," she replies, shaking Chloe's hand lightly, unsure of the confidence a teenager would show.

Ava is met with a surprisingly firm handshake at the same time as the first-period bell rings.

"Welcome back, class. I trust you've all had a lovely holiday, and you made reading *As You Like It* your top priority." A deep voice coming from the front of the classroom interrupts their introduction.

The smell of rich leather and paper with a hint of patchouli fills Ava's nostrils. Its scent evokes feelings of familiarity that she can't put a finger on. Like the déjà vu of a vivid dream.

Small groans elicit from around the classroom. Chloe immediately looks alert and pulls the aforementioned book out of the backpack on the ground next to her. Her dark eyes meet Ava's before flicking to the empty desk next to hers. "Do you have a copy?"

I knew I was forgetting something!

Ava shakes her head regrettably, her nose scrunching up at the mistake. She slides into the desk next to Chloe's and is surprised when the younger girl scoots her desk a few inches closer.

"Here. We can share."

A relieved smile colors Ava's features. "Thank you so much."

The sounds of papers shuffling echo throughout the room as the rest of the students retrieve their copies. Ava takes the moment of respite to finally look up at her first teacher.

Oh my...

Impractically tall, he stands with his back to the classroom, shoulders hunched slightly as he writes on the blackboard. Dark brown, shaggy hair moves of its own accord. When he turns around, PASTORAL COMEDY can be seen, written in thick block letters. "*As You Like It* is an example of a Shakespearean Pastoral Comedy. Did anyone research what that means?"

He turns around now and his eyes catch Ava's with a look of surprise. "I don't think we've met. I'm Nico Adams, although the school strongly suggests not letting my students call me Nico." His casual tone seems at odds with the authoritative energy he exudes.

Mr. Adams' face gives away nothing at first, his thick brows lowering slightly. From the looks of it, this teacher is in his early thirties. He seems to be a hodgepodge of features thrown together, yet somehow they fit. High cheekbones highlight his slightly oval face, punctuated by an aquiline nose. Full lips rest underneath a pronounced cupid's bow, only slightly hidden by his well-kept mustache and goatee. Which is exactly where Ava's eyes are glued at the moment.

He clears his throat, arching one eyebrow at her.

Oh! He's waiting for a response!

"I'm Ava. Eliot. I think the school would be comfortable letting you call me that. Ava, I mean." The words pour out quickly, practically a run-on sentence.

So much for keeping my composure.

It's nowhere near the sort of introduction Ava has been expecting to have one of her teachers. She's a professional, she talks to people for a living. Albeit not usually very interesting people, but still. For some reason, this man's gaze seems to pierce right through and it's tilting her off her axis.

I think it's safe to say I never had a teacher like him when I was in school.

For a moment, Mr. Adams almost seems amused at her reply. But he collects himself quickly, tapping the piece of chalk angled between his first two fingers against the board behind him. "Welcome to English 12, Ava." His gaze leaves hers to scan the classroom. "Again, can anyone explain to the class what a Pastoral Comedy is?"

Someone in the row behind Ava waves their hand and Mr. Adams nods for them to answer. "Pastoral! That's what they do to milk!" An eager, melodic voice states.

A few half-suppressed laughs sound around the classroom.

"That's pasteurization, Quinn," Mr. Adams corrects gently, walking around to the front of his desk to lean against it. "Anyone else?"

His question is met with silence. Ava and Chloe exchange a look before Ava answers without raising her hand, no longer used to the exercise. "Pastoral means set in the countryside, often composed of shepherds. It was first used in the Eclogues of Virgil. It's from the Latin word *pascere*. 'To graze.'"

This catches Mr. Adams off guard. He stands up and paces over to her desk in two long strides. His deep chocolate eyes seem to peer into her very soul as he asks, "Are you sure you're... ?"

Has the ruse been caught onto so quickly? I haven't even started to collect information.

Ava nearly gulps, but by some saving grace manages to keep her countenance unaffected. "I'm seventeen. Just a big fan of the classics." Her voice is the definition of confidence as she repeats, "I'm seventeen."

Two

January 3, continued

The rest of English class goes off without a hitch. Ava keeps her thoughts *mostly* to herself, despite being quite familiar with the required reading. *As You Like It* is one of her favorite Shakespearean plays about a young woman named Rosalind who, disguised as a male shepherd, helps the love interest, Orlando, "cure" himself of his love for her. Ava can feel a newfound camaraderie with Rosalind, temporarily banished from the office and a new disguise of her own.

The instructors of her next three classes, AP Government, Economics, and Fitness, accept Ava as just another transfer student right off the bat. It was only Mr. Adams who took pause.

Note to self: don't answer on a college reading level.

Gotta rein in the nerves.

By the time lunch rolls around, Ava's stomach is audibly complaining of its feeble contents. Eleanor Roosevelt High boasts a thorough curriculum, the finest educators, and a prime location, but its facilities are compact. The cafeteria looks like it can only house half of the senior class at a time, and is quickly filling up as Ava joins in the lunch line.

At least the cafeteria food looks familiar. Questionable, but not inedible.

Her eyes scan the stainless steel island where warm food is fogging up the contamination glass. All the usual suspects are present: rectangular-shaped pizza, deli-style sandwiches, large dill pickles, baskets filled with under-ripe fruit, and a large pot labeled *beef chili*. Better safe than sorry, Ava decides on a sandwich and pickle, her mouth salivating at the thought of food.

A boy queued in front of her turns his head in her direction passively and then circles back, light blue eyes zeroing in. "Hey, teacher's pet."

"Excuse me?"

Ava had ended up in the first row in every one of her classes that morning. Seats were unassigned, but even when she tried to take a seat in the middle, she was shot down. *"We sit here,"* being her favorite line, delivered from the mouth of an intimidating-looking blonde, accompanied by two other girls of equal beauty.

Those same three girls were also in Fitness the same period as her. It immediately struck her how the girls made the gender-neutral uniforms look good, something that Ava's willowy body failed to do.

"Pastoral from the Latin word *suck-up,"* the teenage boy sneers.

Immediately Ava's face flushes, and she dips her head down a touch, causing her shoulder-length brown hair to brush against her heated cheeks.

"Oh. Yeah, I did go a bit ham on my homework over, um, holiday... "

A menacing chortle sounds. "Right. You went *ham*." He shakes his head. "Don't bother trying to get on Mr. Adams' good side with extra research. Every semester, a different girl tries and fails."

Ava draws her eyebrows up in surprise. "Every semester, huh? How many times have you taken English 12?"

Now he's the one looking caught off guard and embarrassed. It brings Ava the tiniest bit of pleasure.

"None of your business, new girl. I was just trying to be nice and give you a fair warning not to waste your time."

"Yes, you've been quite *nice*," Ava deadpans.

"Look, I— Whatever. You'll see for yourself. Mr. Adams prides himself on being unreadable. Middle-aged douche likes to mess with our heads. Very *Mr. Jekyll and Dr. Hyde.*"

Apparently, all the money in the Upper East Side can't buy a brain.

She nods slowly. "Thanks then… ?"

"Logan."

"Thanks, Logan. It looks like it's your turn." During their uncomfortable exchange, they were moving up in the cafeteria line.

"Yeah, no problem." Clearly, he doesn't understand the most basic sarcasm. "What's your name again?"

"Ava."

"Let me know if you need any more ElRo pointers, Ava." Logan offers what he clearly believes to be a charming smile, all white, straight teeth.

Would that have worked on me when I was seventeen?

"You'll be the first person I think of for help."

Logan's smile grows into a grin, his square jaw on full display.

He really isn't reading into this well.

"Oh and Logan?" Ava does her best to match his grin, hoping for once she can manage control of her features and, therefore, her emotions.

"Yeah?"

"It's *Dr. Jekyll and Mr. Hyde.* Read a book."

***

Ava is taking mindless notes in Pre-Calc when she feels a vibration against the chair of her desk.

I really should have put that on silent.

Slouching down in the chair, she glances around the classroom. Her classmates are mostly all facing forward, seemingly paying her no mind.

With all the stealth she can muster, Ava slips a hand into her satchel. Her fingers brush past the loose paper fliers and classroom supply lists she's spent half the day collecting until she finds purchase on her slim phone. In a quick motion, she brings the phone up and onto her lap.

Another pause. The teacher, Ms. Richardson, is writing an equation on the blackboard in precise movements. Math has never been Ava's favorite subject, but she remembers enough pre-calculus to take a brief respite. Ava takes a measured breath before pressing the home button on her phone.

(3) New Messages from Chris

15

The sight of a familiar name brings a smile to her face.

We'd be taking a coffee break right about now.

She presses in her four-digit passcode and clicks the messaging app right away.

—— **Wednesday, January 3** ——

– Chris | 1:08 –

Hey bub, how's the academic life treating you?

Wells has been breathing down my back all morning for updates.

Have you seen or heard anything suspicious yet?

Opposing feelings course through her. So far, today isn't feeling much different from her senior year. It's been a little over six years and not much has changed other than Ava's hairstyle. But senior Ava would never have thought of sneaking around and spying on her teachers, and that is exactly what her job requires now. She imagines Chris at the office stressing out on her behalf and sighs inwardly.

I insisted I could handle this. So, handle it.

Her fingers dance across the screen as she composes a response.

– Ava | 1:09 –

I'm sorry you're stuck with the General! So far, I've only met a few members of faculty. The day is going by way faster than I expected.

But I'm going to try and spend some time checking out the offices when school lets out.

A shadow falls across Ava's desk, making her drop the phone haphazardly on her lap. She attempts to pull her textbook over the edge of the desk to hide the evidence.

"Ava Eliot! Am I boring you?" Ms. Richardson's voice pierces the air. She holds out her right hand lethargically. "Cellphone, please," she breathes out with a sigh.

Looking up at her teacher, Ava can't help but notice how the woman's bright red hair is pulled back, *perhaps too tightly*, making her features appear severe. Ms. Richardson's entire look seems matronly, although in reality, she must only be a few years senior to Ava.

Could she be the culprit?

Embezzling thousands of dollars to what? Fund an early retirement?

"I-I don't have—"Ava stutters and is cut off by the teacher.

"As if I haven't heard that excuse before. Don't make me ask again." She taps her foot impatiently.

Now, for the second time today, Ava is holding the attention of the class. "I'm sorry, Ms. Richardson. I promise I won't use my phone in class again."

"Well, Ava, you've made matters worse for yourself. I was going to hold your phone until the end of class. Now you can pick it up at 4 pm, after detention."

Ava barely contains an eye roll as she begrudgingly hands over her cellphone.

So much for snooping around after class.

At least the screen locked on its own, hiding her words from curious eyes.

***

The sound of the bell rings melodically, releasing the school from the eighth and final period of the day. Well, most of the school. Ava takes her time repacking her satchel in French class. She's in no rush to attend the ridiculous detention she's been sentenced to.

Great job, Thompson. Way to lay waste to the day.

Slinging the bag over her right shoulder, Ava dawdles along the already emptying hallway of the first floor. Many of the classroom doors are now shut, and through the rectangular glass windows, she can see teachers gathering their personal items before heading home themselves.

After Pre-Calc, Ms. Richardson had informed her that they would hold detention in the gymnasium from 2:45 to 4. Being late would only make her stand out yet again, which is the last thing she needs.

The gym is in the southern wing, if I remember correctly.

Best get a move on.

17

She keeps her head down shamefully while she walks in. Earlier for Fitness, the room had seemed much larger. Now it's filled with worse-for-wear old classroom desks and ElRo's special group of degenerates.

Which apparently now also describes me.

"Ms. Eliot. Ava. I must admit, I'm disappointed to see you in this setting." An unmistakable voice draws her attention to the center of the basketball court.

Nico Adams is standing behind a temporarily placed desk. He looks frazzled, as if the day's events were as disorienting to him as to Ava. Even from across the gymnasium, she can spot the bags under his eyes.

Of course. Of course, it would be him. *One mishap apparently isn't enough for the day.*

Mr. Adams sets down his paperback novel and slips the tweed jacket he'd been wearing down his arms in one fluid motion. He carefully folds it in half before laying it over the back of his chair. A nod in her direction, one brow cocked. "Would you care to take a seat?" He asks, running a hand arbitrarily through his hair.

Somehow, this slight movement makes Ava gulp and avert her eyes. At least she doesn't have to sit *directly* under his scrutiny for the next hour and fifteen minutes. Ava takes a seat at an empty desk in the third row of four, offering a solemn nod to the girl next to her. "Hello."

The girl twirls a curly strand of mousy brown hair around her finger indifferently, only offering a low grunt in reply without looking up from her notebook.

"No talking," the teacher's deep voice states.

The other students seem to be familiar with the rules of detention. This is clearly only directed at Ava. She opens her mouth to apologize, thinks better of it, and instead opens her satchel.

Might as well get started on my homework.

The thought feels so alien that Ava can't help the giggle that comes next. All the anxiety of being back in high school, assuming an alias, and the seriousness of her assignment manifest into a fit of laughter.

"Do we have a problem, Ava?" Mr. Adams asks with a sigh. It's been a long day for everyone, and now he's stuck monitoring ElRo's miscreants.

"Not at all," she shakes her head. "Sir."

A noncommittal sound is all he offers before drawing his attention back to his book.

***

Ava spends detention compiling a list of the faculty she's met and, when she's run out of observations, doing homework. Unless she discovers something big, she doesn't have to report in at the office until Friday after class. It's only poor Chris who is stuck there day in and day out with their perfectionist editor-in-chief.

Chris! He's probably going crazy, wondering why I haven't texted back these past few hours.

The anticipation of getting her phone back only makes the punishment of detention feel longer. She notices every voice echoing in the hallway as band practice lets out. Every time Mr. Adams turns a page in his novel. When a fellow student accidentally falls asleep and snores before being prodded by their closest neighbor. The buzzing sound as the heater clicks on every fifteen minutes to keep out the January cold.

Somehow, blessedly, four o'clock does eventually arrive. "Alright, out with you," Mr. Adams' voice booms, startling Ava out of a daze. "We've all served our time here." His metal chair screeches as he pushes back on the linoleum floor. "Collect your personal effects."

From underneath his desk, he produces a black plastic trash bin. He places it on the corner of the desk as an offering and starts to pull his jacket back on.

It takes all the self-restraint Ava can muster not to run to the front of the room. She purposely takes her time as she replaces the books into her bag, winds the yellow scarf around her neck, and buttons up her jacket. Only when most of the students have collected their cellphones and filed out of the room does Ava finally approach the desk.

Mr. Adams peers into the bin, sees her phone as the last item, and takes it in hand. Ava tacks on what she hopes to be an easy-going smile.

Yes, I have all the time in the world.

I refuse to let him enjoy this minor advantage over me.

The bin is replaced under the desk and Mr. Adams casts his eyes downward to meet Ava's gaze. He taps his fingers against the back of the phone case thoughtfully before extending his hand. Their fingers graze as the exchange is made, neither one of them breaking eye contact. A palpable tension fills the surrounding air. The light touch sets Ava's skin ablaze, and she doesn't fail to notice the way his eyes widen.

What the heck was *that?*

He inadvertently takes a step back. "Where did you say you transferred from?" Mr. Adams draws his shoulders straight, his height advantage over her looming.

"I didn't. Say, I mean." Ava clicks the home button on her cellphone and glances down.

(7) New Text Messages from Chris

(2) Missed Calls from Chris

(1) New Voicemail

She pockets the device and turns towards the exit. The school day may be over, but her work is far from finished.

"Well, where did you come from, Ava?" The way he says her name, his voice raising an octave, stops her in her tracks.

This is the kindest he's sounded all day. Jekyll and Hyde, indeed.

Begrudgingly, Ava turns back toward him.

He's just a teacher.

He doesn't suspect you of anything.

Just stick to the story.

"My family just moved here from Central London. My dad works for a commercial real estate firm. It wasn't my decision," she attempts to shrug casually, "but here I am."

Mr. Adams' body seems to relax slightly. Finally, Ava feels she can breathe again.

"Any other questions, or am I free to go?" It's been a long day and Ava needs a drink. She needs to decompress a bit.

Nate had better be home.

Finally, the educator seems to remember where they are. She is a student, detention is over, and they can't exactly stay here alone.

"Right, of course," he nods and takes his book off of the desk. "I'll see you tomorrow in class."

Three

January 3 - 8

"Detention? You?" Nate's hearty laugh echoes into the glass bottle pressed against his lower lip.

Ava and Nate lounge on their worn-in couch, drinking the last two bottles of a six-pack. Their coffee table is littered with plastic takeaway cartons and balled up paper bags from dinner. "It wasn't as bad as I imagined it would be," she decides before taking a swig.

"Wait, stop." Nate sits up straighter, placing a hand on the crook of Ava's nearest arm. "You weren't kidding. This was your first misdemeanor?"

Her eyes roll and she gives his knee a tap with the bottom of her half-empty bottle. "Don't start, please." Ava wrinkles her nose. "I said I wanted to *relax*, remember? If I have to be seventeen during the day, I'm going to be every bit of twenty-four when I'm home."

Nate looks bemused at this, raising a single eyebrow before drawing his hand back.

"*Meaning* I don't want to talk about detention, homework, Mr. Adams, or any other—"

"Mr. Adams, huh?" He baits. "What's he like? That sounds like a hot teacher's name, if you ask me."

Not going there.

A frustrated sound emits from the young woman's throat. Her mouth opens, shuts, and she finishes her beer in one long gulp.

"Oh no, you don't. I should've known it would take you this many drinks to really start talking. Don't hold out on me now, Ace."

"Thanks for the beers, but I should get to work. I want to be able to tell Chris I've at least drafted a game plan for the rest of the week." Ava moves to get up but finds the room moving along with her. She pushes a hand against her forehead, kneading on her temples with the thumb and middle finger. "Or maybe I'll just sit here a bit longer."

"Sorry. I'll drop the interrogation, for now." Nate finishes his drink and sets the bottle down on the scuffed wooden table in front of them. He scoots over until their arms almost touch. "Just take it easy. You had a long day. I can relate. Watson was riding me to finish a new customer's repair a week early." He scoffs. "Old man gets more impatient every day."

"I'm a terrible person. I didn't even ask about your day!" Ava's voice comes out louder than she means it to.

Did we really just kill a whole six-pack?

"It's fine. I just want you to talk to me. All weekend, you were hiding out in your room doing research for this assignment. Just like old high-school-Ava. I remember her pretty well, you know?" Nate's eyes soften as they meet hers. "You spent more time by yourself in the library than most people would consider healthy. If I had a second chance like this, I would use it." More quietly, he adds, "Maybe I'd actually buckle down and get that aeronautical engineering degree. Use my talents in the sky."

Ava's soft gasp comes out mostly as a hiccup. "But you always say you're happy you didn't go to college! Now I feel like the odd man out."

"I didn't want you to feel sorry for me. Besides, I have it pretty good. Look at this castle I got for us." Nate gestures around the small living room grandly.

This earns him a small laugh. His optimism often kept Ava's spirits afloat when they were in the foster system, and it's one trait she loves most about him.

Nate always makes the best of things.

23

"Now look at me and promise me you're going to use this opportunity for the both of us." Nate slides his left leg up the couch and tucks the foot under his right knee, angling his body towards her. "You're going to go in there and bust this embezzlement scheme wide open! Show that bumbling fool Wells what an idiot he was to not have set you loose earlier. You, Ava Thompson, are going to write the best undercover piece *The Times* has ever seen."

Ava nods along vaguely as he talks, wanting desperately to believe him, but lacking Nate's confidence. It's only been a day, but she is on the verge of feeling overwhelmed.

He places both of his hands on her shoulders, planting Ava here in the moment. "I'm serious, Ava. Repeat after me. *I am going to write the best undercover article* The Times *has ever seen.*"

"Nate, this is silly. We're both a little drunk…" She trails off, not meeting his gaze.

"Just say it. Let the words give you power," he insists, giving her arms a squeeze.

Ava sighs, giving in. "I am going to write the best undercover article *The Times* has ever seen."

This earns her a patented Nate Torres grin, his deep-set brown eyes crinkling around the edges. "Atta girl. Louder now."

"I am going to write the best undercover article *The Times* has ever seen!" Nate's positivity feels infectious, and Ava can feel her heart speeding up.

"One more time for good measure?"

"I'm going to write the best undercover articles *The Times* has ever seen!" Ava all but shouts.

A banging on the shared apartment wall behind the television follows her outburst, but it doesn't sully her newfound mood. Ava beams at Nate.

I'm going to show everyone I've got more in me than just fluff articles.

Most importantly, I'm going to prove it to myself.

✳✳✳

The rest of the school week keeps Ava in good spirits. She stays on top of her work, some of which doesn't come as naturally as expected. Interactions with most of her classmates are brief and, by all standards, normal. The phrase *teacher's pet* isn't mentioned anywhere near Ava. Best of all, she saw one of the teachers enter the code for the faculty lounge.

By the time the last bell rings on Friday afternoon, Ava is walking out of the classroom with her new friend and English class savior, Chloe Cuong. "I think you'll get along with everyone else really well! Please, just take the weekend to think it over," Chloe pleads.

Stopping at her locker, Chloe makes quick work of opening the padlock. The inside is decorated with colorful vinyl stickers, including a Vietnamese flag. As Chloe takes books out of her backpack and organizes them, Ava's eyes are drawn to their reflections in the small mirror attached to the locker door. Both girls are wearing similarly cut blouses and leggings, but it doesn't look quite the same on Ava.

It's something more than just having a few inches on Chloe. She can only hope that observation has crossed no one else's mind.

Maybe I should cut my fringe like Chloe's.

"Earth to Ava."

"Oh, yeah, I promise I'll think about it," Ava concedes.

Chloe has been trying to get Ava to sign up for the school's poetry club all day with no luck. Normally, it's the kind of thing with her name written all over it. But as something that doesn't explicitly help her investigation, she's having trouble justifying spending time on it.

Not to mention that the club's supervisor is the peculiar Mr. Nico Adams.

Nothing alarming occurred after Wednesday's detention, but something is compelling Ava to try and limit their interactions. If anything poses a threat to her cover here, it's the strange teacher and his pervading eyes. They seem to be aware of something that the rest of the school is not.

Chloe's face lights up in an enormous smile. "That's all I ask. You won't regret it!" She shuts her locker for the weekend and reattaches the lock.

Ava returns the smile with a modest one of her own. "I'll see you Monday. Enjoy your weekend." She automatically opens her arms for a hug, but stops herself and settles for a flittering wave.

A short giggle escapes Chloe's lips. "You're a funny one, Ava Eliot." She tightens the strap of her leather drawstring backpack and gives her companion a quick once over. In a swift motion, Chloe embraces the taller girl, her rose and citrus perfume encircling Ava.

Just as quickly, Ava is released, and Chloe is offering a funny little wave of her own. "See you Monday!"

***

The *New York Times Building* is a short walk from the Times Square-42nd Street Station. While in college, Ava would make a vision board every semester. Nate teased her about it mercilessly. Still, no matter what changed during those four years at Fordham, working for *The Times* was on every single vision board. Seeing it now, for the first time in a week, makes Ava's heart race with feelings of both excitement and insignificance.

I got myself here. I deserve to be here.

She scans her employee badge upon entering the building and exchanges a courteous smile with an unfamiliar security guard before walking towards the elevators.

Roger must still be on holiday.

Chewing on her cheek, Ava presses the lit *up* button on the panel and produces her cellphone from the bag slung over her shoulder. A brief text is composed and sent to Chris.

—— **Friday, January 5** ——
– **Ava | 3:18** –
In the building. See you soon!

Stainless steel doors open and Ava steps aside to let the few passengers file out before entering alone. She taps *34* and takes a deep breath, holding it until the count of seven before slowly releasing the air through her nostrils. Calmness is key. It's a joke around the office that Wells can smell fear in the air.

There's no way I'll be giving him the pleasure.

"I'm going to write the best undercover article *The Times* has ever seen," she whispers to herself, attempting to gain the feeling of optimism she felt on Wednesday night with Nate.

A small bell chimes and the elevator car lurches, alerting Ava that her ride is now over. Chris is right outside as the lift doors open and he smiles instantly at the sight of her. "Welcome home, bub!"

"Aren't you a sight for sore eyes?" Ava grins, immediately noticing his freshly buzzed head.

I see he's keeping up his routine even without me here to schedule the appointments.

She wraps Chris up in a warm hug and gives his arm an affectionate squeeze before letting go.

"Glad to be of service."

"How are you? How's Finley?" Ava asks, referring to Chris' much adored adopted pup.

If Chris was smiling before, now he is positively beaming. "You've gotta see the video I took of him in the park the other day! I think I've got a champion frisbee player on my hands! Gonna have to find a dog show that accepts mutts."

"Aww! That's fantastic! I miss him so much."

"Maybe you can join us on a walk this weekend." Chris places a hand at the small of her back as they navigate the thirty-fourth floor.

Ava takes in the sight of her office with newfound appreciation. The rows of identical cubicles give her a sense of order, calm and intentional. ElRo was only this quiet during detention. A few people look up to smile or wave at their managing editor, Chris, ignoring Ava as per usual.

When it's my byline on the front page, they'll start paying attention.

"I thought you said you were going to change after class?" Chris whispers.

In all the rush she felt to get here, bringing a change of clothes completely slipped her mind. Ava's current ensemble is nothing like her usual office wear.

Wearing leggings in this part of the city is probably considered a minor felony.

"My brain's a jumbled mess, I'm sorry! I stayed up late last night finishing my French paper and overslept. I barely made it to first period on time!" Ava's words tumble together all in the same breath.

A nervous laugh bubbles from Chris. "Jeez, you really sound like a teenager. Good job, I guess?"

"I'm glad you find my struggles amusing," she chides teasingly.

Both of them adopt serious expressions as they come to a stop in front of editor-in-chief Wells' office. "What's our plan again?" Ava asks, eyes firmly focused on the closed metal door.

"Just leave the chit chat to me and maybe say a prayer that he's in a good mood today." Chris adjusts his slim white tie, already perfectly placed.

"Alright, let's get this over with."

Ava steps forward and knocks *shave and a haircut*. After a moment of silence, she knocks again, *two bits*.

"*Are you amusing yourself out there? Enter!*"

She turns the handle and enters with Chris at her heels.

Cillian Wells looks as intimidating as ever, ginger hair slicked back flawlessly. His considerable height is obvious even as he sits in a rich black leather chair behind a marble and steel desk. His office is a power play in itself. There are no actual seats for guests, just one tiny metal stool next to the large bookshelf that sits between wide windows. An unfinished chess board is the only semblance of character among the monochromatic furnishings.

Keys clack loudly as Wells' fingers fly across the keyboard, making his audience wait for his attention. "What do you have for me?" He demands in a posh Irish accent, eyes still directed at his computer monitor.

Chris answers, careful as always not to let on that his subordinate is also a close friend. "Ava's reports have been promising. She's fitting in well and is working on a plan of action now."

Silence lingers uncomfortably as Wells continues typing. "... And?" He eventually huffs.

"It's only been a week, Mr. Wells. Five days," Chris states calmly.

Wells looks at the pair for the first time, his light green eyes narrowed. "You're not serious."

"Um, well, I've just been invited to join an after-school club," Ava's voice

28

comes out sounding small.

Chris' eyes nearly bulge out of their sockets. This is not part of the plan. *He* is meant to do the talking.

"It's a poetry club. I know that doesn't sound very exciting, but it would give me an excuse to be on school grounds after class," Ava continues. A weak smile flashes, but doesn't reach up to her eyes. "If just give me a bit more time—"

"More *time?* Do you have any idea of the legalities I had to sidestep to even get you this assignment?" Wells' mouth twitches in the corner and he forcefully stands up out of the chair and bounds over to them. He stops right in front of Chris, so close that the younger man is forced to look up at his superior. Wells must have at least four or five inches on him.

"You assured me that Ms. Thompson could handle the assignment. *The Times* is going to break the story on this embezzlement case. Failure is not an option. I'll have *both* of your jobs if she fails." Somehow the fact that Wells has lowered his voice only makes him more intimidating.

"Yes, sir," Chris says, his voice measured.

"Clearly, I can't trust you two with handling something of this magnitude on your own." Wells' gaze directs itself to Ava now. "Your time at Eleanor Roosevelt is going to be monitored and directed."

Monitored? Like I'm a child?

Ava barely keeps her expression blank.

Cillian Wells taps out something on his phone, already turning his back on Ava and Chris. "My secretary will have a minuscule camera and microphone for you to be fitted with on the way out. I'm pulling the bloody strings now."

***

"Exactly how many people will be watching this? Ow—" Ava whimpers into her phone as the back of the small enamel pin presses into her thumb. "Hold on a second." She adjusts her grip, moving the cellphone between her right ear and shoulder. Focusing, Ava carefully tacks the pin onto the collar of her button-down and attaches the rubber back. "There."

To the untrained eye, Ava looks like she's accessorizing with a small spaceship pin. In reality, that pin houses a tiny camera and microphone with a direct feed to *The New York Times*. The sounds of a busy morning at the office become white noise on Chris' end of the phone call. "Let's test this thing out. Wave hello to Mr. Wells, Katherine, and I."

Great, Wells' secretary is in on this too.

Ava stands up a little straighter and attempts a smile at her reflection in the bathroom mirror. She waves with her free hand. "Hello?"

"Excellent, everything appears to be in working order. Good luck today," Chris' tone is suddenly all business. A faint beep sounds in Ava's ear.

Chris hung up without saying goodbye!

With a small sigh, Ava pockets her cellphone. She gives herself a once-over, adjusting the enamel pin, and then turns out the bathroom light. Almost immediately, a familiar tone sounds. Ava digs the phone out of her jeans while making her way down the narrow apartment hallway, stopping in the kitchen. She grabs an apple from the fruit basket and takes a large bite before unlocking her phone.

(1) New Text Message from Chris

A glance at the clock above the stove tells her that the bus will be outside of the building in two minutes. Angling the phone so it's not in sight of her pin, Ava reads the message.

—— **Monday, January 8** ——

– **Chris | 7:42** –

I'm sorry, sensitive ears were listening in to the phone call. Don't worry though, Wells isn't going to watch everything. I literally just heard him say, "this is below my paygrade" before ordering Katherine to bring him the highlights. If it makes you feel any better, I'll be watching your day and rooting for you.

She smiles thoughtfully.

A small solace is better than none.

Her reply is typed as she walks towards the front door, school bag shouldered.

– Ava | 7:43 –

Thanks for believing in me, bub.

Four

January 12

⁓⦿⦿⦿⁓

"Y ou already know Quinn and Isaac from Mr. Adams' class," Chloe says as she and Ava find seats together in the school library's alcove. Ava smiles at the familiar students in acknowledgment. She never would have guessed upon first meeting Quinn that she'd be president of the school's poetry club. But now that they've had a couple weeks of classes together, the younger girl's strengths are clear to see.

"And that's Hunter," Chloe adds, her tone flat.

It isn't hard to catch on to Chloe's apparent dislike for the boy sitting across from them. "I don't think we have any classes together," Ava says to him. "But I'm glad to meet you now! I'm Ava."

"I've seen you around," Hunter replies simply.

"Right. Small school."

She's already lost the boy's attention to his tablet. Taking this as a cue, Ava pulls out the moleskin journal saved from her late teenage years. She thumbs through the pages with a look of quiet contemplation.

I filled this book with the musings of a lonely girl. Things have changed a lot since then.

Haven't they?

"You're not getting it, Nico. Maybe it's a generational thing."

Ava looks up at the sound of her teacher's first name and finds him walking with an unfamiliar looking short-haired girl. Leaning over the armrest of her chair, she quietly asks, "Who's she?"

And why is she talking so informally to Mr. Adams?

"She," the girl answers before Chloe has a chance to, "is called Beatrice Jane McMahon. But I'll usually answer to just Jane."

Mr. Adams, pleased that he's no longer Jane's focus, pulls two more chairs over. The result is a cozy circle that entirely fills the alcove.

"Sorry, Chloe had been giving introductions," Ava says, sounding embarrassed. "You're lucky to share your namesake with the great Ms. Austen!"

This earns her a wide smile from Jane, who takes the seat Mr. Adams has just placed on Ava's other side. "Jane Goodall is my favorite fellow Jane, but Austen has her merits, too."

Returning the smile, Ava agrees, "You've got your pick!"

Jane nods at her before narrowing her eyes at their teacher. "I'm not letting you off the hook yet."

"I'd expect nothing less of you, Ms. McMahon," he declares. Then, shifting his gaze to Ava, adds, "I'm glad to see Chloe convinced you to join our coterie."

Chloe grins, speaking up, "My girl, Ava is going to be the perfect addition!"

Ava laughs softly. "Thanks. Both of you." Clearing her throat, she adds, "Chloe didn't mention you were the club supervisor, Mr. Adams."

Looking up from his tablet, Hunter says, "Isn't that the reason you first joined, Quinn?"

Quinn brushes this off by clearing her throat. "Everyone's accounted for, so we should get started before the Spanish club comes for their session."

"Please feel free to call me Nico outside of class," Mr. Adams' deep voice bellows from behind Ava. He opens the blinds on the alcove's window and adds, "Everyone else does."

A small thread of pleasure weaves itself into Ava's nod. "Alright. Nico."

***

By the time the club's meeting ends, Ava has a newfound appreciation for each of her classmates. They shared their current works-in-progress and bounced ideas off one another for an hour, and then the Spanish club came to claim the space.

Mr. Adams, seemingly in a rush, makes a beeline to the front of the library. Ava tries to put the way his voice sounded when reciting his own poetry — *smoky and honeyed* — out of her mind. The rest of the students don't linger much longer. Chloe, walking with Quinn and Jane, asks, "You coming, Ava?"

Taking a step forward, Ava opens her mouth to speak and then does her best impression of being struck with a new thought. "I just remembered, I need to check out a copy of *Cyrano de Bergerac* for French. Go ahead without me. I'll see you next week!"

The latter two girls incline their heads in response and continue walking. Only Chloe takes pause. "Are you sure? I don't mind waiting. Cello practice isn't for another forty minutes."

She's too nice for her own good.

Offering what she hopes is a gracious smile, Ava shakes her head. "I'm positive."

"Alright..." Chloe says with a little sigh. "If you can't find a copy, let me know. My dad has an amazing library at home."

"Thanks, Chloe. You're the best," Ava says, meaning every word.

She holds the smile until Chloe too disappears from view and breathes out with relief. It's been a long week of waiting for a valid excuse to spend some after-school hours in the building. After a quick glance over her shoulder at the Spanish club now in session, Ava pulls out her phone and opens the notes app. She scrolls through a few entries to find the one she needs.

Faculty Lounge Code: 417291

Repeating the six digits to herself, she takes a side door into the hallway and, finding it empty, continues onward to the stairwell. Ava takes the steps two at a time and attempts to tread lightly. Just as she's reached the second floor, she hears the muffled sound of someone talking. Heart racing, Ava tries the handle on the first classroom door to the right.

Locked.

The deep voice increases in volume, no doubt getting closer. With no other feasible option, Ava pushes the door to the nearest restroom open and rushes into one of the stalls. It's only when she's locking said stall that she spots urinals on the opposite wall.

Just my luck. I wonder if Chris and Katherine saw that.

For a few heartbeats, all is silent. Ava draws her hair up off her neck and into a ponytail. She takes a deep breath and holds it, eyeing the spaceship pin on her sweater. The thought of any of her coworkers watching her hideout in the men's room makes her skin crawl.

She's contemplating sending a text message to Chris when the door to the bathroom swings open.

"It's fine Pamela, I told you everything is under control."

There's no doubt in her mind that this is the voice she'd heard in the hall! But it isn't one Ava can place. Attempting to block out the sound of the mystery man using the urinal, she leans forward and peeks through a gap in the stall door frame.

"No, no, of course not."

All she can see is the back of him, golden blonde hair and well-tailored trousers. Besides her group of teachers, Ava's met the principal, Mr. Steele, and has observed a few of the male custodians.

None of them have blonde hair.

A flush sounds, and Ava takes a step backward into the stall. She can't make out the man's next words over the sound of a faucet running. It isn't long before the room is quiet again and his footsteps can be heard heading toward the exit. Still breathing shallowly, Ava reaches for the lock. Her cellphone vibrates a sharp burst from within her pocket. The footsteps stop. *"Is someone there?"*

Ava curses to herself and freezes in place.

"Hello?"

She musters a deep cough, letting her presence be known. The next few moments seem to spread out for ages. Neither Ava nor the man makes another sound. Not knowing what else to do, Ava flushes the toilet in her stall.

"No, not you. I was just taken by surprise—" the unknown blonde says, the sound of his voice trailing off as he disappears out the door.

Curiosity leads Ava to waste no time digging out her phone.

(1) New Message From Chloe Cuong

—— **Friday, January 12** ——
– **Chloe Cuong** | 4:02 –
Was it just me or did Isaac's poem sound like an actual Mad Lib?

Laughing shakily, she sends a reaction heart back and steels herself.

Ok, focus, Thompson. Faculty lounge, 417291.

Back to the task at hand, Ava walks out of the stall, quickly washes her hands and dries them on her jeans. She nods at her reflection in the mirror in passing and exits back to the hallway. This time, it is truly silent.

Ava takes long strides down the hall and stops in front of the door labeled *faculty only.* Pressing her ear against the solid wood, she ascertains that if anyone is inside, they're being awfully quiet. She thumbs the code in and smiles to herself when the keypad lights up green and clicks open. Stepping inside, Ava quickly shuts the door behind her and takes a moment to scan the room.

This is nicer than my entire flat.

Lush sofas and comfortable-looking chairs occupy one large portion of the space. The adjoining kitchenette appears to be equipped with all the usual suspects, plus a shiny espresso machine. No doubt the source of the room's warm aroma. "They keep this place awfully tidy," she whispers for the benefit of anyone watching at the office.

Ambling slowly through the room, Ava keeps a lookout for any belongings someone may have left behind. While richly furnished, the room is mostly void of clues to its unique occupants. The only papers lying around seem to be memos to the staff about upcoming school events and a recent copy of the *Washington Post.* Unable to help herself, Ava briefly skims the cover article on New York's favorite journalist turned CEO, Thea Lewis-Woodard. Her motor vehicle company seems to always be in the news these days — whether for its charitable works or company acquisitions.

36

She *is exactly who I aspire to be.*

Returning to the task at hand, Ava opens draws and cabinets in the kitchenette. One such cabinet is filled with mismatched mugs and boxes of tea and coffee. A smile comes unbidden to her when her gaze lands on a tin of Earl Grey tea. *Nico Adams* is written on a piece of scotch tape, securing the contents.

Tea. Earl Grey. Hot!

Ava closes the cabinet and purses her lips. While that discovery *does* tell her something about a certain teacher, it's far from being helpful for writing this article. Which leaves the adjoining offices to peruse. Taking a steadying breath, Ava sets her sights on the first private room, marked *School Treasurer - Genevieve Navarro.*

***

Buttoning up her coat, Ava walks with purpose out the front door of Eleanor Roosevelt High. She's taken pictures of any documents she could get her hands on in Mrs. Navarro's office, to go over in the safety and privacy of her flat. Next week after the poetry club meeting, she plans to search the adjacent office - one belonging to Vice Principal Jordan Lambert.

All of that will come in short order, but right now I'm late meeting Chris in Central Park.

She attaches earbuds to her phone while she saunters down the sidewalk, and soon her world is soundtracked by indie folk music.

The towering trees of Central Park drip with melting snow in the late afternoon sunshine. Its paths are full of fellow New Yorkers and off-season tourists taking in the unusually warm weather. Pausing the music, Ava presses Chris' name on the phone app. He picks up on the second ring. "Hey bub! I was just about to start worrying you'd stood me up."

"No, never! Sorry, I got held up longer than expected. I just crossed 5th Ave where it meets East 76th, where are you?"

"Almost to you! Just got a little snack to share with Finley after our run."

Ava laughs and turns toward the nearest food carts. Spotting her friend and his dog, she jogs over to them. "I know little about dogs, but kebabs don't seem like very healthy treats," she says as she plucks out her earbuds.

Chris holds a finger to his lips. "Shh, don't let him hear you say that! He's very sensitive about his extra winter fluff."

"Aww, I'm sorry, Finley!" Ava bends down to scratch the floppy-eared dog's head. "Your dad tells me you're a frisbee champ these days."

"He'll be back in top shape come springtime. Won't you, boy?"

"I have no doubts," Ava agrees. "Shall we?"

"Yeah, let me just…" Chris kneels down to tighten the laces on his athletic shoes. "There we go!" Standing back up, he gives Finley's leash a gentle tug toward the fenced walkway into the park.

They take leisurely strides along the foliage-lined pathway, allowing Finley to sniff around to his heart's content. Ava buries her hands in her coat pockets to stay warm and glances over at her companion. His dark skin glistens with sweat from his aforementioned run. She can smell his familiar scent - sandalwood, oak moss and something both herbal and floral.

Lavender, maybe?

"So tell me about your findings this week. Any suspicions?" Chris breaks the comfortable silence.

Ava proceeds to tell him about the strange bathroom encounter, the bits of conversion she heard, and the photos she plans to pour over this weekend. "Though to be honest, I sensed nothing off about Mrs. Navarro," Ava admits. "Not that I'm just working from my gut feeling!"

"Hey, sometimes you just gotta go with your gut. Those inclinations can be the best," Chris states. "But still check everything out! We've gotta show Wells that he did the right thing assigning you to this investigation."

"Absolutely."

"It sounds like you're on the right track. I'd suggest going over the school website again tonight. See if you can match up any of the faculty members' pictures with that guy you saw."

"I hadn't thought of that! Chris, you're a genius," Ava says.

Chris shrugs nonchalantly, then seems to think better of it. "They didn't make me the managing editor because of my good looks."

So humble.

Rolling her eyes, Ava leads them over to a bench. Finley immediately rubs his nose against her and she obliges him with more pets. "Remind me not to compliment your dad," she murmurs.

In a high-pitched voice to mimic Finley, Chris answers, "Not a chance!"

Five

January 22

"All the world's a stage, and all the men and women merely players." Chloe finishes the reading with a reverential sigh and takes her seat.

Ava sits at the desk next to her, eyes somewhat glazed over, still lost in the narrative. Distantly, she recognizes a voice interrupting her thoughts.

"What did Shakespeare mean by that?" Mr. Adams asks, lowering his copy of *As You Like It*.

His free hand comes up and absentmindedly strokes his chin, chocolate brown eyes scanning the classroom. Between class on Friday and today, he had shaved. Ava has spent most of first period trying and failing to keep her thoughts about his new look in check.

He looks so much younger now.

Not that he looked old *before.*

I kind of miss the scruff.

The teacher paces the classroom, walking between rows and desks, peering down at the students. His restlessness is something Ava became aware of on her first day at ElRo, more than a month ago.

He's like a tiger, marching endlessly from one end of its cage to the other.

When no one volunteers an answer, Mr. Adams continues. "It's about disguise. Playing a part. This is one of the major themes in *As You Like It*. Where do we see this?" From the middle of the classroom, a hand hesitantly raises. "Yes, Hallie?"

Hallie straightens in her seat and tucks a strand of curly hair behind her ear. "Well, Rosalind disguises herself as a man and escapes into the forest."

This earns her a smile. Ava doesn't fail to take notice. "Correct. It's when Rosalind is in costume that she finally feels liberated enough to express her love for Orlando." Mr. Adams stops pacing in the back corner of the classroom, forcing heads to turn. "Shakespeare's showing that when we're disguised, we feel freer. We do things we wouldn't normally do in our own lives." His words resonate with Ava in a way she's never felt while reading Shakespeare.

This man could easily see through my disguise, and yet he fails to.

She begins to lightly chew on her bottom lip.

Do I feel freer? Or more shackled than usual?

Mr. Adams resumes his saunter, this time walking around the room's perimeter. "Logan, what happens when you go out on the football field in your uniform?"

The rude boy from the cafeteria responds immediately. "We win!" He pumps his fist in the air proudly, the gesture repeated by a few other kids around the room.

Unconstrained whoops of delight echo to the sound of *"Go Huskies!"*

Mr. Adams' hand cuts the air with a swivel of his wrist and the room silences. "You push people. You yell. Societal rules no longer apply. Sometimes you even touch other guys' butts."

Logan's pleased expression falters. The classroom erupts in laughter. Stopping in front of Logan's desk, Mr. Adams allows a chortle of his own. "That's okay though, because you're in uniform. Disguise changes the rules."

Ava abruptly bites down on her lip, sharp teeth finding purchase in the tender skin violently enough to draw blood. She instinctively runs her tongue along the puncture and swallows back the metallic-tasting liquid.

The rules became more restrictive with my disguise.

Mr. Adams resumes his normal stance in front of his desk. An unhindered smile lights up his face. "When I was seven, I went through a superhero phase. One day, my father brought home a Spider-Man pajama set with a matching mask. I was positive that it gave me superpowers. I wore it every day for about a month, even to school," he laughs in a soft, nostalgic way.

At her desk, Ava finds herself mirroring his relaxed expression.

Seeing him smile is contagious.

"Believe it or not, I was a pretty shy kid. But when I wore my Spider-Man costume, I felt invincible. I was making friends at recess and participating more in class, finally acting like the son my father expected me to be." Mr. Adams' smile falters briefly. "On the playground one day, I tried to use my "superpowers" to jump from the top of the jungle gym onto the slide."

"Did you make it?" Quinn calls out.

"To the nurses' office and the Emergency Room," he replies with a coy smile. "The point here is that disguise can be wildly liberating. So much so that it can even get you to do things you never thought possible." Mr. Adams gestures with his copy of the play. "And for our fair Rosalind, her male costume opens the door to finding the great love of her life."

It's too bad that love always leads to loss.

Happily ever after is a fallacy.

Ava's fingers cover her spaceship pin impulsively. A few seconds pass before she catches herself, and opts to trace the cold metal instead.

If Katherine is watching, I hope she's losing interest.

"Ava, read for the class from Act 5, Scene 2, Rosalind's speech."

"For your brother and my sister—" she begins.

"Standing," he states shortly, and then adds, "please."

There he goes with that tone again. Like we're the only two people in this room.

The rest of the classroom has their heads down, ready to follow along. But as Ava stands up from her seat, Mr. Adams peers intently at her.

He's much better at tempering his expressions.

She clears her throat before continuing. "No sooner met but they looked; no sooner looked but they loved; no sooner loved but they sighed; no sooner sighed but they asked one another the reason; no sooner knew the reason but they sought the remedy; and in these degrees have they made a pair of stairs to marriage… ”

***

The bell sounds, effectively ending first period. Pandemonium ensues as students flock out into the hallway. Ava still stands, clutching her copy of *As You Like It* tightly.

Wow, I zoned out there.

“Ms. Eliot, a word?”

Why does he keep going back and forth, addressing me both distantly and familiarly?

“Yes, Mr. Adams?” She repacks her satchel with her back to him.

“Please, I’ve asked you to call me Nico outside of class,” his voice sounds from a mere yard behind her.

Hearing his first name again is mildly disorienting. Almost as if he’s just a regular man she could’ve met anywhere.

But you didn’t!

Instead of responding directly, Ava raises an eyebrow as she turns back around and places her bag on the desk. “Aren’t we still in class?” She presses her lips together firmly to hold back a smirk.

“Yes, but — Right now I’m just talking to you as your poetry club supervisor.” There his hand goes again, kneading at the smooth skin of a now bare chin.

Filing this one under: Things You Shouldn’t Notice About Your Teacher(s).

“I’ll call you Nico if you agree to only refer to me as Ava.”

“Fair enough, *Ava.* I wanted to ask about the poem you read for the group on Friday.”

Her heart speeds up. She’s been pointedly only sharing pieces she wrote as an undergrad, hoping they would sound more juvenile than her more recent works. “Hmm?”

“The emotive language you use is quite powerful. I know it’s not my place to ask, but I’m not especially good at following social cues…” Mr. Adams — Nico’s — eyes seem to soften. He doesn’t break their contact, and for once this doesn’t leave Ava feeling uncomfortable. “Have you… er, lost someone

43

close to you?"

Ava can't help but force her eyes shut. They stay that way for a moment, and then she blinks rapidly. This does nothing to stop full tears from forming.

Ava Eliot moved to Manhattan with her parents. This doesn't fit in with my story. What a bloody idiot I am!

Nico misinterprets her tears, taking one large step to close the gap between his desk and hers. He sits lightly on the desk Chloe had previously been occupying, so that their faces are level. "I'm sorry, I shouldn't have asked. I should have just complimented your poem and left it at that." Hesitantly, he reaches out and brushes his thumb and first three fingers against her shoulder. Just as quickly, his touch is withdrawn.

"It's alright," Ava almost manages to control the quiver in her voice. A fat tear rolls down her cheek. She wipes it away roughly and drops her gaze.

You have to lie now.

"When I was eight, I did. Lose someone. It felt like the end of the world, like the tightness in my chest would always be there. Marking me as different. But life kept going on around me and I realized I had to either join in or be left behind permanently. So I went through the motions, and one day I realized I couldn't remember the, uh, face of… that person, anymore. The pain never went away, but it became more of a dull throbbing. Easier to bury and ignore."

She lifts her head, embarrassed she's said so much. Somehow she managed to tell him the truth, leaving out only that it was two people, not one. Both her parents.

Ava finds understanding in Nico's eyes. Her pain reflected impeccably. He doesn't need to say anything, to tell her of his own suffering.

Brrrrrnnnnngggg!

The sound of the second bell pulls them from the trance. Nico is the first one to react, jumping up from the desk. Looming over Ava, he once again looks like the authority figure that he should be.

That he is.

"I'm sorry, I have to get to second period," she says at the same moment that he speaks.

"Thank you for trusting me."

Ava nods lightly, suddenly feeling the need to be somewhere, anywhere other than here. She throws her bag over her shoulder and heads for the door as fast as her feet can carry her.

"You have so much talent, Ava. Keep writing the truth."

***

For the rest of the day, Ava's phone is unusually silent. It's not until she's sprawled on her twin bed, dinner eaten and classwork finished, that her phone springs to life.

Cillian "The General" Wells is Calling...

"Oh, crud," she mutters.

Maybe if I ignore him, he'll think I went to sleep.

The phone seems to ring longer than usual before the screen goes black. For a moment, Ava feels relieved. Until it rings again.

Cillian "The General" Wells is Calling...

Swallowing hard, Ava reaches for the device on her desk. She breathes in deeply and slides a finger across the screen to accept the call. "Hello?"

Wells immediately talks over her. "Jordan Lambert was arrested for embezzlement this morning. I'd be flaming if Katherine hadn't shown me this."

The vice-principal?

She sits up on her bed, leaning against the wall. Her entire world feels like it's been turned upside down. Someone else found the embezzler, someone likely *not* undercover at the high school. "I'm sorry?"

Her phone immediately buzzes with a text. Ava clicks it open on impulse. A large, pixelated image of Nico pops up. In the picture, he's leaning towards her, his arm out of the shot. Her stomach turns. "Mr. Wells, I don't know what you're saying—"

How was Jordan Lambert arrested? What was he doing with all that money?

"He's your story. It's got everything an editorial needs - sex and intrigue, all wrapped up in this country's education system." He somehow sounds proud and bored all in the same breath. As if this is all so obvious.

"I can't, he's my teacher," her voice is softer now, almost pleading.

Wells laughs in one quick burst. "That's the best part! I can see the headline now: *Teacher-Student Relations: How Close is Too Close?* We're going to blow the lid off this thing and go viral in one fell swoop!"

"No, there is no lid," Ava insists. "Nothing is going on between Nico and me. Er, Mr. Adams and me."

A groan sounds. "Not yet, maybe. But something is there. Every person on the floor has been watching you two. It's like a bloody Regency film!"

Ava's jaw unhinges. The phone almost slips out of her dampening palm. "The entire office is watching?"

"This isn't a joke, Ms. Thompson. *He* is your story now." Wells' tone is finite. "Good night."

Six

January 24

~~~❦~~~

"…I can't bear to be around him anymore, Chris. Nico is a good man, and he didn't ask to be swept up in this." Ava fidgets with the straw in her drink. "You were right. I'm not ready." Almost as an afterthought, she mumbles, "I quit."

Chris sits at the large chair next to hers in the Midtown lounge. Earlier in the afternoon, she'd sent him a text, telling him she needed a drink, but somewhere she wouldn't risk being recognized. Chris had polled some of his rock climbing buddies and eventually come up with Raines Law Room at The William, a boutique hotel not far from the office. Its Prohibition Era atmosphere and cozy seating had put Ava at ease immediately.

Surely, no one from the uptown high school would be here.

At least not on a weeknight.

So she'd changed out of her school clothes, ditched the spaceship pin, and met Chris just shy of seven in the evening. Her hair is in a loose bun atop her head, and her freckled skin is blissfully free of makeup, save for some carefully applied sable eyeliner. The form-fitting dress she's wearing is one picked out by the shop girl at Zara.

Honestly, a welcome change from the adolescent outfits I've spent three weeks living in.

Ava's companion takes a small sip from his snifter glass, savoring the caramel-colored liquid. Replacing the drink on the marble coffee table in front of them, Chris shakes his head. "You keep saying you want to be a reporter, right?"

This sounds like the beginnings of a Chris Price pep talk.

Ava hesitantly replies, "Yes."

"Then you need to *think* like a reporter. This doesn't have to be personal, in fact, it shouldn't be. Being a talented journalist is all about knowing your audience and following a story through to the end." He carefully plucks a dog hair off his jacket, leaning on his elbow against the plush pink armrest. Chris sighs. "My instincts are telling me you're already too attached."

"C'mon, bub," she implores, offering him a polished smile. "You know me better than that. In all the time you've known me, have I ever been keen on someone?"

"No... "

"Exactly. So why would I, after a few short of weeks, suddenly become besotted with an emotionally unavailable teacher?" Ava gulps down an inch of her drink, forfeiting the straw. This isn't entirely true, but what Chris doesn't know in this particular case can't hurt him.

She reaches out to place her free hand against his forearm. Chris drops his look of scrutiny, now focusing on her small hand. In a detached section of her brain, Ava realizes that playing on her friend's emotions is wrong. Chris has always been more than a work superior to her, but she's never let it go any further. There have been small moments, easy to overlook, where Chris has hinted at wanting something more. When that happens, she consistently plays coy and changes the subject, or physically takes a step back.

You're selfish.

Ava pushes this thought back with another swig of her drink.

But avoiding relationships means avoiding love. If I don't fall in love, no one can hurt me.

"That doesn't sound like you, you're right." Chris doesn't sound entirely convinced, but at least his demeanor has softened.

This answer earns him a bright smile. "There, was agreeing with me so difficult?"

"I'm not entirely persuaded, but we can leave your personal sentiments aside for now." Chris cups a hand over hers, delicately stroking his thumb across her knuckles.

The touch feels only familial to Ava, so she doesn't pull away.

"I have to agree with Wells here," Chris laughs sourly. "I can't believe I just said that."

She mirrors his laugh while shrugging one shoulder, tugging the skirt of her dress down closer to her knees. Her pale winter skin looks ashen in the dim lighting of the lounge. "Neither can I."

"Please stick with the story. The more time you spend with him, the quicker it'll be over." His eyes are pitch-black in the candlelight.

Ava sighs, defeated. There's not much she can do to stop this, short of skipping town. But then all the hard work from her past two years at *The Times* will have been for nothing.

"What do you think of all this? I know you've been watching, too." She distracts herself by chewing on the cocktail straw.

"I... Know you better than most people at work," Chris prefaces. "I'd be lying if I said you haven't changed recently."

She wrinkles her nose. "Changed, in what way?"

"Not in a bad way!" He rushes to add. "Is the term 'blossoming' too strange?"

Unsure how to think of this, Ava crosses and uncrosses her ankles, visually scanning the large bookshelves occupying the opposite end of the room. "It depends on how you mean it."

"Putting Wells breathing down our necks aside, this seems to be a good experience for you. You've made new friends, albeit young ones, and you've been much more outgoing when you pop in at the office. Also, *poetry club?* Ava Thompson, taking part in a voluntary after-school activity." They share a mutual chuckle. "A little extroversion suits you."

"Thank you, then."

"*Ava?*"

A familiar voice interrupts their conversation from behind. Ava subconsciously snatches her hand back from Chris and they both turn their heads towards the figure in the doorway. She slides her nearly finished glass next to a candle on the side table between her and Chris.

Nico Adams stands with a look of curiosity etched on his brows. He's dressed down from his usual work attire, a thick slate-colored sweater casually half-tucked into a pair of dark denim jeans. The left sleeve of his sweater is inched up slightly, revealing a wide silver watch. The subdued light of the room casts a dark shadow across his cheeks, no longer smooth from his morning shave.

Why is he so unnervingly good-looking?

It takes Ava an embarrassingly long moment to notice the woman standing beside him. Judging from her rouged cheeks and the way her arm snakes through Nico's, Ava ascertains the pair are on a date.

"Hello, Mr. Adams."

The wounded look that flashes across his face is unmissable. *Good.* She has no right to feel vindictive, but the emotion persists.

"I'm surprised to see you here," Nico remarks, as if they are the only two people in the room. He studies her intently, no doubt trying to marry the image of the girl in the juvenile halls of ElRo and the elegant woman that currently sits before him.

"I could say the same."

It's the truth. When Ava pictures Nico in his personal life, she imagines him as the type to frequent a crowded bar. The kind of tucked-away joint in DUMBO where the bartender would have his drink of choice memorized. But now that he stands before her in this posh setting, it seems just as fitting.

From the chair next to Ava, Chris clears his throat loudly.

"Oh. Mr. Adams, this is Chris. My..." Ava whips her head in her friend's direction, eyes pleading with Chris to supply an answer.

"Her boyfriend," Chris finishes.

He says it with such ease that it takes Ava by surprise. Still, she nods, hoping this suffices. "My boyfriend," Ava repeats.

Nico doesn't seem perturbed by this. "Pleased to meet you, Chris," he steps further into the room, his date following. Finally, Nico seems to remember her presence. "Isobel, this is one of my students, Ava Eliot."

The petite brunette offers a smile, comfortable now that the seated girl no longer poses a threat. "Nico and I go to the same tennis club," she says, by way of introduction.

Nico nods. "Ava, I'll pretend I didn't see you here if you keep this chance encounter to yourself as well."

Ava fights a heavy eye roll, plastering on what she hopes they will construe as a gracious smile.

"Good to meet you both," Isobel says.

"You too." Ava can't help but notice the physical similarities between her and Nico's date. Similar English accent, shoulder-length dark hair, small build also dwarfed next to Nico's stature. Only lucid green eyes contrast with Ava's brown ones.

Interesting...

A feeling of restlessness captures Ava now, and she scoots to the front of her seat.

"Please, don't leave on our account," Nico requests. "In fact, may we sit for a moment?" He uses the first two fingers of his right hand to gesture to the matching pink plush seats across from Chris and Ava.

"Go right ahead," Chris speaks up. He slides to the side of his chair, nearing Ava, and lightly places a hand over her knee.

Ava gives him a frosty side-eye, which only makes him smile.

Weasel!

Nico and Isobel take their seats, much to Isobel's obvious dismay.

"Chris, I don't recognize you from any of my classes. Do you attend another school in the city?"

"Sort of, I'm a sophomore at… Fordham," he replies, supplying Ava's alma mater.

"Great place. Keating Hall has some beautiful grounds." Nico focuses back on Ava, fidgeting in her chair. "Will you be joining him in the fall?"

"I wasn't planning on going to college," she says weakly.

Disapproval scores the lines around his eyes and forehead. He leans over the coffee table, his head cocked to the side. "What? Of course, you are. Ava, you owe it to yourself — to your writing — to go to college. You're a gifted writer." In a softer tone, he adds, "You just have to find your story."

If only he could recognize the irony in his words.

The room seems to warm up without notice, Ava's nerves causing sweat to prickle under her arms. A lump forms in her throat that she can't swallow down. Not caring that Nico thinks she's seventeen, Ava reaches for the drink she'd tucked away, knocks back the remaining liquid, and stands up forcefully. "I just remembered that it's a weeknight and I have a, um, curfew. Chris," Ava drops her eyes and pulls the confining material of her dress down, "walk me to the subway?"

With a far too pleased expression, Chris stands up as well. "Of course, bub." He reaches for her hand, finding the palm already clammy.

"Enjoy the rest of your date." Ava presses her lips into a strained smile.

Isobel smiles, tight-lipped, leaning closer to Nico to wrap a possessive hand around his bicep. Nico's gaze flits between Ava's face, the pair's clasped hands, and, briefly, down the length of Ava's cocktail dress. Her cheeks heat under his scrutiny, and she silently prays that this goes unnoticed in the dim lighting. "Indeed," Nico finally agrees, releasing Ava from the interaction.

She exhales the breath she didn't know she'd been holding in and tugs Chris' hand towards the exit, eager to escape.

Why does it feel like I'm always running away from him?

"Oh, and Ava?"

"Yes?"

"I trust your evening won't impede upon the essay due tomorrow." The way he enunciates *evening* leaves little to the imagination.

Ava would swear she almost detects a growl in his voice.

Is he jealous? Of Chris?

"Of course not," she replies and then walks through the doorway without another glance behind.

***

"I'm so angry with Chris," Ava huffs as she paces from one end of the quaint living room to the other. "He's supposed to be my friend! The last time I

52

checked, friendship includes not letting someone suffer unnecessarily! Not suggesting unethical behavior!"

Nate sits hunched over the coffee table with a sketchbook in his lap. His square jaw is set as he says, "Uh-huh."

"I know I got myself into this, but the least he could do is take my side!"

"Mm, yep."

"And why'd he say he was my boyfriend? There are a dozen other aliases he could've used!"

"Alias, good show," Nate replies vaguely.

Ava stops pacing and lets out a fatigued sigh. "Nate Torres. I thought you were listening to me."

Sitting up from his work-in-progress, Nate pats the cushion next to him. "Sorry, Ace."

She kicks off her shoes before joining him, sinking onto the comfortably worn couch. Ava tucks her knees together underneath her and works her bun loose. "How was work today? Watson decide to pull his weight yet?"

"Nah, but that's nothing new. Old man's getting close to retirement age. I'm playing a long game of 'yes, sir', and hoping he'll give up his half of the business under market value when the time comes."

"Or you could go back to school," Ava offers, her tone conspiratorial.

"And what? Live in a household of two students? Explain to me how that'd work," Nate chuckles.

Ava's hair cascades around her face, kinked from the hair tie. She runs a hand through it thoughtfully. "I won't be undercover forever. I may not even finish the semester."

"What, why not?"

"You know I can't do what Wells wants. I'm not going to ruin this man's life."

"Ava," he playfully pokes her side, "in case you've forgotten, you're a grown woman. Not an actual teenager."

"He doesn't know that, Nate. I think…" Ava purses her lips for a moment, "I think somewhere, deep down, he knows something's off. But I can't keep leading him on with a piece of fiction."

Nate nods, his freshly washed wavy hair sweeping across his forehead. "Then don't lead him on. Be a reporter. Act like you're doing Mr. Wells' bidding, but keep digging for your own story. And then, when this is all over," he shrugs, "who knows? Maybe Nico Adams isn't just a footnote in the story of Ava Thompson."

Without meaning to, Ava smiles a wide, toothy grin. Nate catches her with a knowing smile of his own. "What's that smile for?" Ava attempts to push down the fluttering in her stomach. "That was good advice. The first part, I mean."

Shaking his head, Nate curves back over his drawing. "Yeah, whatever. You can't fool me, Ava. I've known you for the better part of my life and I knew this day was bound to come eventually." He picks up the charcoal pencil and traces back over a line he'd already made, darkening it.

"Oh, and what day is that?" Ava's voice comes breathily, her heartbeat increasing.

"The day you finally let down your guard and fall for someone." Nate replies without missing a beat, the words unmistakable.

Seven

February 7

⁓◦⟨∘⟩◦⁓

Ava and Chloe sit together at the wooden table in the library, both girls huddled over their homework. It's a custom they put in place when they realized that over half of their classes are shared. Now they pool ideas and bounce theories off one another for an hour after school each day. Mild gossip also ensues. "Is it just me, or is the English sub even scarier than Mr. Adams?" Chloe asks as she finishes writing a paragraph.

Scary isn't quite how I would describe Nico.

Ava stifles a giggle by biting down into the eraser of her pencil. "He certainly drones on more than Mr. Adams ever has."

"You've got that right," Chloe agrees, blowing air up into her bangs, making them flutter before settling back down onto her forehead. "I wonder where Mr. Adams has been all week."

The sentence is spoken casually, a passing remark. As if that isn't the exact thing Ava herself has been wondering, try not to as she might. After the embarrassing encounter at The William, Ava had made herself scarce. She'd sat in the back of English class without comment and made up a weak excuse to get out of the poetry club's weekly meeting.

Now it appears that Nico is doing the same thing. He's been absent since class the previous Friday. Wild thoughts on his whereabouts have been filling Ava's mind far more than she cares to admit. So far the top contender is that Nico and Isobel are cocooned in a love nest somewhere, throwing caution and their responsibilities to the wind.

"Does your pencil taste good?" Chloe teases.

Ava pulls the pencil from her mouth with a *pop* and smiles sheepishly. "Not as tasty as I imagined it would be." Her stomach growls audibly, punctuating the statement.

Closing her notebook, Chloe's dark eyes widen. "You should come over for dinner! My mom's making *bún chả*."

"I wouldn't want to intrude upon a family dinner," Ava says carefully.

She's become close to Chloe over the past month, but getting together off school grounds could present new challenges. The environment wouldn't be controlled and there was sure to be lots of small talk. Ava would need to be very in-character to pass a parental examination.

"It's barely a family dinner. My sister Victoria is bringing her new boyfriend over," Chloe sticks her tongue out distastefully. "If anything, you'll make the evening *less* awkward." Clasping her hands together, she exaggeratedly makes her lower lip quiver. "Please?"

If I can convince a whole faculty of teachers that I'm just another student, what danger can one family pose?

"Alright, you've persuaded me," Ava agrees. "Your lunches always smell so good that I've been secretly wanting to try some of your mom's cooking, anyway. What can I bring?"

***

Morton Williams Supermarket is bustling with life. The smell of freshly trimmed herbs and meat roasting immediately flood Ava's senses. Well-dressed patrons courteously move past her while she stands, taking it in. The 1st and 72nd Street location is situated in the heart of Manhattan, and most importantly, close to the Cuong family residence. Chloe had said she didn't need to bring anything, but coming to dinner empty-handed seemed impolite.

Isn't this place posh?

With a basket slung over her arm, she meanders through the prepared foods section. After she and Chloe left the library, Ava had spent the better part of the afternoon rummaging through her closet. She wanted to look youthful, but not childish. Mature but not entirely grown-up. It turns out that striking the perfect balance had been much easier in theory. The only thing Ava feels truly confident about is her hairstyle. It's one she often wore back in school — three buns cascading down her head.

As she turns a corner, Ava catches a whiff of cinnamon and nutmeg.

If I hadn't spent so long getting dressed, I could have baked something!

Here's hoping the Cuongs have a sweet tooth.

With newfound determination, Ava weaves past other customers to create the shortest path to the bakery… and manages to shoulder someone unwittingly in the process. "Excuse me! Are you alright?" Her apology comes instantaneously.

Rubbing her shoulder, Ava looks up at her accidental victim, and her mouth falls agape.

Nico!

"Ava," Nico says simply. It's obvious he wasn't expecting to see her.

The relief Ava feels at beholding him comes without her bidding. It's like all the tension in her body is flooding out. Her knees literally go weak. She staggers backward and almost goes down, but Nico's hand shoots out to steady her elbow in the nick of time.

"Whoa, there. Did you wind yourself while trying to knock me out?" He starts to laugh and finishes it with a deep cough.

Ava nods vigorously, trying and failing to form words. Nico in turn clears his throat, the sound phlegmy, and withdraws his hand. Blinking, she takes in the sight of the man clearly now. Hair more disheveled than usual, redness around his nose, the scruffy beard of a few days without shaving - *the poor bloke has obviously come down with something.*

Perhaps there was no love nest after all.

Further evidence of this theory comes in his strange choice of attire. Normally, Nico looks practiced and put-together. But now he stands before her in thick red flannel pants, quite possibly pajamas, and a black hoodie zipped halfway over a t-shirt advertising the band *Radiohead*. Two cans of soup and a Gatorade sit in the basket on his arm.

"Sorry about that. I have a one-track mind when it comes to desserts," she explains vaguely.

Nico shifts his head to the side, perplexed.

Pointing to the refrigerated case behind them, Ava repeats, "Desserts."

He turns to look and nods. "Ah. All the DayQuil I've been taking makes my head a little fuzzy." Another cough into the sleeve of his hoodie.

"So, you're sick?" Ava asks, despite the proof before her.

"Yeah, I came down with something over the weekend," Nico shrugs. "It's nothing to worry over, but the school board insisted I use up some sick time. Contamination prevention and all that."

"Right," Ava nods and they consider one another silently for a few moments.

Without the scrutiny of a building full of students and teachers, or a bar with our separate dates, how am I supposed to interact with him?

"I'm glad you're—"

"You look nice—"

The awkward feeling subsides as they try to speak at the same moment, and laughter takes its place.

"What were you going to say?" Nico asks first.

"Just that I'm glad you're not, you know, dead on the side of the road somewhere," she says, a coy smile on her lips.

Or in a love nest with Isobel.

Nico's face breaks out in a boyish grin, baring his perfectly imperfect teeth. "You were worried about me."

Why have I never noticed his dimples before?

Being this adorable while sick should be illegal.

Bashfully, Ava nods once, her cheeks warm. "Maybe just a little." She rocks back on her heels lightly. "What were you about to say?"

"You're dressed up nicely," Nico states. "And I like the, uh," he gestures along the back of his head, "hairdo."

If her cheeks weren't painfully red before, they are now. His compliments, however small, make Ava's whole body tingle with excitement. "Thank you, I used to wear it like this all the time in—" abruptly she catches herself, "middle school."

Close one, genius.

The mention of such a young age registers on Nico's face as if he's remembering who exactly she is. His student. "Another date with Chris tonight?"

Ava straightens, shaking her head. "No, actually. Dinner with Chloe and her family," she points to the bakery case weakly, "I'm bringing dessert."

"That's very courteous of you," he says shortly. Nico's voice is colder now than it was just seconds before.

The conversation has clearly reached its end, the mental gap between them widened into a trench. Still, Ava resents the tone in his voice.

How can he toy with me like this?

One moment he's charming and the next he's suddenly the picture of apathy.

"I may be young, but I'm not uncivilized, you know. I've been taught manners and social cues."

Following the pattern she's set for herself, Ava turns on her heels and marches the remaining few yards to the bakery display. Her fist clenches and releases as she tries to focus on picking something out. Not ten seconds pass before a hand plants itself firmly on her shoulder. "I'm sorry, I didn't mean to imply anything that would upset you," Nico says with an inadvertent sniffle.

No, that isn't going to work. He doesn't get me to feel sorry for him.

"That is what you think of me, though, isn't it? I'm just another one of your immature students?" Ava brushes his hand off and faces him again. Her anger demands to be felt.

"Ava, that's the last thing I'd ever think of you," Nico scoffs at his own words. Lowering his voice, he adds, "I shouldn't even be thinking of you at all."

The conflict etched into his lips, colored into his eyes — it's all more than Ava can bear. Pressure from Wells, from Chris, even a different kind from Nate — is finally catching up with her.

"Then don't. Go home and let *Isobel* nurse you back to health." She blinks back traitorous tears and raises her voice so that the woman behind the counter can hear her when she twists back around. "May I have the chocolate one, please?"

"You're mistaken…" Nico speaks deliberately, sounding wounded.

Shaking her head, Ava refuses to look at him again. "Please, just go."

He doesn't deserve to see the effects of his clandestine hold over me.

***

"Welcome, Ava! Come in from the cold," Mrs. Cuong beckons her into the foyer.

Ava gratefully steps into the warmth of the brownstone. "Thank you for having me," she says as the older woman takes the boxed cake from her and hands it to Chloe.

Mrs. Cuong promptly wraps Ava up in a hug. "The pleasure is ours! Our Clover has nothing but wonderful things to say about you."

Over the woman's shoulder, Ava and Chloe make eye contact. Ava mouths *"Clover?"* and is shot a playful glare.

"Should I take off my shoes?" Ava asks once she's released from the embrace, still grinning at her friend.

There is a small rack in the entryway with neatly arranged shoes of varying styles and sizes. Next to that is a round table topped with a beige crocheted doily. A digital photo frame displays family pictures that change over at ten-second intervals. More photos are trailing up the wall of the staircase in the back of the entrance. Chloe and what must be Victoria at various ages in cello and piano recitals, in the kitchen with Mrs. Cuong, wearing colorful silk *ao dai.* In every picture, unposed smiles light up their faces.

This is exactly how I home should feel.

Ava's foster homes all had a very impersonal air about them, a silent statement not to get too comfortable and forget it was all temporary.

"That's unnecessary." Mrs. Cuong assures her.

Chloe interjects, patting a hand against Ava's shoulder. "That's Mama for 'yes.'"

Mrs. Cuong doesn't correct her daughter.

60

"Shoes off it is," Ava says with a laugh. She kicks back one leg, removes the shoe, and then does the same with the other one. Heels in hand, Ava looks questioningly at her friend.

"Oh, the floor next to the shelf is fine." Chloe passes the cake off to her mother and takes Ava's arm once she's placed her pumps on the tiled floor. "C'mon, I want to show you around before dinner!"

***

"This is an amazing library, Chloe. I've never seen so many first editions in person before." Ava says reverently.

The pair stand in an upstairs room, dwarfed by wall-to-wall bookshelves. The books have been organized by topic, year of publication, paperback, and hardcover. A navy leather couch and loveseat frame two sides of a gold patterned rug with crisp vacuum lines. Even with the bright reading lamps, Ava can't see a single spot of dust in the room.

"Dad's the real collector. He prides himself on having found a lot of these at second-hand shops." Chloe runs her fingertips over the spine of *The Martian Chronicles* by Ray Bradbury. "He's always said that persistence is the greatest virtue."

"Energy and persistence conquer all things," Ava agrees.

"Benjamin Franklin said that," the younger girl remarks.

"Spot on." Ava smiles fondly at her friend.

So much of what Chloe says and does has given Ava a hopeful outlook on the younger generation. She is passionate and optimistic, but not naïve. The world is, thankfully, full of more than just Logans.

"Girls!" Mrs. Cuong calls from somewhere downstairs. "*Victoria is home. Come down for dinner!*"

"It's about time," Chloe says, immediately beelining for the door into the hallway.

Ava takes one last look around the room before following after her. Indiscernible voices can be heard from the dining room as the girls pad down the staircase and across the cold tile floor, getting louder the closer they get to the dining room.

"Victoria didn't tell me how handsome you are," Mrs. Cuong practically coos.

Congregated in a small circle by the dinner table are Mr. and Mrs. Cuong, a young woman Ava recognizes from the family photos as Victoria, and—

"Nate?" Ava nearly chokes out.

Eight

February 7 & 8

A va's eyes widen at the sight of her foster brother. He's more dressed up than she's ever seen him, in a maroon button-down shirt that brings out his dark eyes and naturally tan skin. Nate has styled with his wavy black hair with just enough product to tame it, is sporting a fresh shave, and—

Is that cologne?

Usually he comes home from work smelling of motor oil and coffee, but now Ava is getting notes of something warm and peppery. Nate is truly the last person Ava could have anticipated showing up to this dinner.

Why didn't he tell me he was seeing someone?

Her obvious familiarity with Nate has caught the Cuong family off guard. For what logical reason would this "teenage girl" know the new beau of their beloved eldest daughter?

Luckily, Nate is quick about his wits. He pretends to study her for a few moments, as if trying to place her face. Then, all at once, his umber-colored eyes zero in with recognition.

"Oh! You're Duncan Eliot's kid, right?"

Trying not to appear dumbstruck, Ava nods her agreement. "Yep, that's my dad."

Looking around the room at the Cuong's confused faces, Nate continues. "I just finished up some work on his fleet of *Lewisson Cruisers*. Ava, is it?"

She again nods compliantly.

"Ava came in with her father a few of times to check on the progress." He shrugs. "What a small world."

"Ahh, quite the coincidence indeed," Mr. Cuong answers for the family.

Waving Ava further into the room, the distinguished older man smiles now. "This makes introductions easier. You must be the Ava Eliot I've heard so much about. I'm Chloe's father, Tuan Cuong. You may call me Tuan."

Ava gives him a firm handshake and a smile. "Thank you for inviting me into your home, sir."

"The more the merrier," Mr. Cuong insists. "And this is Victoria."

Victoria steps forward. The similarities between her and Chloe are obvious. In a few years, Chloe will probably be a mirror image of her sister, but for now, a more pronounced brow and fuller lips set Victoria apart.

"It's nice to finally put a name to the face," Ava says as the two of them exchange pleasant smiles from their respective spots. "Are you enjoying your classes at Columbia this semester?"

Victoria lights up at the question. "Yes! All of my professors this year are fantastic. In fact," she meets the eyes of everyone in the room. "Professor Greene pulled some strings, and I made the list for the summer program in Italy!"

At the news, Nate reaches out to rub his hand over her arm affectionately. "I knew you could do it! Congratulations, Tori!"

She mouths a pleased *'thanks'* in return.

"Let's sit and eat. The pork is going to get cold," Mrs. Cuong insists. She looks to her husband to take his seat first.

Tuan Cuong pats a hand lightly against Nate's shoulder. "You can sit next to me, at the head of the table."

Pressing her lips together to prevent a smile, Ava shoots her brother an encouraging glance.

This will be a humbling experience for the sometimes cocky, always confident Nate.

64

The men take their seats and Mr. Cuong gestures for his wife to sit next to him.

Victoria is quick to pull out a chair beside Nate, and Chloe takes the seat next to her. This puts Ava between her friend and Mrs. Cuong, completing the circular table for six.

White porcelain bowls sit atop red silk placemats at each setting. Chopsticks and wide spoons rest on a thick cotton napkin. Each person's bowl is filled halfway with a tawny liquid. On the center of the table sits a large plate of rice noodles, a steaming bowl of grilled pork pieces, and smaller bowls filled with mixed herbs and pickled vegetables.

Mrs. Cuong serves her husband first, adding particular amounts of each food to her husband's bowl. Once he has picked up both spoon and chopsticks, the rest of the table begins to do the same.

Ava mimics Chloe, using her chopsticks to get a bit of everything into one bite. The dish is both sweet and sour, rich and earthy.

Yes, this was an excellent decision.

Once everyone is a few bites in, Ava inquires further about Victoria. "So, what will you be doing in Italy?"

"Archaeological fieldwork at Hadrian's Villa, in Tivoli," Victoria replies as she replaces her spoon in the bowl. "On the weekends, we're allowed to explore the city and anywhere else in Rome we can get to. I'm so excited!"

"Yes, yes," Mrs. Cuong says with a sigh. "I still think you're too young to be spending that long away from home."

"Victoria has a good head on her shoulders," her husband speaks in such a way that suggests they have had this conversation many times before.

"It sounds like you're going to have a great time," Ava meets Nate's eyes across the table pointedly, the rest of them bent over their bowls. "Will Nate be joining you?"

Chloe coughs into her chopsticks and slides her foot into Ava's under the table, kicking her lightly.

Nate manages a short scowl at his foster sister before all eyes turn to him expectantly. "No, no. I wouldn't want to get in the way of Tori's research," he blurts.

Mr. and Mrs. Cuong seem to let out a collective sigh of relief.

"We only just starting seeing each other," Victoria agrees, her cheeks darkening.

"How *did* you two meet, Vee?" Chloe asks, taking advantage of the timely opportunity.

Ava perks up in her seat.

Now this *I desperately need to know!*

The couple shares a look, silently hashing out which one of them will have to recount the story. Evidently, Nate wins, because Victoria clears her throat before regaling the dining room.

"A few weeks ago, I was having lunch alone between classes at Friedman's, that diner near campus. Nate sat at the booth next to me, and every few minutes he would lean over with some preposterous story of what the other customers were talking about." They share a smile before Victoria continues.

"It was amusing, but I thought little of it. By the time we both got our checks, I was in a rush to get to my Nineteenth-Century Criticism class. So I go outside and while I'm waiting to cross the street, standing there in the frigid cold, Nate appears next to me. He looks like the biting air couldn't bother him in the least, and there I am, teeth chattering like an idiot." Victoria laughs softly to herself. "It couldn't have been a good look. But anyway, Nate starts to unwind the scarf from around his neck, and I'm trying not to pay him any attention. It's hard because now the wind gusts past me, carrying his scent. All of the sudden, Nate hands me his scarf. I think I just stared at it blankly for a while because he had to clear his throat before I took it. He said something along the lines of 'You look like you could use this a lot more than me.'"

Nate purses his lips before nodding his consent.

"So I awkwardly wrap his scarf around my neck and immediately sigh from the warmth." Victoria drops her eyes to the bowl in front of her. "Anyway, then the crosswalk changes, and I blurt out, 'How will I get this back to you?'. Nate just shakes his head and tells me to keep it, saying that it 'suits me' before he heads off in the opposite direction. It was kind of bittersweet because now I wouldn't get to see him again. *Until,*" she emphasizes, purposely captivating

Nate's gaze.

"Until," he repeats, taking this as a sign to continue the story, "a couple of minutes later. Victoria was halfway across the quad, and I'd been trying to decide if approaching her again could be taken as stalkerish. Something told me to just go for it, so when I'd almost caught up, I called out, 'Mrs. Hollandaise'—"

"The name he'd made up for the woman in Friedman's who scarfed down her eggs benedict in two minutes flat," Victoria interjects.

A sheepish smile materializes on Nate's lips. "Right. So, I call out to her, and Victoria turns around and we both just start laughing. I jogged the last few yards to her and asked how she felt about kismet."

From a few seats over, a snort slips out. Ava tries to play it off as a cough and brings her napkin up to her mouth. "Excuse me."

Shaking his head, Nate chuckles to himself. "Tell them what you said, Tori."

"I told him that depended on how many times he'd used that line today," Victoria smiles at her sister. "Always make sure you call a guy out. It sorts the losers from the gentlemen."

"Duly noted," Chloe agrees, lifting the spoon to her lips.

"Nate looked sort of wounded at this and shook his head repeatedly as he told me he would do no such thing. Then he asked how often I eat at Friedman's. In truth, I'd only gone a handful of times before. He said that if we happened to meet there again, it would be the universe trying to send us a message. And then he walked off. I was so surprised that he didn't ask for my number or Snapchat. But with a newfound incentive, I made sure to go to Friedman's the very next day for lunch. And there he was, in the same booth."

Nate's hand finds Victoria's on top of the table and he gives it an encouraging squeeze.

Conflicting feelings of happiness and minor envy flow through Ava. "That was a really sweet story."

"It also doubles as ammunition when you don't want to let me borrow your clothes, *Mrs. Hollandaise*," Chloe grins resolutely.

"*Ha ha,*" Victoria deadpans.

"I think it's romantic," Mrs. Cuong insists.

Mr. Cuong just continues to focus on his dinner, a small grumbling sound his only reply.

***

"Dinner was delicious, Mrs. Cuong, thank you for having me," Ava praises, standing in the foyer as she puts her shoes back on.

After dinner, the six of them had settled into the living room for a lively game of Phase 10 and more questioning of Nate. In the end, it turned out that Ava had little attention cast on her and her pretend story.

"It's been our pleasure, Ava. You were so thoughtful to bring dessert!" Mrs. Cuong gives her the second hug of the evening.

"It was no trouble at all! I'm just sorry I didn't bring something homemade."

Mrs. Cuong simply shakes her head at this, as Chloe says, "You'll have to come over again soon. We can bake together!"

"And bring your parents! I'd very much like to meet them," Mr. Cuong requests.

Ava manages a convincing smile. "Of course."

Swooping in to redirect the conversation, Nate pipes in, "I should head home, too. Work in the morning."

It's clear that Victoria isn't ready for him to go, perhaps wishing for some time alone with her new sweetheart. "Yeah... I have class."

"Excellent. Nate can accompany Ava to the subway. A young girl shouldn't be walking around the city alone this late at night." Tuan Cuong's words are firm.

"I'll see you tomorrow, Chloe," Ava says, giving her friend a side hug.

"See ya."

Ava turns the knob of the door and pauses, giving Nate and Victoria a moment to say goodbye.

"Call you tomorrow," Nate promises, his voice soft. He presses a chaste, family-friendly kiss to Victoria's cheek.

"You'd better," she murmurs, leaving hand lingering on his hip.

They stand like that for a moment, having a private conversation with their eyes.

Mrs. Cuong takes her husband's arm and pulls him out of the room, waving Chloe along with them.

With a final smile, Ava opens the front door. She zips her coat up and steps out into the dark winter night.

The door almost shuts behind her and then reopens as Nate emerges. His voice is higher than usual as he asks, "So, what part of town does your family live in?"

"We've got a flat on the Upper East Side."

Once they're a few yards from the now-closed door, they drop the facade.

"Okay, what the hell, Nate?! You could have given me a little warning or something!"

"I'm sorry! You never told me Chloe's last name, or even that you had dinner plans tonight," Nate points out.

"I— Ugh, yeah, you're right," Ava exhales, her breath a cloudy fog. "We could stand to communicate better."

"Yeah," Nate agrees. "We've both been so busy, I couldn't find the right time to tell you I met someone."

"True... But I don't know how this is going to work, Nate. After graduation, my cover will be blown. I can't keep up the act forever," Ava sighs tiredly. "Are you serious about her?"

It doesn't take Nate long to reply. "Yeah, I think I really am. She's so incredibly smart and kriff," he can't fight back a toothy smile, "she challenges me, makes me think from sides I've never considered before. It's crazy, Ava, I never thought I'd feel like this."

This lowers Ava's defenses. Her foster brother makes selfless sacrifices often. Be it for her, for them, or even a stranger on the subway.

If anyone deserves happiness, it's Nate.

"Well, if she's anything like Chloe, you have great taste. I'm happy for you, honestly." They brush shoulders as they walk towards the subway station. "You shouldn't have to suffer because of *my* job... We'll just cross that road when we come to it."

"Thanks, sis. I really am sorry I caught you off guard, though. Let's have, I don't know, weekly house meetings to discuss the big headlines of our personal lives," Nate chortles at the idea. "Save us from any further surprises."

Ava nods along. "Alright, deal."

***

When Ava walks into first period the following day, there is a small folded note placed on her usual desk. She balks at the sight of it, immediately looking around for Chloe, to no avail. In fact, the classroom is empty, save for a couple talking closely at their desks in the fifth row.

Weird.

She slips her leather satchel over the back of the chair and sits down. Hunching over, Ava brings the note into her lap, feeling strangely conspicuous.

In familiar block letters, her name is written out on top of the paper. Gulping, Ava carefully unfolds the note. Her heartbeat increases pace as she reads the simple words:

It didn't work out with Isobel.

Immediately, Ava sneezes into the stationery.

Nine

February 8 & 9

"Gesundheit," Nico appears in the doorway of the classroom, holding a steaming metal tumbler.

Ava brings the paper to her chest, effectively crushing it. "Thank you." Her instinct tells her to look away, but she resists.

With a fresh shave and clean hair, Nico looks much improved since they saw one another at the grocery store yesterday evening. He nods once and strides into the room, other students hot on his heels. Just like that, any opportunity to ask how the note mysteriously appeared on her desk vanish.

As Nico gets situated at his desk, Ava balls the note up in her fist. She considers throwing it away but decides against it. This would be incriminating evidence, with her name plastered on it in Mr. Adams' obvious penmanship. Instead, Ava pushes the compact paper ball into the bottom of her satchel.

There. I'll get rid of it at home.

The rest of the class floods in and finds their seats. Ava spends the remaining time until English starts staring glass-eyed at the blackboard.

How can I spin this to Wells?

She hasn't been wearing the pin after class. When they ran into each other at Raines Law Room and Morton Williams, it was without the prying eyes of her editor-in-chief. But there hadn't been a way to hide the unexpected note.

As if on cue, Ava's leather bag vibrates against her chair. Hoping it's just Chris or Nate, Ava ignores it for the time being.

Brrrrrnnnnggggg!

Chloe just manages to walk into the classroom as the first-period bell rings. The girls exchange friendly smiles, and Nico moves to close the door. "I've been told that Mr. Gorman kept you up to date with the coursework," Nico addresses his students.

"I'll be grading your papers over the weekend. Today, we're going to start our discussion on *Jane Eyre*. By a show of hands, how many of you have read this previously?" He picks the book up off his desk, holding the cover up.

Ava turns her head to look around the room and is surprised to see several hands shoot up. She raises her hand as well, facing the front of the classroom once more.

Nico seems pleased with this, a small smile gracing his mouth. "Any major takeaways from the relationship between Jane and Rochester?" He points to a raised hand. "Isaac?"

"Attraction isn't always physical. Mr. Rochester and Jane's connection is based heavily upon their intellectual communion," Isaac says confidently.

A voice somewhere behind Ava whispers, "Isaac's appeal definitely isn't physical."

"Interesting thought, Isaac," Nico nods. He lightly tosses the book from one hand to the other, beginning his usual pacing. "Yes, Hallie?"

"It's so romantic. Jane needs someone to love her, and Rochester needs someone to see beyond his past. They save each other, in a way." Hallie sighs happily.

"Attraction, romance — these are instruments that often drive a plot." Nico broadcasts his voice from the corner of the room.

While having enjoyed the book in past readings, Ava has a lingering feeling that she knows why Nico chose this particular book. For some reason, this irritates her.

Ava shoots a hand into the air.

Nico hesitates for a few seconds before he calls on her. "… Ava?"

"Mr. Rochester is kind of a jerk. He baits Jane by saying how much he will miss her after getting married, and that soon she'll forget him." She clears her throat, but can't seem to get the irritation to budge. "He basically manipulated her, so that usually self-controlled Jane would confess her feelings for him. That doesn't sound romantic to me." She doesn't turn to see if her words elicit a physical reaction.

"Now that's thinking outside the box," Nico announces carefully.

Is it my imagination or did the grandeur disappear from his voice?

Out of the corner of her eye, she sees Chloe raise a hand. Ava's nose begins to drip, and she absentmindedly rubs it away with her sleeve.

Nico is making his way back to the front when he calls on her. "Yes, Chloe?"

"No one has mentioned the vast age difference between Jane and Mr. Rochester yet. I think it's interesting that at first, it's a plot device that they use to mentally separate themselves. But as the book goes on, they cease to acknowledge age. He stops referring to her as Ms. Eyre and calls her Jane. Even though Rochester is majorly flawed," Chloe pauses for a millisecond to glance over at Ava, "he is redeemable as a character."

Ava leans back at her desk, surprised at her friend's point of view.

Chloe's right, of course.

The second sneeze of the day escapes Ava. She directs it mostly into her elbow, sniffling immediately afterward.

Pausing in front of the classroom, Nico moves his eyes from the face of one student to the next. He lingers on Ava for a couple of seconds, no doubt taking in her ruffled state.

"Thank you, Ms. Cuong. That was a great introduction to our discussion of the Byronic hero." Nico takes a tissue out of the box at the front of his desk and hands it to Ava.

***

"Don't forget that the fundraiser for the senior class trip is next Friday! We still need volunteers. Please see Mrs. Asher for details." An announcement buzzes

through the speakers of the cafeteria.

"Are you sure you're feeling okay?" Chloe asks, peeling an orange.

Ava and Chloe are sitting at their usual end of one of the long, rectangular tables. Hallie, from English class, is eating with them today, along with two of her friends, Krista and Shawn.

"I'll be fine. I think I just need to take it easy after school today," Ava replies.

"It sounds like you're coming down with something. I hope your desk got disinfected after class," Hallie wriggles her nose in disgust. "Just don't give me any of your germs. I've got a date tonight."

Krista rolls her eyes playfully. "Yeah, with some guy you met at Starbucks."

"At least he's got a job!" Hallie retorts. "No offense, Shawn."

"None taken," Shawn says into his slice of pizza.

Ava smiles at the surrounding conversation. Everything is so simple when your biggest life responsibilities are passing a class and doing chores around the house. A sip of milk is sliding down her throat when her body protests. Ava's stomach heaves and her eyes widen.

I will not throw up in a high school cafeteria.

I will not *throw up in a high school cafeteria.*

"*Mmm,*" she sounds through closed lips, her head turning to Chloe for help.

"Hey! Let's get you out of here," Chloe directs, placing a hand across Ava's back. She guides her off the bench and turns her head over her shoulder. "I'm gonna take her to the bathroom. Don't wait up for me."

***

Ava sits propped up in bed by a great number of pillows, with her favorite penguin plush tucked next to her. A box of tissues is within reach and a trashcan sits on the ground, practically overflowing.

So much for not getting sick.

She lets out a frustrated sound and pounds the backspace key multiple times. "No, no, no! This isn't coming out right at all."

Yesterday at lunchtime, Chloe had escorted Ava both to the restroom and the nurse's office before they ultimately sent home her with the beginnings of the flu. Her symptoms are textbook: fever, cough, runny nose, sore throat, achy muscles, and fatigue. They're also eerily similar to what Nico had come down with.

Earlier in the day, Chloe called, offering to bring Ava her homework for the weekend. Ava's excuse had been a weak one, manly arguing that she didn't want to infect her friend. This was only partially true, as Ava didn't think she could explain away her East Harlem apartment with missing family members in her current state. Graciously, Chloe accepted this and told her friend to feel better soon.

So Ava has been spending the better part of the afternoon chugging liquids and attempting to write a first draft of the story she's secretly working on.

Attempting is the keyword because all the over-the-counter medicine Ava has been popping is severely messing with her head. She's already fallen once in the kitchen and then a second time on her way back to the bedroom.

The built-in laptop speakers sound in a ringing trill.

Skype Call From Chris

Ava clicks to accept it and a pixelated version of Chris' face pops up. "Hiiii!" Ava waves a hand excitedly at her webcam.

"Ava? I—school—... ay?" His voice cuts out and fades.

Based on the way Chris' head moves rhythmically in and out of frame, Ava assumes he's walking. She sniffles and smiles blankly at her screen until he stops moving so much.

"Sorry, I was just getting off the subway. Had to drop Finley at the vet," he explains. "What happened yesterday? The audio cut out of your feed right after lunch. Katherine mentioned that Wells texted you a few times and hasn't heard back."

It's kind of adorable, the way Chris is holding his phone out at an angle like he's getting ready to snap a selfie.

This thought makes Ava burst into a fit of giggles.

Chris blinks like he can't believe what just happened. "Ohhhkayyy." He pauses and brings the phone closer to his face, recognition now dawning in his eyes. "Bub, are you sick?"

That was a perplexing sentence. "Why are you talking about bubbles,

Chris?" She asks, cocking her head to the side.

"What? No, Ava, *you're* my bub. Just like I'm yours."

"But that doesn't make any—*achoo!*" Ava sneezes all over the laptop, covering the screen in little droplets of sick.

"You really are sick." Chris furrows his brow. "Is Nate home with you?"

"Nate's at work." Ava takes a half-used tissue and wipes the laptop screen.

Chris shakes his head, looking concerned. "I was heading to see you at the high school. Keeping up appearances and all that. But if you're home sick, I'll just—"

"Wait! Class just let out for the day. You have to bring me my homework. Please, Chris?" Ava sits up straighter against her pillows, the change in elevation making her feel dizzy once more. She takes a few deep breaths before continuing. "Chloe offered to drop it by but I couldn't have her poking around here. Pretty please? I can't keep my cover up if I'm falling behind."

The view of Chris on her screen shifts as he switches hands. "I... I guess it couldn't hurt."

"Thank you! Just head straight for the main office and they'll give you what you need." Ava speaks into her cup of water.

"What? Ok, I'll figure it out," Chris nods. "Hey, do I look like office-Chris or college-boyfriend-Chris right now?"

Replacing the cup on her bedside table, Ava attempts a shrug. "I don't know? Are you wearing slacks or jeans?"

"Jeans."

"Sounds like college-Chris to me."

"Good. Alright, I'll get your homework. Anything else I can bring you?"

Ava's hand pats around the bottom of the tissue box. "More tissues, please."

***

Chris waves in a way he hopes will come across as casual to a girl in the hallway. "This is kind of freaky," he mutters to himself, taking in the sterile surroundings of the high school.

Ava was right. School had just ended a few minutes before. As Chris walked up to the building, students had flooded past him on their way to weekend freedom. Now he is trying to inconspicuously locate the school's main office.

That could be... upstairs, right?

Shrugging once to himself, Chris bounds up the staircase.

And maybe to the right?

He only gets a couple of feet when Chris sees a familiar face walking out of a classroom. "Hey, Mr. Adams!"

The teacher's mouth twitches in recognition. "Chris?"

"It's lucky that I ran into you. Ava sent me to pick up her homework. I was just looking for the office." Chris explains.

A few different emotions seem to flash across Mr. Adams' face before settling on curiosity. "Ava wasn't in my class today. Is everything alright?"

Somehow Chris both nods and shrugs at the same time. "She's pretty sick."

Mr. Adams runs a hand through his dark, unkempt hair. "I'm very sorry to hear that. Do you know what's wrong with her?"

"Ava was sneezing and talking crazy on Skype, but it's probably just your typical fever," he says, unfazed.

The slightly older man presses his lips together firmly for a couple of seconds. "Does she need anything?"

Chris narrows his eyes, feeling more than a little annoyed. "No, man. That's what she has me for. I'm her boyfriend." Saying the words aloud feels thrilling.

Mr. Adams doesn't back down from the statement. "Then see that she's well taken care of," he nearly growls. As an afterthought, he adds in a softer voice, "Ava doesn't deserve to suffer."

Taking a step back from the much taller man, Chris nods once. "Just tell me where I can pick up her homework."

Ten

February 9 - 15

L oud knocking rouses Ava from drug-induced slumber. The sound
is disorienting at first.

    What time is it?

It's still light out.

Ava fishes around her sheets until her hand presses against a small, cold
rectangle of metal and plastic. She draws the phone out and holds it close to
her face.

(4) New Text Messages from Chris

—— **Friday, February 9** ——

  – **Chris** | 3:35 –

Got it. Omw.

  – **Chris** | 3:48 –

Almost at your place.

  – **Chris** | 3:52 –

I'm here.

  – **Chris** | 3:54 –

Ava, wake up!

Right. Chris went to ElRo for my homework.

"I'm coming!" Ava calls out as loudly as her parched throat can muster. Despite the protest in her muscles, Ava sits up and slides out of bed. She takes a moment to get oriented to the new vertical position her body is in, running a hand through her matted hair.

Ava tosses her cellphone back onto her bed and takes a quick look at what she's wearing. Pajama bottoms and a bleach-stained old t-shirt advertising Tapper's Outpost, a dive bar that closed down years ago. "Chris has seen me in worse," she decides with a shrug.

Another series of knocks sound from the front of the apartment.

"I said I'm coming!" Ava walks quickly across the strips of carpet and linoleum floor in her socked feet until she reaches the front door. Nate installed a couple of after-market deadbolts, so she takes a few moments to get the door unlocked.

She opens it to find Chris leaning against the doorframe, looking mildly perturbed until he sees her.

"Bub, you look terrible," Chris says with a smile that tells her he's mostly joking.

"Yeah, well, you look…" Ava takes in the sight of her friend, attempting to find fault. His crisp blue button-down is tucked into a pair of fitted light-wash jeans, contrasting nicely with his dark skin.

It's not a bad look.

When Ava leaves the sentence unfinished, Chris holds out a small stack of papers as an offering.

"Thank you! You're a lifesaver," Ava smiles, taking the papers and holding them against her chest.

"And these," Chris adds, producing a box of Kleenex from behind his back.

Laughing, Ava steps away from the door. "Do you want to come in for a bit?" A loud sneeze interrupts her laugh. "I should warn you, there's probably a good chance you could catch whatever I have."

"I'm up to date on all my shots."

Ava leads the way past the kitchen and into the living room. "Make yourself at home." She places the stack of homework onto the coffee table and curls herself up into a corner of the couch with one of the throw pillows.

Chris follows suit, takes a seat a couple of feet away from her, and places the tissue box between them.

"Were you able to find the office alright?" Ava asks, taking a tissue. "Oh, of course you did. Duh." She looks over at her friend with a sly grin, only to find his face tense. "What's wrong, bub?"

"I don't like that guy, Ava."

"What guy?" Her fingers comb through the fringe around the pillow.

"The teacher. *Nico.*"

Ava draws back. "Wait, why don't you like him?"

"He likes you. Ava, the guy thinks you're a teenager, and he doesn't even do a good job of pretending to be indifferent about you in front of your fake boyfriend."

"I don't know what you're talking about, Chris."

"Like hell, you don't."

"Um, the last time I checked, *you* were the one begging me to stay on this story!" Ava flings the pillow at Chris' lap. "So I don't appreciate the attitude you're taking with me *doing. My. Job.*"

Chris catches the pillow and defensively throws it on the ground. "There's such a thing as being too involved, Ava."

"I think you should go." Ava wipes at her nose. "I don't want us to say things we don't mean."

"Ava, think about this logically

"Chris! I said that you should go."

Chris stares at the blank television screen across the room for a few long seconds. Abruptly, he stands up. "Feel better, Ava. That's from the teacher and me."

***

The flu keeps Ava out of commission for the entire weekend and most of the next week. This proves to be of great annoyance to Cillian Wells and the rest of the thirty-fourth-floor office.

After their almost-fight, the conversation between Chris and Ava is at worst strained, and at best professional.

Chris sends Ava daily updates of their coworkers' complaints. Most are along the lines of *'When is she going to get back to flirting with her sexy teacher?'*. Even Chris himself seems to show a more clinical attitude towards Mr. Adams, referring to him as *'the teacher.*

Needless to say, Ava isn't in any hurry to get back to her undercover gig.

When she wakes up Thursday to find most of her symptoms virtually gone, Ava knows she has to face the music. Stalling for time, she pushes a plastic slat of her bedroom blinds down and peers out the window. Sunlight floods into the room, warming her waxen skin. "It looks like Spring is finally making an appearance," she murmurs to herself.

Outside, the morning is in full swing. Cars and buses speed up as they pass by her window. Ava watches a woman carefully cross the road, holding her toddler's hand and a precarious stack of books. One of the middle books looks dangerously close to toppling the whole thing over. Ava bites into her bottom lip, transfixed on the woman, until the two make it safely to the other side. She breathes out, relieved, as the woman corrects the stack and continues down the sidewalk.

Letting go of the blind, Ava turns around and takes in the sight of her messy bedroom. A week's worth of laundry spills out of its basket, various bottles clutter her desk, and her bed is a complete disaster. Ava's cellphone display shows the time: *7:41.*

With a bracing sigh, she goes to face her closet. Only a few tops are still neatly hung on their hangers. For the sake of time, Ava grabs the first thing she sees. She strips off her bedclothes and pulls the top on over her head.

A few more takes around the room, and the outfit is finished with a black denim skirt, stockings, and a pair of booties.

Plowing into the bathroom, Ava makes quick work of brushing her teeth and hair. Her hands mindlessly style her dark tresses into three buns down the back of her head, then spritzes her perfume. As an afterthought, Ava strides back into her bedroom and adds the spaceship pin to the right pocket of the blouse. "Grab a coffee, the All-Humiliation Network has returned for an encore," Ava mutters to the pin.

She collects her laptop and the coursework Chris brought on Friday and heads to the living room. On top of her leather satchel rests a small scrap of paper and Ava's heart immediately speeds up.

Nico obviously wasn't in the house. I would have remembered that.

... Wouldn't I?

Ava snatches the paper up, now recognizing Nate's handwriting.

Have a great day at school, sis. Remember our talk. Also, Tori said Chloe signed you both up for the fundraiser tomorrow. So please make yourself scarce, if you catch my drift.

"Subtle," Ava says, a smile on her lips.

Good for Nate.

"Looks like I need to arrange a sleepover."

***

The bus isn't outside at its normal time, so Ava waits an extra few minutes, thinking it just got held up. But more time goes by and at 8:07 there's still no sign of the bus, leaving Ava no choice but to walk to school.

When she enters the building at 8:32, the hallways are silent, first period having started twelve minutes prior. Flustered, Ava makes her way up the staircase and down the hall to English 12.

The door is closed, and when Ava turns the handle and pushes it open with a wretched creaking sound, effectively turning all heads in her direction. Chloe smiles brightly at her friend and offers a small, encouraging wave.

"How good of you to grace us with your presence," Nico says impassively from his seat. His feet are propped up on the desk in front of him and both hands cradle a hardcover book.

At first, Ava finds this odd, but as she takes in the classroom before her, she realizes she's walked in during a test. "I'm sorry, my bus never showed up, so I had to come on foot," Ava explains, approaching her teacher's desk.

"Tardiness is not permitted, whatever the cause. Your classmates have just begun a written exam." Nico slides his feet down off the desk and back onto the floor, sitting up in his chair. "A word in the hallway, Ms. Eliot, to discuss the consequences of your disrespectful conduct." Nico's tone is cold, yet professional. His eyes tell an entirely different story.

Ava nods and drops her gaze to the floor, letting him lead the way out of the classroom. "It won't happen again, sir," she enunciates carefully, the door shutting closed behind them.

The teacher looks both ways down the hall before gesturing for Ava to follow him. They walk a few yards away from the classroom and stop in front of the audio/video supply closet.

"I didn't mean to cause a disruption," Ava says, looking up at the much taller man. She is pleased to see that he's let the scruff grow back above his lips and across his chin.

In a confusing turn of events, Nico smiles. Tiny lines around his eyes emerge and his cheeks scrunch up, displaying the dimples Ava so rarely see.

Ava's brows knit, and she returns his smile with a perplexed one of her own. "Am I not in trouble?"

Nico laughs softly and drops his head, pushing a hand against the back of his neck. "Trouble? No, of course not." He kneads his neck and looks down at Ava once again. "I just wanted, no, *needed,* to explain myself to you."

"Alright," Ava speaks hesitantly. She toys with the spaceship pin as an outlet for her nerves.

"First, I believe it's my fault that you got sick, and I'm deeply sorry for that." Nico's eyes dance over her face, taking in every feature as if he's seeing them for the first time. "Second, the note I left on your desk." His line of sight narrows in on Ava's lips for a few impossibly long seconds.

Her breath comes out ragged, and she nods for him to continue.

"That was *highly* inappropriate."

Ava presses her lips together in a frown but still forces herself to nod.

"My personal life shouldn't be of any concern to you, just as yours shouldn't affect me." Even as he says the words, Nico's eyes betray him.

"Yes." The singular word is the only thing Ava can call to mind at the moment.

"And finally, if I have acted in any way that could undermine my professionalism, I apologize. You are my student and it is my duty to treat you as such. If my actions have suggested otherwise, that was never my intention." Nico states, sounding like this is something he's rehearsed.

"Yes- I mean, I forgive you. For everything," Ava offers a smile that doesn't reach her eyes. "That is, if you'll forgive me for acting so juvenile."

"Absolutely."

They remain locked in a stare, clearly at a standstill. Both of them are on the verge of saying something unwarranted or improper. Somewhere down the hall, a door opens. Ava jumps at the sound, her arm brushing against Nico's.

"Shouldn't we get back to class, Mr. Adams?" The name feels wrong as it leaves her lips.

"Yes, we should." Nico draws his arm back and walks in the classroom's direction.

He didn't correct me.

***

"*Yes!*" Chloe squeals. "I would love that!"

"Me too. I kind of really love your parents," Ava says with a smile.

"This is gonna be great! We'll do our couple hours of volunteering tomorrow and then have the rest of the night to enjoy the fair."

"What *did* you sign us up for, exactly?"

"Oh," Chloe suddenly looks very interested in her chocolate pudding. "I meant to tell you, I couldn't get us signed up for the same thing."

"Okay, and?"

"I'm running the dunking booth with Hallie," Chloe brings the spoon to her mouth, talking into it. "And you're working the refreshments stand."

"That's not as bad as I was expecting," Ava says with an encouraging nod.

"With Mr. Adams."

Eleven

February 16

ꙮ

The school day ends on Friday and, instead of rushing home, most of the senior class walk down York Avenue to Carl Schurz Park. The East River runs alongside the park, offering a beautiful backdrop for the fundraising fair.

Ava walks with Chloe and Hallie, the three girls making idle chatter about the evening's events. "I heard that last year, some boys jumped into the river and they got disqualified from the senior class trip. Their parents were really upset, but Principal Steele wouldn't change his mind." Hallie's tone is low and cautious.

Unable to stop herself, Ava asks, "Are you worried that you're accidentally going to jump in too?"

Chloe nudges her with an elbow but keeps her eyes ahead discreetly.

"No... I was just saying," Hallie says quietly.

They lapse into quiet observation for the remaining couple of blocks. When the park comes into view, Chloe reaches out and grabs Ava's arm. "It's beautiful."

"Someone's been busy," she agrees. The lawn of Carl Schurz Park is covered with booths offering typical carnival attractions: a ring toss, dunk tank, face painting, skeeball, water gun racing, even a kissing booth. A few rides are set up too, including a small bumper car track, teacups, swings, and a gigantic Ferris wheel in the middle of it all. Fairy lights and colored lanterns hang from the gazebos. Little carts and tents are scattered throughout, with pictures of food and drink items identifying them as refreshment stands.

As students enter the park, Ms. Richardson stands with a clipboard, marking the volunteers as present. "Chloe Cuong and… Hallie Hodge, dunk tank," Ms. Richardson puts check-marks next to their names. She reaches into her fanny pack, fishing around for their name tags. "There we are." Ms. Richardson holds the stickers out to the girls. "You can check in with Mr. Martino at your booth."

Chloe and Hallie remove the wax paper from the back of the name tags and press them onto their shirts.

"Ava Eliot," Ms. Richardson scans the paper for her name. "Ah. You're working Refreshment Stand Two with Mr. Adams." She produces a name tag for Ava and gestures behind her. "That's the one with the Icee machine. You can't miss it."

"Thanks," echo from the lips of all three young women as they march past Ms. Richardson and step onto the lawn.

Other students and faculty are finding their posts or testing out the games and rides. The fair doesn't open to the public for another thirty minutes. "Do you think we're going to raise enough money?" Chloe asks, heading towards the dunk tank.

"I really hope so. I haven't been to Disney World since seventh grade," Hallie says. "But even if we don't, I'm sure some of the non-scholarship parents will step in. ElRo always sends their seniors on a trip."

"Is attending the trip a required activity?" Ava plays with the lowest bun on her head, right at the base of her neck.

"What? Don't you want to go?!" Chloe looks bemused.

"I do. I'm just not sure if my parents want me to go all the way to Florida without them," Ava quickly answers.

"Oh," Chloe softens. "It's totally chaperoned, if that's what they're worried about. I could get my parents to talk to them, too."

"No!" Ava blurts out. "I mean, no, that won't be necessary. If it's chaperoned, I'm sure they'll be cool with it."

They stop in front of the large blue dunk tank. It's caged, housing a small black seat that resembles a diving board. Off to the side are two plastic folding chairs and a basket full of balls.

Hallie picks up a ball and aims it for the red circle on the vinyl sheet next to the tank. She throws, and the ball hits the black circle encasing the red, missing the target. "Which one of you wants to get in there and test this thing out?" Hallie smiles, reaching down for another ball.

"Everything appears to be in working order." Mr. Martino emerges from somewhere behind the booth and walks around to the front. "Oh, hello, girls. Let me show you what you'll be doing."

Taking this as her cue to leave, Ava brushes her fingertips across Chloe's arm. "Okay, so I'll meet you by the Ferris wheel when our replacements come."

"Sounds good. Have fun with Mr. Adams," Chloe says with a broad smile.

"Yeah, yeah. You owe me for this."

Walking off towards her assignment, Ava's stomach feels like it's being tied into intricate knots. After their conversation yesterday, she's not sure how to approach Nico.

It feels like we trekked a great precipice together, and then he went off and ran away.

Ms. Richardson had been right, Refreshment Stand Two sets itself apart with a large ICEE logo on the banner. Already, Nico is standing under the small tent, unwrapping the plastic from sleeves of cups and stacking them neatly. The small area where Ava will spend her next few hours is comprised of a high-top table covered in cups of differing sizes, a money box, and the Icee machine on another tiny table behind that. No chairs to be seen. Just eight square feet of space for them to occupy.

Nico looks out at the park, taking in the excitement around him casually. His eyes seem to do a double-take when he spots Ava, and his peaceful expression vanishes.

Half of Ava's mouth pulls up in a small smile. "Hi. Ms. Richardson sent me."

He hums a curt response and takes a step closer to the front table so that Ava can walk around him.

She pretends to be very interested in watching the Icee machine churn its liquid. Behind her, Nico finishes setting up all the plastic cups and makes busy work of counting out the bills and coins in the metal box. Minutes pass by in silence.

Fine, I don't want to talk either.

Ava takes one of the smallest cups, deciding to test the drink. She presses the cup against the red side of the Icee machine until it's filled about a quarter of the way up.

Leaning against the front table, Ava drinks a sip. "Not quite frozen," she says, mainly to herself. Shrugging one shoulder, she finishes the rest of the drink in one gulp.

Bad idea.

A concentrated pain announces its presence right between Ava's eyebrows. She squeezes her eyes together tightly and bounces on her heels.

"Press your tongue against the roof of your mouth," Nico instructs, his voice barely audible.

Ava does as directed, in too much discomfort to be surprised. After a long few seconds, the intense feeling subsides and Ava's eyes flutter back open.

Nico stands looking down at her, his eyes clouded with concern. Doing the first thing that comes to mind, Ava sticks out the tip of her tongue. "What color is my tongue?"

"Red."

She draws her tongue back. "Spider-Man red?" A sheepish smile spreads across her lips.

Nico furrows his brows for a few seconds, then raises them. "You remember that story?"

"I remember everything that you say," Ava says, without thinking. "In your classroom," she adds.

To her relief, Ava's smile is matched by one from Nico. "Can I ask you something?"

Ava nods her consent, trying not to notice the way her heart is pounding heavily.

"Do you think I tell too many stories in class?"

This is not the kind of question I was expecting.

She shakes her head once. "No. That's what makes you interesting. As a teacher, I mean."

Nico gives a low laugh, running his fingers through his trimmed beard. "God, I would love to think I'm an interesting teacher. I had… maybe one or two teachers in high school who had any passion at all."

"You do seem to have passion," Ava's words come unhindered. "In the classroom."

Their borderline unseemly conversation is interrupted when Logan approaches the stand. He looks at Ava thoughtfully for a second before saying, "One large blue slushie."

"Sure." Ava grabs a cup and turns around to fill the order while Nico takes the payment. "Here you go," she attaches a lid and hands the drink over.

Logan unwraps a straw and takes a long swallow before burping loudly. He smiles at Ava and winks, then walks off.

"Teenage boys," Nico's tone is laced with disgust.

"I know."

"I'd like to tell you it's something we all grow out of it, but that's a lie." Nico shakes his head and takes a step back from the front table.

Ava follows suit as if the extra foot of space will make their conversation more private.

"You probably knew as much already, though I can't see Chris acting that way around you."

"We… broke up," Ava decides on the words easily. One less lie to tell will only make her life easier.

Nico presses his lips together briefly. "I'm sorry to hear that."

Ava brushes his words off with a fluttering gesture of her fingertips. "Can I ask you something now?"

Averting his eyes, Nico agrees. "I suppose so."

"About a month ago, you asked me if I'd lost someone close to me," Ava's eyes shut of their own accord at the memory. She takes a slow breath before continuing, "I told you something that I rarely share with people. I guess I… let you in." Ava's eyes find Nico's. "I think it's only fair if you do the same."

"As your English teacher, I feel the need to inform you that none of that was posed as a question." One eyebrow shifts upward.

"Are you teasing me?" A self-deprecating laugh.

"Perhaps."

"*Nico.*" Ava extends a hand on impulse, only just managing to stop herself from touching him. Instead, her hand rests awkwardly on the side of the Icee machine between them.

"Hey, Mr. Adams. Ava."

Both heads turn simultaneously. Isaac stands in front of the counter, a small line forming behind him.

For the next hour, Ava and Nico work in tandem. She pours the drinks; he takes the money and makes change. They stay busy and only make light conversation. Only once the fair publicly opens and rides start to operate does the refreshment stand begin slowing down.

"You're going to hate me if I tell you," Nico says quietly, after their most recent customer walks off.

Impossible.

"I… I don't think that's possible." Ava busies herself with wiping down the drink nozzles. Their backs are to one another.

He clears his throat loudly before speaking again. "It happened when I was a little younger than you are now."

Ava makes a small noncommittal sound.

"I begged my parents for *weeks* to let me practice for my learner's permit. Dad was the one who gave in first and decided to take me out." The strain in Nico's voice makes Ava's heart ache.

"Everything went well for the first week or so. Dad would pick me up from school and we'd find a semi-empty parking lot, and I'd drive around. But it wasn't enough for me. I wanted to go *fast*, I wanted it to be real," he inhales sharply. "I finally wore him down, and he let me drive out onto State Route 25."

For the second time today, Ava's stomach turns to knots. This time, it's not for herself.

I have a terrible feeling about the direction his story is taking.

"Dad was so proud of me, saying he couldn't wait to tell my mother that he'd done such a great job training me in so short a time frame." Nico turns around now to look at Ava. The pain she saw in his eyes when she vaguely shared her story with him stares across at her once more.

"But you know New York weather, cloudless one moment and pouring rain the next. Dad told me to pull off and let him take over, but I was headstrong. Proud, just like he raised me to be. I insisted I could handle anything." His eyes press together tightly, and Ava can imagine the scene playing out in his mind.

"I didn't have time to react when the car in front of me slammed on its brakes. Dad screamed for me to stop, and instead, I swerved to the left."

"Nico, it's okay, you don't have to finish," Ava whispers.

He shakes his head firmly and laughs once, low and sullen. "It's all so ridiculous. That's not even my real name."

"What are you talking about?"

"*Nico Adams.* I was a coward when I changed my name. I guess I still am."

Ava furrows her brow, confused and upset for him. *By* him.

"He died, Ava. I was an arrogant little brat who bit off more than I could chew, and my father died because of it."

The words don't surprise her at this point, but they still make Ava want to cry for him. Unable to hold back from offering comfort any longer, Ava reaches out and wraps her right hand around his forearm. Her thumb strokes the smooth skin of his wrist. "I'm so sorry…" she trails off, not wanting to repeat the redundant words people always said to her.

"Daniel. My name was Daniel Woodard before I turned eighteen and changed it to protect my mother's public image." He looks down, eyes focused on where their skin is touching. But he doesn't move.

Why does that name sound familiar?

"Daniel," Ava repeats slowly, trying the name out. Somehow, it seems to suit him even better than Nico ever did.

This seems to strike a nerve because when he looks back up, his chocolate eyes look bright and animated. "She's the only one who has called me that in the past decade. When we actually talk. I make little habit of keeping in contact with the people who love me."

Everything suddenly clicks into place.

Thea Lewis-Woodard, former journalist and CEO of Lewisson Motors.

That has to be his mother.

When Daniel pulls away from Ava's touch, for the first time he does so gently. Just creating space, not pushing her away. "I told her I changed my name so that I wouldn't sully her reputation any further. But really, I think it was to help her forget about me. I took the person she loved most in the world away, and she's never looked at me the same." Daniel rubs the back of his neck, looking out at the fair activities. "Not that I can blame her for that."

Ava's mind races to catch up with all the new information he's just given her. For the first time in the past three months, it truly feels like they are just two people having a conversation. "Thank you for trusting me," she says, repeating what he'd said to her a month ago.

Daniel picks up a paper straw wrapper that someone had discarded on the counter and rolls it into a ball between his thumb and index finger. "I do trust you, Ava. I can't seem to figure out *why* exactly that is. But it's there."

Her lips open and shut, wanting to tell him the truth, but knowing she can only give something resembling it. "I want to let you in, too. But that's not as easy as it sounds."

"There's something different about you. I could feel it the first day you showed up in my class." He flicks the paper ball into the trashcan under the table. "Are you going to tell me what that is, or do I have to find out on my own?"

Ava's chest tightens.

Am I truly that transparent?

"Changing of the guard!" Krista announces, rescuing Ava from both Daniel and herself.

Shawn has an arm draped comfortably over her shoulder, and he gives Ava a friendly smile. "You've done your time."

"Yes, and you two are right on time," Daniel says after a glance down at his watch. "Everything has been going smoothly. There are plenty of cups left and if you need more change, flag down Ms. Richardson or Mr. Martino."

Daniel and Ava walk out the back of the small tent, allowing Krista and Shawn to take their place. "I promised Chloe I would meet her by the Ferris wheel," Ava says, wrapping her arms around herself.

"Of course, best not to keep Chloe waiting."

"Yeah," Ava nods, wishing their conversations didn't always have to end so abruptly. "What should I call you now? When we're not in class."

"Whichever name you prefer," he says with a shrug.

He always tries to act casual, but his eyes always betray him.

"I like Daniel, if you don't mind." *Like* is putting it mildly. It's a safe word, one that could never sum up how it feels to be opened up to. *Like* is an appropriate word, but only just. *Like* is all Ava is currently able to admit to.

"I don't mind. I like hearing you say it."

Like *could easily be the death of me.*

Twelve

February 16 & 17

"You're seventeen. You're busy being carefree. Your friends are the most important thing in your life. Teachers are *old* and not in a sexy, illicit way," Ava mutters to herself as she walks across the lawn.

All around her are the sounds of joy and laughter, and Ava needs to shake off the conversation she's just had and join in. Pronto.

"There you are!" Chloe shouts from a couple of yards away. She stands alone, clutching a strip of tickets.

The smile that erupts on Ava's face is genuine. Her friendship with Chloe is the only thing that doesn't hurt her conscience as of late. "How was working the dunk tank?" she asks, crossing the distance between them.

"Pretty exciting, actually. We have a lot of talented pitchers. Somehow, Hallie talked Mr. Martino into getting into the tank." Chloe's eyes go wide. "I wish you could've seen it! Logan Trite knocked him in on the first try."

"It sounds like Logan's been making his rounds tonight," Ava says with a shake of her head. "I'm glad you had a good time." She gestures to the Ferris wheel in front of them. "Shall we?"

"Yes!" Chloe breaks off two tickets and hands them to Ava.

"Thank you."

There isn't much of a line for the ride, so the girls can walk right up. Mr. Steele is overseeing the operations. "Having a good evening, girls?" he asks, taking their tickets.

"Yes."

"Everything's great."

"I'm glad to hear that," the principal smiles. He opens the gate and lets them take their seats before closing it behind them. "Enjoy."

Sitting back, Chloe smiles over at her companion. "I'm a little bit afraid of heights. Just a warning."

"What?" Ava laughs once, softly. "Why did you want to ride the Ferris wheel, the tallest thing here?"

"I don't know. I've always wanted to."

"Take a deep breath and hold it until the count of seven, and then slowly release it. That usually helps me when I'm nervous."

Nodding, Chloe breathes in through her nose. Deciding to join her, Ava counts out the seconds with her fingers. When she shakes her fingers out, both girls exhale. "I feel... Calmer," Chloe decides. "You always have an answer, Ava. I think you're the most mature girl in our grade."

Ava smiles graciously. "Thanks, but I'd say it's a tie. I feel like I'm learning from you half of the time in class. What you said about *Jane Eyre*? Well beyond your years."

"You do that, sometimes. Say things that make it sound like you're older than me," Chloe giggles. "I just turned eighteen."

Smooth move, Thompson.

"Sorry! Only child syndrome. You're right, I don't turn eighteen until right before graduation." The time frame comes to Ava with little thought.

Chloe makes a small humming sound. Initially, Ava assumes it's because the Ferris wheel is nearing the top. But when she looks more closely at her friend, she finds her grinning. "What?"

Waggling her eyebrows up and down teasingly, Chloe shakes her head. "Oh, nothing."

"Chloe, tell me!"

"I was just wondering if a certain teacher knows the date of your upcoming

95

turn about the sun."

The gasp that escapes Ava is both in character and entirely natural. "Chloe Cuong! Did you sign me up for the refreshments stand on purpose?"

"A lady never tells," Chloe insists, pretending to zip her lips shut.

Of course. Chloe is perceptive. I should have seen this coming.

"Well, whatever you're scheming, it didn't work."

"I'm not implying that Mr. Adams would ever do anything unethical, but I wasn't born yesterday. I notice how he looks at you when he thinks no one's watching."

"Eww."

Chloe narrows her eyes. "*Uh-huh*, sure."

Inside her pocket, Ava's phone vibrates. She presses a button through the jeans, silencing it. "Let's talk about something fun and *real*. Like, what are we doing tonight?"

"Fine, we'll put this conversation on pause because I actually have something fun planned."

Leaning in, Ava nods eagerly. "Tell me more."

"Hallie's new boyfriend Josh found this club in Brooklyn that doesn't check IDs."

Ava squints, pressing her lips to the side. "A club?"

"Not my typical idea of a good time, yes. But one night of dancing isn't going to do any major damage."

Still not looking convinced, Ava sits back. "I don't know."

"It'll be fun, Ava, I promise. Besides, Victoria is spending the night with Nate, and in exchange for keeping her secret, she's included me in her cover story. We'll be 'on the Island,'" Chloe makes exaggerated quotation marks with her first two fingers, "at our cousin Bianca's house."

"Your parents aren't going to want to verify that with Bianca?"

"Already taken care of." Chloe nudges Ava with her shoulder. "Come on, when's the last time you let loose and had fun?"

Honestly, longer than I care to remember.

Ava looks out at the fairgrounds, lit up by the multicolored lanterns. Her eyes scan the crowd for a few moments before she realizes she's inadvertently looking for Daniel. "I guess… Where will we be sleeping, though?"

"At Hallie's. See? The plan is foolproof."

Ava spots Daniel playing darts with a few other members of the faculty standing around him. They're all smiles and laughter.

He's living his life just fine. I should do the same.

"Alright, I'm in," Ava agrees, her lips pulled up in a minuscule smile.

Chloe claps her hands together. "I feel like our entire friendship consists of me convincing you to do things you don't want to do."

"Or secretly want to do."

"That sounds better, okay."

The Ferris wheel is making its final descent, and once again, Ava's phone vibrates against her leg. The tight fit of her jeans makes it difficult to slide out, but with some effort, Ava frees it.

Cillian "The General" Wells is Calling…

Ava gives Chloe an awkward smile and presses the phone against her chest. "It's… my dad. He worries."

"Trust me, I get it."

As soon as their car comes to a stop, Ava rushes to get out for some privacy. "Be right back," she calls over her shoulder, already taking long strides towards a less lit area. Ava slides her finger to accept the call. "Hi, Dad… I miss you too."

"Thompson, are you purposely trying to disgust me?" Wells snarls into her ear.

"Sorry, sir. I'm trying to maintain a cover."

"Is that what you'd call the love fest you just broadcast?"

"I—"

"A false identity? The son of Thea Lewis-Woodard? This is better than I ever expected it to be."

Is this what Wells sounds like when he's happy?

"Your methods are very questionable, Thompson, but they seem to be quite effective."

"Thank you?"

"Obviously, you've been undercover much longer than anticipated, but now you should have enough information for the story."

"What?"

"Keep up, Ms. Thompson. I'm pulling you out of Eleanor Roosevelt High as of this Monday. You can finish the piece here, at the office."

Ava's eyes widen, and she nearly drops the phone. "No, I—"

"What do you mean 'no'?"

If you would let me finish for once...

"I mean, yes, I got a lot of, er, information tonight. But I have a plan."

I do?

"You do?"

"Yes. I need to stay on at least another month until the senior class trip."

Silence for a few painstakingly long moments. "Is this teacher of yours one of the chaperones on the trip?"

Is he?

"Yes, definitely. That's… why I need more time. To take the trip with him."

Wells breathes deeply into the phone, making the hairs on the back of Ava's neck rise. "Fine. One month, and not a day more."

"Thank you, sir! You'll—" A beep sounds in her ear, letting her know Wells has ended the call.

What did I just sign myself up for?

***

A few hours later, Ava stands shivering on a barely lit street in Brooklyn. She's now wearing a sequined dress, borrowed from Hallie, that only just covers her rump. Fishnet stockings offer no practicality or warmth from the cool February air, and the open-toed sandals with thick metallic block heels aren't exactly made for walking. Ava's only solace in the ensemble is that it does not include her spaceship pin. She left that under her discarded clothes in a pile on Hallie's bedroom floor.

"Okay, act casual, like we belong here," Hallie's boyfriend, Josh, instructs the group.

Krista and Shawn have decided to join in at the last minute, making it a party of six. Chloe smooths out her own dress, a bodycon with a sweetheart neckline, and tries to relax her facial expression. "My birthday? March 4, 1996," she practices.

Focusing on a fresh piece of gum on the wall, Ava tries not to laugh. If Chloe really were asked that question, it would be a stretch for her to pass as 22. Ava's birthday, just around the corner, could easily be called to mind. *April 10, 1993.* Although it probably wouldn't be wise to give that exact year.

"Our turn," Hallie stage whispers.

They approach a tall woman with elaborately braided blue hair. She stands with her arms crossed, leaning against the building. Dark eyes pass over the group with a look of boredom. Wordlessly, she nods, and they walk past her hastily.

Bright neon lights direct them into a large room filled with the pulsating beat of a remixed Top 40 hit. The air is foggy and thick with smoke and the breath of so many bodies. Ava surveys the crowd, mostly under-aged kids, with a few exceptions. The majority of the people are dancing in various stages of intoxication. A hand latches onto her arm. "Should we get a drink?" Chloe asks, looking as young as Ava has ever seen her.

"Let's dance first," Ava replies.

I have no control over any of these kids drinking, but I won't be the one to hand it to them.

Chloe looks relieved. "Yeah!"

The pair squeeze their way through warm bodies until they find a small square of space. They regard each other with meek smiles, nodding along to the beat.

"C'mon," Ava says, taking both of Chloe's hands. She starts to step side-to-side, shimmying their arms back and forth. Chloe mirrors the moves. After a minute of this, Ava lets go of one of Chloe's hands and spins her around. When she turns back around, Chloe is grinning.

Now loosened up, they fall into an easy routine. Songs come and go quickly, and Ava finds she's losing track of the time.

"Hey guys, can we join?" Krista has a half-finished drink in her hand.

"The more the merrier," Chloe agrees.

Hallie, Josh, and Shawn also have suspicious-looking drinks when they make their way over into what is now a dance circle. As a group, they continue to dance, though it's easy to notice when the couples begin to pair up. A pang of longing twists inside of Ava and she presses her lips against Chloe's ear. "I'll be right back."

Chloe nods and keeps dancing, a blissfully sweaty mess.

Ava works her way over to the bar and falls onto a stool.

"What'll it be?" A twenty-something young woman asks.

"Dealer's choice."

The bartender smiles. "Bad day?"

Ava hesitates at the question. Under any other circumstances, getting to know more about a handsome, mysterious man would have made it a good day. She settles on a wordless shrug.

"Dating problems, huh? I've got just the trick." She gets to work, pouring from different bottles into a shaker.

Ava resigns herself to people-watching while she waits. When a tall, broad-shouldered man with dark hair walks in, her heart speeds up. Ava has to force herself to stay seated. Only as he nears the bar does she realize he is someone inconsequential to her.

Daniel wouldn't be here. Don't be ridiculous!

"Do you want to start a tab?" The bartender asks, placing a tall glass filled with green liquid in front of Ava.

Turning back around, Ava nods and fishes a card out from her bra. She hands it over to the woman and takes a long drink.

Ooh, this is strong.

"Here you go," the woman says, extending the credit card.

"Thanks." Ava replaces the card and finishes the drink, feeling an insistent need to get back onto the dance floor. Her mind hadn't been reeling when it was filled with music and movement.

Scooting her chair back, Ava takes a moment to find her footing in the ridiculous heels before she rejoins her friends. "Heeey," Ava yells above the music, wedging her way back into the circle.

"Whoa there," Chloe shouts back, waving her hand in front of her nose. "Had a little drink, did we?"

Ava smiles and nods eagerly. "Yup. I deserved it."

"And you didn't bring me anything? I'm offended."

"Wounded?"

"Just a bit."

They share a laugh and fall back into motion, Ava dancing closer now.

I can live my life and have fun, too.

An indeterminable amount of time later, Ava feels a tapping against her shoulder. She turns to see Josh and Hallie, grinning like idiots as they hold a tray of shots out. "Help yourselves," Josh shouts.

Chloe seems to hesitate before taking a small glass, and she nurses it between her hands. Ava, on the other hand, reaches out for a glass and downs it quickly.

"Ahh!"

"Ava knows what she's doing," Hallie yells, looking impressed.

Nodding loosely, Ava replies, "You bet I do. I can drink anyone in here under the table."

*⁎⁎⁎

Nausea wakes Ava from a dreamless slumber.

Where am I?

She rolls over too quickly and falls onto the cold hardwood floor, landing painfully against her shoulder. "Ow!"

"*Shhhhh!*" A familiar voice whispers from across the room.

Pushing herself up into a sitting position, Ava takes stock of her surroundings. The room she's in is dimly lit by the light coming in through a large window.

It's morning.

Two other bodies are spread out on air mattresses nearby and she's able to make out someone snoring on a bed in the room's corner.

Chloe, Krista, Hallie.

Ava's stomach gurgles and she urgently pushes herself into a standing position, only to feel the room move around her.

Slowly.

Taking her time and using a small end table to balance herself, Ava comes to her feet.

Bathroom. Now.

Ava's feet seem to know where to go better than her mind does, as she walks out the bedroom and down the hallway to a small bathroom. She falls to her knees in front of a porcelain toilet and pushes the seat up. Ava braces herself with both hands on the bowl and dry heaves. The pain in her throat announces itself.

Apparently, I've already done this at least once before.

Ava doesn't bother trying to move for a few minutes. She just sits on the tile floor and breathes deeply.

What happened last night?

Gradually, images pop into her head. Dancing at the club. Dancing with her friends. Taking a shot. More shots. More dancing. Dancing with strangers. Another drink- no, it was a competition. And she'd won. After that point, her memory fades into black.

Great. Real family-friendly fun you got into with a bunch of teenagers.

Deciding that she's already thrown up the contents of her stomach, Ava closes the toilet lid and carefully stands up. She moves to the sink and splashes water on her face. The cold sensation triggers a headache.

Wonderful. Anything else, world?

Ava exits the bathroom and attempts to tip-toe back to Hallie's bedroom. At least she isn't stomping around.

The three girls still lay sleeping. Knowing she can't fall back asleep, Ava locates her backpack. She pulls out the t-shirt she'd meant to sleep in and pulls it over the sequined mini dress. Squinting in the early morning light, Ava strolls around the room until she's able to find both her wallet and cellphone. "I'm gonna run to the store. Does anyone need anything?" she whispers.

No response.

"Alright then."

With her personal items in hand, Ava walks through the house. She's relieved to find her boots by the door and slips them on before hitting the street.

One good thing about New York is that no matter where you are, you're never far from a corner store. All Ava has to do is pick a direction to walk. On a whim, she chooses left and walks a block and a half before finding a Corner News and Grocery. The bells chime as she walks into the brightly lit convenience store. Ava nearly gags the smell of hot dogs and taquitos ambushing her nose.

No food.

She pads over to the refrigerated cases and takes a minute to peruse the Gatorade selection.

"No way, *Tapper's Outpost*? I used to go there all the time before they closed." The voice behind her is too loud for whatever time of morning this is.

"Same here. It's a travesty the health department shut them down." Ava turns around, about to ask the guy why he's so chipper on a Saturday morning.

"Ava?"

Oh, bloody hell.

Daniel stands there with a roll of paper towels tucked under one arm and a newspaper in the other.

"Hi, Daniel," she says lamely.

His nose wrinkles when her breath hits him. Eyes roam across her face and over her outfit. "Are you hungover?"

II

No Sooner Looked

"No sooner looked but they loved,"
- William Shakespeare, As You Like It

Thirteen

February 17 - 19

~⚬⚭⚬~

"**D**on't be ridiculous," Ava answers. Her words come out more confident than she's currently feeling.

She turns back to the refrigerated case and opens it as if ignoring Daniel will make this whole untimely meeting go away. Ava is just selecting a water bottle when Daniel's hand touches her shoulder, gently easing her around to face him.

With the sunlight flooding into the convenience store, Daniel's eyes seem lighter. Flecks of warm caramel surround the pupil of his chocolate-colored eyes. He is entirely too put together considering the time of day. Checkered flannel half-tucked into charcoal jeans and a faded denim jacket.

Obviously a morning person.

"Ava," he murmurs, shaking his head.

When Daniel looks at her, it's as if he's looking right through her. She feels so exposed in front of him, still dressed in last night's outfit with some strange modifications. Her hair is no doubt a giant mess, but the three buns are still somewhat intact. At least she hadn't been wearing any makeup, or that would be smudged around her eyes as well.

Even if she was currently stone-cold sober, lying to Daniel would be a difficult task. Right now -head pounding, nauseous, and dying of thirst- Ava stands no chance. Twisting the top off the water bottle, she brings it to her lips and takes a long drink. Ava wipes her mouth with the back of her hand, recaps the bottle, and a hiccup escapes.

"Kriff, you *are* hungover." Daniel's eyes are so disappointed that it doesn't seem fair.

Thanks, universe, for never letting me have any fun.

"You're hungover," he reiterates, "in a Midtown grocery store, wearing a t-shirt for a dive bar over—what is that? A child's dress?"

It's almost like she can see him piecing this together in his mind.

"A dive bar that closed down when you should have been in, what, middle school?" Daniel's voice is raised slightly, like when he's scolding someone in class.

Ava's mouth feels like it's full of cotton, dry, and too full to speak.

"But how can that be? You just told me you used to go all the time."

She shakes her head, willing him to stop talking. To stop thinking.

Pressing a thumb against his bottom lip, Daniel studies her face in the most unnerving way. The surprised look he'd worn not a minute before is now replaced with skepticism. Ava fidgets, bouncing from one foot to the other. Thoughts of running out the door die when Daniel's brows shoot up.

What is this look?

Recognition.

Oh, bloody hell.

"I've seen you there. Four years ago," his confident tone leaves no room for questioning. "You were doing karaoke in the corner... with a dark-haired shorter guy." Daniel runs a hand through his shaggy mane. "I *knew* I'd seen you before. I recognized you the first day of the semester, but I just couldn't place *where* I knew you from."

Tears well in Ava's eyes, yet she remains frozen.

"You *lied* to me, to everyone. For what purpose?" He demands.

Words. Where are my words?

You can still save this, brain.

Ava only averts her gaze, looking around the small convenience store. Apart from a woman behind the counter in the back, they are alone. For the first time, this knowledge does not fill Ava with deliciously nervous tension.

"I told you things that no one else knows. I *trusted* you, Ava." Daniel's voice seems to crack, breaking both of them in one fell swoop. "Is Ava even your real name?"

The saline liquid leaves a shiny trail as it slides down her cheeks.

"For kriff's sake, say something!"

"It was never personal," she finally says, whispering. "I work for *The New York Times*."

Daniel takes a step back into a shelf full of trail mix and corn nuts.

"I'm a junior writer, just trying to catch a break. My boss offered me an undercover assignment, and I jumped at the chance."

"To do what? Spy on the prodigal son of *Lewisson Motors*?" He hisses.

"*No!* Well, it didn't start that way... But I would never betray you, Daniel."

His face hardens as if she'd just slapped him. "Don't you dare call me that."

Ava gives in to the tears now, her voice hitching. "I'm sorry. I wanted to tell you so badly. I just thought... if I could come up with a different story to write and then tell you on my own, you'd be... "

"What? That I'd be *happy*? Because it turns out that all along I was allowed to be attracted to you?"

She sniffles, wiping at her cheeks. Those are the words she's assumed but desperately needed to hear. "You were attracted to me?"

"For kriff's sake, Ava, you set me up for a story!" Daniel crushes the newspaper into his fist.

"No, I—"

"Just drop the act. Do you have any idea what I went through, thinking I was attracted to a seventeen-year-old girl? It was unethical, and I spent my nights pondering what the hell I was going to do when I couldn't teach anymore!" A bitter laugh. "I mean, every word out of your mouth has been a complete lie," he trails off. Anger replaced with betrayal. "I don't know you at all."

"But you do know me. You know me better than almost anyone," she pleads. "Some part of you knew the poem was about my parents."

Daniel flinches at the last word, staring at her. The softness in his eyes that she's grown so accustomed to is nowhere to be seen. After a few moments, he wordlessly shakes his head and walks towards the check-out counter. Ava attempts to keep up with his long strides as she follows him, needing to pay for her water.

"Thanks, have a good day," Daniel says to the woman after he's paid. He turns and heads for the door, not even acknowledging Ava's presence in line.

Feebly, Ava reaches out and catches the tail of his jacket. "Wait, please don't walk away."

Barely turning his head so that he can look at her from the corner of his eyes, Daniel sighs, "I just can't look at you the same way."

***

Ava spends the rest of Saturday near the phone. Every time it sounds with an alert, for a sickening moment she thinks it's Wells calling to fire her. She sets a Google alert for 'Lewisson', 'Lewis' and 'Woodard'. Nothing other than news of *Lewisson* Motors acquiring *Marth Aeronautics* comes up.

Sitting in a booth at a Greek diner on Sunday, Ava stirs a packet of sugar into her coffee. Nate is across from her, texting away with a grin plastered on his face. This is the first time they've been together in close to a week, and both foster siblings are only present physically.

"You're a talkative couple," the waitress comments as she fills their water glasses.

"Huh?" Ava asks, looking up from her coffee. The server has already moved along to another table. "Nate."

Laughing at something on his screen, Nate looks up. "Yeah?"

"I don't know. It's weird not to be talking."

"Sorry," he says, placing the phone face down on the table. "Tori can wait."

"Did you two have a nice time on Friday?"

Nate's smile grows, unbridled. "*Yes.* Thank you for letting us have the apartment."

"No problem," Ava replies. She takes a sip of her coffee, purses her lips, and adds a splash of cream. On second taste, she nods thoughtfully.

Just the way I like it.

"What about you? How was your slumber party?"

Groaning, Ava covers her face with her left hand.

"That bad, huh?"

"I broke my cover," she mumbles.

"I'm sorry. What did you say? Because it sounded like you said you *broke your cover.*"

Ava slowly slides her hand down her face, stopping to rest her index finger between her lips and her thumb under her chin. "I did."

"What?!"

"Not with Chloe, don't freak out," she says. "Although I might as well have. Everyone's going to know tomorrow."

The waitress arrives with their breakfast. Ava spares no detail as she explains yesterday's events in between bites of food. Once she's finished, Nate leans back against the plush booth, biting the tines of his fork. After a little while, he says, "It might not be over yet."

"You didn't see his face, Nate. I really screwed him up."

He waves this sentiment away. "I mean at school and with your story. You haven't actually heard otherwise, have you?"

Pursing her lips, Ava shakes her head. "No, but only time will tell. Daniel has no reason to keep my secret."

"Are you sure about that? You're right, I wasn't there to see how everything went down. But what I do know is that he can't be a total prick. You'd never be interested in someone who was," Nate says matter-of-factly. He clasps his hands together on top of the table. "So, is he mad as hell? Yes. But I don't think you should assume he's going to get you fired. Even if, no offense, he probably should."

Unable to argue with that logic, Ava resigns herself to finishing her coffee.

∗∗∗

The next morning, Ava wakes feeling like many teenagers do—restless and having no desire to go to class.

I've had enough with Wells, Katherine, and god knows who else being witness to every embarrassing moment of my life.

She picks the spaceship pin up from her desk and holds it in her palm, contemplating how to get rid of the thing without too much suspicion. For the time being, Ava pins it to her top as if this were just another day.

On the bus to school, she figures out what to do. The vehicle stops and Ava waits until her fellow students have exited to take her turn. As she walks down onto the sidewalk from the elevated position, Ava pretends to stumble. Not enough so that she falls to the ground, but so she slams into the door frame. Her pin presses against the metal and she swiftly reaches through the neck of her shirt to pull off the rubber back. Now freed, the pin clatters onto the asphalt. Ava presses her lips into a smile and walks towards the school. Only once the bus rolls past does she look behind her to check that it's been run over.

Let them find fault with that.

Ava heads into the building and shortly thereafter finds Chloe at her locker. After she'd returned to Hallie's on Saturday, the four girls made pancakes and watched re-runs until Ava deemed them sober enough to face their parents.

"Good morning, dancing queen."

"Hi!" Chloe smiles, peppy as always. "You were pretty great out there yourself."

"Thanks, we were definitely all in rare form."

Chloe closes her locker and reattaches the padlock. "Yeah. I'm gonna need some time before we make a repeat performance."

Shaking her head dramatically, Ava laughs, "My dancing shoes are permanently retired."

They walk to the staircase and pad up together. "What a shame for the rest of the world," Chloe teases. "Or maybe just one person in particular."

"Mhm," Ava hums a neutral sound.

As per usual, the door to English 12 is wide open and welcoming. Ava's heartbeat picks up when she trails in behind Chloe. When she's imagined this moment, Ava thought she would walk right to her desk without a glance in Daniel's direction. But now that the time has come, she finds her eyes drawn to his desk like a pair of magnets.

Physically, nothing has changed about this infuriatingly mesmerizing teacher. Perfectly mussed hair, firmly set jaw, and downcast eyes as he reads over the day's lesson. Daniel's mouth twitches upward in the corner, alerted to Ava's presence when she walks past him. Still, he keeps his eyes fixed on the page.

Look at me. Please.

"Good morning, Mr. Adams!" Chloe chirps, placing a notebook and pencil *just so* on her desk.

He raises his head and pointedly looks just at Chloe. "Good morning. Did you have a pleasant weekend?"

"*The best.* Ava and I went dancing. Do you dance, Mr. Adams?"

"Decidedly not."

"Not even if you had a really good dance partner? Ava—"

"No, never," he cuts her off.

"Leave the man alone," Ava says with a sigh, taking her seat.

Only now does Daniel risk a glance at her, his eyes void of expression. "What excellent advice."

Fourteen

February 19 – March 2

"What excellent advice."

Those words echo in Ava's mind during every waking hour and sometimes in her dreams. As does the detached look in Daniel's eyes as he said them. She had truly hurt him and broken the small circle of trust they'd built up over the past months.

Without their regular conversations to distract her, it doesn't take long for Ava to realize just how much she's come to care for Daniel. The attraction she feels for him is so much deeper than physical looks. He is, in many ways, her equal—mentally and emotionally. Not that she would admit that to anyone else.

So for that entire week, Ava tries to heed her own advice of "leaving the man alone". She keeps her thoughts to herself in class, keeps her head down when they pass each other in the hallway, and keeps her eyes to the paper when it's her turn to read aloud in poetry club.

By the following Monday, Ava is feeling hopeful that maybe time was all Daniel needed. The cool disregard with which he treats her lets Ava know just how wrong she is.

In the convenience store, he told her he didn't really know her. If Ava is going to make things right, sitting back idly will not get her anywhere.

Ever perceptive Chloe assumes that something has happened between them, and it takes all of Ava's restraint not to further break cover and tell her. It's not until Wednesday evening, sitting cross-legged on the floor of the Cuong family library, that an idea occurs to Ava. "Chloe!" Ava breaks the comfortable silence in which they've been working.

"Hmm?" Chloe asks, still hunched over the cello bow she's wiping clean.

"How much attachment does your dad have to the books that *aren't* first-editions?"

Chloe lifts one shoulder in a shrug. "I don't know. Why?"

"I just had an idea. It's probably dumb. Forget I asked."

Placing the bow on the floor beside her, Chloe shakes her head. "There's no such thing as an entirely bad idea."

Ava sighs softly. "Okay, you know how Mr. Adams has been giving me the cold shoulder?"

This catches Chloe's attention. "Yes!" She leans in closer to Ava.

"I was thinking, maybe I could get back in his good graces with a few well-planned gifts."

"I don't think you can bribe Mr. Adams," Chloe says, her eyelids closing slightly.

"No, not a bribe! I... I wish I could explain exactly what happened, but for now, can we just keep it really simple?"

Eager nodding.

"He gave me a secret to keep, and I unintentionally betrayed his trust," Ava frowns, blowing out a long sigh. "I feel terrible and I want things to be right between us again. He's my... favorite teacher."

A toothy grin forms on Chloe's lips. "I *knew* you didn't dislike him as much as you pretended to! So, what's your idea?"

"Remember the lectures he's been giving on the Byronic hero?"

"Of course, he's kind of obsessed."

"I want to give him a special copy of some of those books. As a thank-you, for managing to *slightly* change my opinion," Ava looks down bashfully.

"Ohmygod, I love that idea!" Chloe squeals. She gets to her feet and walks over to the section of paperbacks. "Which ones did you have in mind?"

She looks up at the shelves from her seated position. "All the most angsty novels. *Pride and Prejudice, Wuthering Heights, The Phantom of the Opera,* and *Jane Eyre,* of course. Can't forget how much he loves that one," Ava laughs thoughtfully.

Chloe pulls copies from the bookshelves as Ava names them and then plops back down on the floor, offering them to her friend. "Are you sure your dad won't mind?" Ava hesitantly asks.

"They're not first-editions and they aren't hardcovers. Which means they *aren't* worth a small fortune," Chloe says, placing the books on Ava's lap. "I'm confident he would give you these himself."

"Thank you so much." Ava runs her fingertips lightly over the book covers. "I hope he'll accept them from me."

"Just put them on his desk 'anonymously'," Chloe says, making finger quotations. "Then he'll have no choice."

"Chloe Cuong, what would I do without you?" Ava asks honestly.

"Let's hope we never have to find out."

***

Later that evening, as she's sitting down to eat a very limp-looking salad brought home by Nate, Ava's phone lights up.

(2) New Text Messages from Chris

Spearing a tomato with her fork, she unlocks the phone.

—— **Wednesday, February 28** ——

– **Chris** | 7:35 –

Hey, bub. Katherine wants to know what kind of pin you want.
Since the spaceship had its "accident".

Ava's nose wriggles with displeasure. Her only solace about things with Daniel has been that no one was watching him ignore her. She's been hoping that maybe Wells lost interest, given what he's already seen. Clearly, the assumption is wrong. She types out a reply.

– Ava | 7:36 –

How about an invisible pin?
A weightless, invisible pin.

His response comes immediately.

– Chris | 7:36 –

In other words, you don't want a new one?

Ava smiles and murmurs, "Smart boy."

– Ava | 7:37 –

Ding, ding, ding! We have a WINNER.
Also, when did Katherine ask?
Because office hours are over.
– Ava | 7:40 –
Chris?
– Ava | 7:55 –
CHRISTOPHER whatever your middle name is PRICE!

Her phone is unusually silent as she finishes her dinner. Ava does the dishes that have been collecting in the sink and has started to write a note for the first book when Chris finally responds.

– Chris | 8:52 –

I plead the Fifth.

***

Despite the effort it takes to pry herself out of bed early, Ava decides it was well worth it. For once, she has beaten Daniel to class.

Ava approaches his unoccupied desk reverentially. If viewed objectively, it's nothing spectacular. The desk calendar is filled in sparsely, only with dates of upcoming lessons and tests. Metal paper trays sit empty. Pencil cups are overfilled with various highlighters and writing instruments. Only a small tennis placard on the edge of the desk offers insight into the desk's usual occupant.

Standing in front of Daniel's chair, Ava carefully places the copy of *Jane Eyre* on the center of the desk. Tucked just inside the cover is a note written last night:

N.A./D.W.,

> *You told me you can't look at*
> *me the same anymore,*
> *and I don't blame you.*
> *I had to create a piece of fiction,*
> *but most of the details were true.*
> *Here are some more truths:*

> *-My middle name is Charlotte.*
> *-I graduated from Fordham University in May 2016.*
> *-My favorite color is green. Sometimes I favor sage,*
> *others emerald, but always green.*
> *-I don't deserve your forgiveness,*
> *but I'll regret it for the rest of my life if I don't try.*

She knows there is risk involved in leaving this lying around. Chloe could pick it up, or even another member of the faculty. But in this case, the outcome will make it worthwhile. Ava gives the book one last meaningful look before she steps back and goes to take her seat. She removes her English notebook and a retractable pencil from her leather satchel. Rereading the drafted essay inside, Ava motions like she's underlining the words as she goes.

Heavy footsteps echo down the hallway, getting closer until the teacher enters the classroom. Ava's steady breathing hitches, even as she keeps her head down.

Daniel sets his messenger bag down on the floor beside his desk and takes his seat. "Where...?" He quietly asks no one in particular.

Daring a quick glance up, Ava watches him pick up the book. She drops her chin once more, seeing the notecard flutter out and land beneath his desk. His chair skids back and he bends down to retrieve the note. Moments stretch out, heat creeping up Ava's neck as she knows he's reading her words. Students begin to file into the classroom and find their seats, and the quiet quickly turns to chatter.

Dropping her pencil on the desk, Ava turns in her seat to greet her friends. She does not fail to notice Daniel wordlessly depositing both the note and book into his bag.

***

"Did you pick up your tickets from the office yet?" Chloe asks. Her legs are tucked under her as she lounges in one of the school library's oversized chairs.

"I got them after lunch," Ava replies.

The senior class trip to Walt Disney World leaves in exactly two weeks, on Friday the 16th. Ideas of suntans and rollercoasters are all anyone can seem to talk about. For some of these kids, it'll be their first big trip *without* direct parental supervision.

So far, a good number of teachers have signed up to chaperone along with family members over the age of 21. It took a lot of pleading and bargaining, but Chloe managed to convince Victoria to leave Nate to his own devices for the weekend and come along. Ava was instructed to ask her parents if they'd like to sign up as well, and she quickly shut that one down with excuses of important work obligations.

"Doesn't Disney sound juvenile to anyone else? We're all practically legal adults," Isaac mutters to the currently present members of the poetry club.

Jane replies first. "Don't be so ageist. There are plenty of mature attractions. Haven't you ever been to Epcot?"

"Some of us are here on a scholarship and weren't fortunate enough to vacation in Florida every summer," Chloe adds.

Or at all.

"No one's forcing you to go," Quinn says quietly, not lifting her eyes from the book in front of her.

Frustrated, Isaac exhales loudly. "Whatever. None of you share my intellectual sentiments."

"You sound heavily burdened," Daniel's deep voice announces his presence.

Ava tries to look over at him casually. As if she hasn't spent the past day and a half wondering how he's feeling about her gift and the attached musings.

"We're talking about the senior trip, Mr. Adams," Chloe says. "Are you going to be chaperoning?"

For once, Chloe's meddling falls on grateful ears. Ava has been trying in vain to find out that very thing.

Please say yes.

Daniel pulls a wooden chair towards the group and takes a seat. "How could I turn down a free vacation?" His tone is even, emotionless.

Ava finds herself smiling and quickly presses her lips together, feigning indifference.

"Now that Mr. Adams is here, we can begin," Quinn announces, sitting up in her chair. "Last time the club met, we tried something different. Instead of sharing our own works, today we'll be sharing published poetry that has touched us."

Clutching her moleskin notebook tightly, Ava takes in a deep breath.

"And based on where we left off the last session," Quinn says, visually scanning a list, "Ava's up first."

Ava clears her throat and glances around the circle of chairs at her fellow literature nerds. "I've gone a little outside of the box and chosen song lyrics," she begins, bringing the notebook closer to her eyes. "This is a section taken from *Muscle Memory* written by Lights."

Five sets of eyes stare intently at her, making Ava's pulse race.

This should feel easier than sharing something I've written myself.

Just read the words.

"When I am alone, I/See you in the dark, I/Talk into the empty/Like you were with me," Ava dares a peek up from the paper. Four sets of eyes still watch her, but not the one whose attention she really wants.

Daniel sits slouched down in his seat, making the already small chair look comically tiny in comparison to his body. One hand is balled up into a fist in his lap, the other presses against the side of his face, partially obstructing his view. Dropping her gaze, Ava continues. "Started on a cold night/Felt you in the low light/Noticing the reflex/Taking over me/I see you when I reach/Muscle memory/I feel you when I sleep/Muscle memory."

Ava closes the notebook firmly and wraps both hands around it, bringing it down onto her lap. Her cheeks are red, but at least her pulse has slowed, the hardest part now over.

"That was... kind of sexy," Quinn decides with a small grin.

"I didn't know you had a boyfriend," Hunter quips, finally contributing to the conversation.

Chloe looks at Ava curiously and Ava shrugs. "Well, um... "

Releasing his fist with a sigh, Daniel chimes in, "Chris, right?" He looks at the confused faces of the students and continues, "One of my old students."

It's all Ava can do to nod, grateful that he's saved her. "Ex-boyfriend, but yeah. Chris."

"Interesting. I want to hear about that later," Quinn states. "Next up is Jane."

A faint smile pulls at Ava's lips.

While the other students look eagerly at Jane, Ava finally catches Daniel's eyes. She mouths *'thanks'* and when he nods his acceptance, Daniel almost smiles back.

✳✳✳

Daniel waits around until the poetry club students have all left the library, busying himself with returning chairs to their proper places and re-shelving books. Once he's confident he is alone, he props his messenger bag up on a small table and rifles through it until he locates the copy of *Jane Eyre*. An unsolicited smile presses up into his cheeks as he looks down at the book. Opening the front cover, Daniel's eyes reread the short note for the fourth time today. "Kriff, this girl," he murmurs to himself before putting the contents safely back into his bag.

Does she have any idea how quickly she's crumbling the walls I've worked so

121

hard to maintain?

He makes his way out of the library, through the school hallways, and out the main entrance. Once he's on the sidewalk, starting toward the nearest subway station, Daniel pulls out his phone. Not the type to save contact information, Daniel has no trouble tapping in the number he wants from memory. On the second ring, the call is accepted.

"Daniel, is that you? I'm so glad to hear from you! It's been months since—"

"Mother," he firmly cuts her off, "I think I need some advice."

Fifteen

March 5 - 9

On Monday, Ava leaves the copy of *Pride and Prejudice* on Daniel's desk. Just as before, there is a notecard tucked under the cover:

*-I've never had any pets
because they weren't allowed in my
foster homes, and Nate's allergic,
but I quite like cats.
-I'll be 25 next month.
-I live in East Harlem with my foster brother, Nate.
(Nate is dating Chloe's older sister,
so this is especially sensitive information.)
-I wish you'd come to say hello when you
saw me at Tapper's. Or that I'd noticed you.*

When Daniel saunters into the classroom shortly thereafter, he does a double-take at his desk before peering directly at Ava. A sheepish smile makes itself known to him before she bites into her lower lip and looks away, silently urging him to pick it up.

During class, Ava finally risks raising her hand and Daniel calls on her without much hesitation. When she speaks, he looks at her instead of around the classroom.

On Wednesday, *The Phantom of the Opera* by Gaston Leroux is gifted. Its note reads:

-I think you'd like Nate, once you see past
his overconfidence, he's a great man.
-Chris never was my boyfriend.
He's my best friend and boss.
-Besides meeting you, Chloe has been
the best part of this experience for me.
-You really are the best teacher I've had.
My first, actual, high school experience
was pretty awful. I never stayed at one
school for more than three months at a time.

This time, Daniel picks up the book and walks around to the front of his desk before opening it. He leans against the counter in that easygoing way of his. Not only is there a note inside the cover, but a small child's valentine is placed behind it. It's a red rectangular card with a comic-style Spider-Man and a pre-printed inscription that reads: *My spidey-sense isn't the only thing that's tingling.*

When he sees the valentine, Daniel actually laughs out loud. A delicious, unselfconscious laugh. To Ava's surprise, he addresses her directly. "Have you ever read *The Phantom of the Opera*, Ms. Eliot?"

Being called by her fake name doesn't even bother Ava because he's finally talking to her unprompted. "No, but I like the musical quite a bit."

"As do I," Daniel replies. "But don't go spreading that around." His lips press together in a small, conspiratorial smile.

Ava matches it with one of her own. "Your secret is safe with me, Mr. Adams."

On Friday, Ava brings in the last book. *Wuthering Heights* by Emily Brontë. This one she holds onto until the end of first period, wanting to hand it to Daniel directly. "I'll see you at lunch," she tells Chloe, taking the paperback novel out of her satchel.

Chloe gives her a knowing smile. "See you then."

Despite being one to meddle in the past, Chloe has been surprisingly quiet on the subject of Mr. Adams this week. It's just curious enough to make Ava take pause, but not so much that she's worried. If anything, she's grateful for the privacy. "Mr. Adams," Ava says carefully, his chosen name feeling strange on her tongue. She approaches his desk with the book extended towards him, a small barrier between them.

Daniel looks around the classroom. "Another one, Ava?" His eyebrows arch slightly and he accepts the book.

"It's the last one."

Used to the pattern by now, Daniel begins to lift the cover.

"Wait!" Ava says loudly, reaching out on impulse to grab his hand.

They lock eyes; her grasp having successfully stopped him from reading the note. Ava's breath comes shallow now, and she lets her hand linger for a few long seconds before finally letting go. "I just… I don't want you to read it in front of me," she whispers.

Daniel nods once, his usual facade crumbling in the wake of their touch.

She manages a shaky smile. "Thank you."

"You didn't have to do… this."

"I didn't know what else to do," Ava says with a small sigh. "I'm already failing at my first investigative assignment. Chris is angry with me. Nate's spending his free time with Victoria. Not that I can blame him. I… I don't really have anyone else."

He blinks a few times, allowing her to continue.

"Not that I indifferently just want *someone else*," she quickly adds. Ava focuses her eyes down on Daniel's hands, holding the book like it is something precious. "Is it too far-fetched of me to hope that you'd want to try again after this is all over?"

"Um—"

"Or maybe try again isn't the right phrase! We never had anything, I just thought…" Ava trails off, looking back up. "Nevermind. That's not important right now."

"Ava… "

Embarrassed and finding him too hard to read, Ava turns to go. "This one tells you what you need to know. What you probably already gathered…

125

This is my heaviest burden."

***

Daniel watches as Ava hurries out of the classroom, his mouth agape. She hadn't left him much room to speak and tell her what *he* wanted. Carefully lifting the cover, his brown eyes absorb the words:

It happened on November 12, 2001. I was eight.
They were flying to the Dominican Republic,
but they didn't even make it out of the state.
The plane crashed in Queens.
251 passengers, 9 crew members dead.
Duncan and Gwendolyn Thompson were their names.

His chest tightens as the message sinks in. All of this time he's been worried about what Ava would do with the information about his family, and for what? Her loss had been just as brutal as his, maybe even more so.

Suddenly, certain lines from her poetry take on new meaning. Daniel closes the book and brings it up to rest against his forehead, taking ragged breaths.

She didn't deserve this.

He stays like that for a couple of minutes, just trying to calm himself down and process the new information rationally. Second-period students start to pour into the classroom and Daniel knows his personal time is over. Without thinking, he presses a feather-light kiss to the book before placing it into his bag for safekeeping.

***

It starts as mere curiosity. Daniel just so happens to be leaving the building at the end of the day when Ava does. He walks to the left towards the subway station, and she's just ahead of him, heading for the bus stop. When Ava checks her phone, no doubt realizing she's got a long wait before the next bus, Daniel thinks this is the last he'll see of her until Monday. But she just keeps walking down the sidewalk, towards his usual subway terminal.

As she walks, Ava seems to shed her school persona. Her shoulders pull back proudly. The March afternoon breeze brushes by her, making her tresses rise and fall ethereally. She seems so much freer than Daniel has ever seen her. He doesn't even notice when he's walked right past his stop.

At this point, he should turn back around. Or at least make his presence a few yards back known to Ava. But something inclines him to just keep on. They walk out of the business class district of Manhattan and into diverse East Harlem. The notes she's left him all week make Daniel assume she's heading for her apartment.

He's a little surprised when she ducks into a storefront with red neon lighting. A sandwich board outside encourages passersby to 'come on in'.

Alright creep, this is your chance to leave.

She didn't see you yet, so this doesn't have to be weird.

Internally, Daniel debates whether he should head home or walk inside. More people of various age groups and ethnicities go into what Daniel has gathered is a bar called *Lion Lion.* After a few minutes of standing outside, garnering more unwanted attention, he bites the bullet and heads inside.

More red lighting, this time placed at intervals along the ceiling. It takes Daniel's eyes a little while to adjust to the dim lighting. Two bars are back to back, lined with stools. Further inside are booths lit by candlelight. Patrons in various stages of intoxication talk loudly above the nondescript music. It only takes Daniel a moment to find Ava. She sits on a barstool facing the shelves of liquor bottles, nursing a beer.

Now that he's here, Daniel draws a blank on how to proceed. He could play coy and sit down a few seats away and act surprised to see her, but the way Ava is lounging comfortably makes him think this is a regular haunt of hers. She'd know seeing him here is no coincidence.

Just rip the band-aid off.

Opting for the direct route, Daniel strides over to the bar and swiftly pulls out a stool. "I followed you here," he says bluntly, taking a seat.

Ava spits out the liquid in her mouth, spraying the counter in front of her. Eyes wide, she turns to Daniel and laughs.

Does she make a habit of laughing at stalkers?

Furrowing his brow, Daniel asks, "What's so funny?"

"You!"

"I'm afraid I don't understand. I just felt it was best to be straightforward... I don't know what came over me."

"I know, Dan—," she cuts herself off. "I noticed you trailing me when I walked past the bus stop. It was actually nice to have a tall man following me, in case I needed any type of protection." Ava lifts the bottle to her lips, a laugh echoing into it.

Running a hand back through his hair, Daniel almost smiles. "Are you... You're making a joke, right?"

Ava turns toward him, the brash red lighting of the room amplifying the green flecks in her hazel eyes. "Just a bit, yeah."

In this setting, it's hard to imagine Ava ever passing as seventeen. This thought only serves the purpose of making Daniel feel nervous, out of his element. At school, he is used to having the upper hand.

"To be honest, I'm glad you're here. It makes me think my last note didn't entirely scare you away," she says, her gaze unrelenting.

"No," Daniel shakes his head once. "I don't scare easily. Not from a kindred spirit."

Ava seems to mull this over, taking another sip of her beer. After a minute, Ava places the bottle on the table. "We already know so much about each other, but I'm just realizing we've never had a real, uninterrupted conversation."

Daniel's words come to him automatically. "Ava, would you like to have a drink with me?"

Sixteen

March 9

A va's eyes widen at the proposition. It is both what she's been wishing for and, given their current circumstances, a terrible idea. Her left hand grazes the side of his arm for a brief moment, and she gives him a wistful smile. "Would I like to? Yes, truly. But I don't know if mixing alcohol and public places is a wise plan right now." She arches an eyebrow carefully.

Daniel purses his lips, breaking their gaze to glance down at the leather satchel by the feet of the barstool. The same one she brings to a *high school* five days a week. "Right. That was foolish of me."

He starts to push back in his seat and Ava stops him, this time placing a hand firmly on his shoulder. "I still want to talk, just not here."

"Oh," he says dumbly, beginning to smile.

"Let me just…" Ava bends down to retrieve her bag. Pulling it into her lap, she fishes out a $5 bill and places it underneath the nearly finished beer bottle. "There." She slips off the stool and shoulders the satchel, quirking her head towards the door. "Shall we?"

Daniel nods, at this point ready to follow her anywhere. They make their way out of the bar and back onto the streets, the late afternoon sunlight temporarily blinding. Ava seems used to it, walking with haste down the sidewalk. It takes Daniel a moment to catch up before he is easily matching her shorter strides. "Where are we going?" Daniel inclines his head down toward her.

Ava keeps her head forward as she responds, "My place." Her cheeks heat under his scrutiny. "I can guarantee you no one from ElRo lives there."

Smiling to himself, Daniel looks ahead once more. It's only a few short blocks to Ava's flat. She opens to door to the shared entrance and Daniel walks in behind her. "Up here," she murmurs, heading for the staircase.

They take the stairs two at a time, Ava leading the way until she stops in front of a door. She fishes around her bag for her keyring and produces it with a triumphant grin before inserting a silvery key into the matched lock. With no fanfare, Ava turns the handle and pushes open the door. "So... this is it." She walks inside and drops her bag by the door, waving Daniel on with a gesture over her shoulder.

Ava pauses when the hallway splits into a living room and a small kitchen. "Where would you like to sit?"

"Um," he clears his throat, out of his element.

"Kitchen table?"

"Sure."

At the end of the galley kitchen sits a small round particleboard table, painted white. Ava pulls out one of its four matched chairs and Daniel does the same, taking a seat across from her. "Hello," Ava gives a pageant wave, coaxing a smile out of Daniel.

"Hello," he repeats, now taking the time to look around the small room. "This is nice. Homey."

"Thanks, it's mostly Nate's doing. He brings the stuff home and I generally keep it clean."

"That sounds like a pretty good arrangement," Daniel says, resting his elbows against the table.

"Yeah," she agrees. "Oh! We need drinks!" Ava pops up and rushes over to the fridge. Over her shoulder, she calls out, "Ale or stout?"

"Stout, please."

Ava grabs two bottles of Guinness and pops the lids off. She takes a sip of hers while walking back over to the table. Extending a bottle, Ava takes her seat.

"Thank you kindly," Daniel says, taking the bottle. He gulps down a good few inches of the liquid before resting it down on the table. "So, Ava Thompson, huh? That's going to take some getting used to."

Ava tucks a lock of wavy brown hair behind her ear. "Don't get comfortable saying it yet. My boss has me enrolled until after the Florida trip."

"This boss of yours, what's his angle?"

She purses her lips, searching for the most fitting words, and takes another drink. "Wells is... Great at his job. Best editor-in-chief *The Times* has seen this decade, or so they say. He's not a great people person, though, to put it lightly."

"That must be difficult," Daniel says. He's nursing the beer bottle with one hand and absentmindedly stroking his chin with the other.

"It presents its challenges," Ava nods. "To be honest with you, Wells thinks I'm on board with his idea of a story about your family."

Daniel's eyebrow twitches. "What *are* you writing about?"

"Currently, I'm working on a piece about the life of upper-class adolescents. But it doesn't feel complete." Ava lifts the bottle to her lips and sighs. "Part of me wants to write about how much different my experience has been with everyone thinking I'm from a normal family. Having two parents and a Manhattan zip code really seems to matter to these kids."

"I know what you mean," he frowns. "Unfortunately, I come from the negative side of your story. Kindergarten to twelfth grade in a private school like Eleanor Roosevelt turned me into quite the pompous hellion."

"I don't know if *pompous* is the right word," she teases.

"Pretentious?"

She hums her disapproval.

"Arrogant?"

"No... "

"Patronizing?"

"Mm, a little."

Daniel's foot searches for hers underneath the table. Upon finding it, he gives her a light tap. "You're goading me."

Grinning, Ava taps his foot in return. "I'm sorry. Would you believe me if I said it's a nervous habit?"

"Not really, but I'll let you have your fun," he smiles, bringing the bottle to his mouth again. "For now."

"How chivalrous of you," Ava's voice echoes with laughter.

"Yes, well," Daniel's jaw hangs open, trying and failing to come up with a retort.

Victorious, Ava takes a long sip.

"I've been meaning to say thank you, by the way. For the books and... the rest of it." Daniel's eyes meet hers and hold their gaze steadily. Even now, in privacy, his eyes convey more than he lets on.

Ava fights the urge to look away, despite the uncomfortable feeling churning inside her.

He means the secrets.

He means my parents.

"You're welcome," she whispers.

"And I'm sorry for practically yelling at you that day after the fair, I just..." Daniel exhales loudly, blinking. "It was a lot."

"I know," Ava hesitantly reaches across the table, fingers brushing against the hand he's got wrapped around the bottle. "I'm sorry too."

Daniel laughs once, the sound low, and looks down at her hand. So petite next to his own. "Every time you do that, I feel you've stolen some part of my soul. And I am defenseless." His fingers, slick with condensation, stretch out and dust over hers. "Defenseless and desperate," he all but whispers. Daniel turns her hand over to trace across her palm.

Ava swallows hard, her heart hammering so loudly it feels like it's moments away from bursting out of her chest.

It's just a touch. Calm yourself.

Try as she might, Ava cannot convince herself that her nerve endings are not on fire. Burning from a simple caress.

"Daniel, I—," The sound of a lock turning interrupts her train of thought.

"*Ava, are you home?*" Nate's voice reverberates down the narrow hallway.

"In the kitchen!" Bashful, Ava draws her hand back and mouths '*Nate*'.

Nate's work boots drop to the floor with a thud. "*How was your day? Did ole Danny boy like your love notes?*"

This makes Daniel grin, the toothiest smile Ava has ever seen him wear. "Love notes?" he whispers.

Ava kicks him firmly under the table. "Nate! Would you please shut up?!"

"*What, why?*" Nate now makes an entrance, looking down as he unbuttons his work shirt. "He didn't like 'em?" He slips the shirt off, revealing an olive green t-shirt. Finally, he looks over at the kitchen table. "Oh! Hi Ava and… Danny?" Nate cocks his head to the side, looking mildly amused at this new development.

"Just Daniel is fine." He slides his chair back on the linoleum and strides over to Nate, hand extended. "You must be Nate."

Ava crosses an arm below her chest and anchors the elbow of her other arm on it, resting her chin to the back of that hand. Her lips press together, suppressing a giggle. Nate has to tilt his head back to look at Daniel. "Nate Torres," he says, taking Daniel's hand firmly.

Daniel's expression is cool, unreadable, and he lets Nate shake his hand for entirely too long. Unable to hold her laughter in any longer, Ava releases it and gently chides, "Boys."

Nate lets go of Daniel's hand and puts on a patented Nate Torres grin. "I take it you're staying for dinner. Tell me, Danny, are you a Mets fan?"

***

Hours later, after a dinner of takeaway Thai and a few more beers, Daniel declares it's time for him to head home. Nate protests from his spot, lounging on the floor in front of the television and using the throw pillows for cushions. "But I didn't get to show you the pictures yet!"

"What pictures?" Ava asks, narrowing her eyes at him.

"Your pictures," Nate says before looking to Daniel. "Ace wasn't always the graceful swan that stands before us today."

"*Oh.* I like pictures," Daniel smiles pointedly at Ava and takes a step back into the living room.

Ava scowls over at Nate and moves deftly in front of Daniel. *"No pictures."*

Dropping his head to the floor, Nate laughs with abandon, the way only an excessive amount of beer can draw out of someone.

"Raincheck on the pictures, Torres."

"Introducing you two was a misjudgment on my part," Ava mutters.

"Does it truly count as an introduction if he also lives here?"

"Goodnight, Danny boy! Text me," Nate yells before falling prey to another fit of laughter.

"I don't even... have," Daniel chuckles and shakes his head. "It's late. I overstayed my welcome."

"No," Ava says firmly. "If anything, Nate overstayed *his* welcome in the common areas of our flat," she smiles and nods towards the hallway. "I'll walk you out?"

"I'd like that."

The television light guides their way into the darkness of the hallway. Ava walks with a hand along the wall until her fingers find the light switch. She flips it on and they both instinctively shut their eyes. Without preamble, Ava counts to ten in a whispered voice, opening her eyes once she's finished counting. Daniel gazes down at her, a dorky smile on his lips.

"What?" she asks, finding herself looking up at boundless brown eyes.

"My mother used to do that. When I was little, she would tuck me in every night. After a story, she'd go to turn off the light, and I'd always protest that it was *too dark*. But she promised that if I closed my eyes while she counted to ten, the darkness wouldn't be so bad." He takes his lower lip between his teeth, eyes leaving hers to travel her face. "She was right, of course."

With bated breath, Ava realizes that this is the closest they've ever been physically. "What are you looking at?"

"Your freckles," Daniel replies, the trail of his eyes leave making her skin flush. "They're beautiful."

Ava drops her chin, attempting to distract herself by looking at his feet. "Daniel..."

"Too much?"

"No, never," she murmurs, inhaling deeply. Working up the courage to meet his eyes, she adds, "I just don't know how I'm going to be able to look at you appropriately on Monday if you keep saying things like that."

"Ah," he says, slowly nodding. "I'll rein it in until our next date, then."

Her brows shoot up. "This was a date?"

"What, don't all your dates start with gangly men following you across town?" Daniel teases.

"Oh, is that how you met Isobel?" she counters.

"*Ouch.*" Pressing a hand to his chest, Daniel playfully stumbles towards the door. "Fine. Can we compromise and call this a practice date?"

"That sounds fair."

"Alright then. To rephrase my previous statement, I'll rein it in until I can take you on a *first* date. After that, I make no promises."

Now Ava is the one smiling, dumbfounded.

Daniel presses his thumb against his lips. "Goodnight, Ava." He reaches for the doorknob and twists it.

"Goodnight, Daniel."

Seventeen

March 12 - 15

O n the bus ride to school, Ava's phone nearly falls off her lap, vibrating insistently. She takes firm hold of the bag right before it falls to the ground, and promptly locates her cellphone.

Cillian "The General" Wells is Calling...

Ava's stomach knots at the name and she forces herself to take a deep, cleansing breath before answering. "Good morning, Mr. Wells."

"Ms. Thompson, I trust you're well."

This greeting makes gives her pause.

When has he ever asked that?

"Y-yes, sir. Thank you. And yourself?"

"Just fine," he says crisply. "Alright, enough small talk. I'm calling to check in on your story. Without that handy camera, you've left things up to my imagination. Is everything still going according to plan?"

According to your *plan? Absolutely not.*

"Yes, sir. Just putting the final touches on my last draft before the class trip," Ava's voice sounds collected, believable even.

"Excellent," Wells almost sounds pleased. "I'll hold off on congratulating you until I have the final copy in my hands."

"Of course."

"That's all I called to discuss. Thank you, Ms. Thompson."

He ends the call before she can reply.

I don't think he's ever said 'thank you' either.

Fighting off feelings of guilt, Ava clicks the screen of her phone off and tosses it back inside her bag.

I have nothing to be sorry for. Writing the article he wants would be a conflict of interest now.

He'll still get a great story, just not the one he's expecting.

She presses her lips firmly together, distracting herself with thoughts of Friday evening. Despite the mistakes she's made, Daniel has shown he's willing to give her a chance. Old Ava might have scoffed at that and sided with her employer, but there's no more denying that these past two and a half months have changed her. For better or worse.

When the bus stops a block away from ElRo, Ava gets up to leave with the other students.

Act normal. No excessive smiling.

Especially around Daniel.

And Chloe. That girl is too smart for her own good.

Ava is so focused on her mental preparation that she doesn't notice Daniel loitering outside of the school. "Ms. Eliot," he says, as she nearly walks right past him. His voice is neutral, just a teacher addressing his student.

Her head turns sharply, and her eyes zero in on Daniel. He's dressed down from his usual work clothes, his tweed jacket replaced with a navy blue cable-knit sweater. The sleeves are rolled up once, revealing a black and white gingham shirt, which also peeks out at the collar.

Stop staring! Pick your jaw up off the floor before someone sees.

"Good morning, Mr. Adams." She enunciates his name carefully.

"Did you finish your assignment?" Daniel asks, louder than he needs to be.

"Yes, sir."

"Good. Since you're early, you can help me pass out today's exam," he says before walking up closer. Lowering his voice, he adds, "I couldn't wait until class to see you. I've been thinking about you all weekend."

A pleased smile spreads out across Ava's features as they walk together into the building. "I've been doing much of the same," she admits.

"I don't even have your phone number," he says with a sigh. Daniel is walking half a pace ahead of her down the hallway, giving the illusion that he's exercising authority.

"What if someone got a hold of your phone?"

"I won't save you as a contact," he says, starting up the staircase.

Ava frowns at the back of his head. "Am I that temporary to you?"

Stopping right in the middle of the stairwell, Daniel shifts his body halfway towards her. "No."

He meets her eyes with such intensity that Ava has no reason to do anything but nod.

"I'll save your name as something else," he suggests. Daniel runs a hand back through his hair as he thinks. "Rosalind?"

"That's... kind of perfect," she agrees, awarding him with a smile. "You can be Orlando."

As You Like It *is officially my favorite play.*

Daniel matches her smile and pulls his phone out of his messenger bag. "What's your number?"

She recites it to him. They both wear contented expressions for the rest of the short walk to English 12. The first to arrive, Daniel turns the handle and holds the door open for her.

"Thank you," Ava says, bowing her neck in a mock curtsy before entering.

Walking into the room, their body language changes automatically. Ava walks over to her desk and Daniel to his, each without further regard for the other. It feels strange given the exchange they just had, but necessary.

Other students come in as the clock ticks closer to the first-period bell. "Whoa," Chloe announces as she enters the room.

Both Ava and Daniel turn their heads to look at the younger girl.

"This room feels..." Chloe holds her index finger out in the air and looks up, trying to decide on a word. "Weird."

Ava laughs and gestures to her wristwatch. "Yeah, because everyone's mentally checked out. We leave on Friday!"

Bringing the finger against her lips, Chloe ponders this. "Mm, I don't think that's it."

Daniel shakes his head softly to himself and turns to the blackboard.

"I think you're too energetic for this early in the morning, and on a Monday no less," Ava counters.

Taking her seat, Chloe groans. "I woke up early with cramps from the netherworld. My current existence is courtesy of cà phê sữa đá and Midol."

Comprehension brightens Ava's eyes. "That's it! Our cycles must have synced up."

"Ohhh," she nods, her dubious look disappearing. "Yeah, that makes sense."

Relieved that she's gotten out of that one easily enough, Ava's shoulders release their tension. "Do you want to skip the library and do our homework at the cafe down the street today? We can gorge ourselves on hot chocolate and pastries."

"Yes! That sounds perfect."

***

Ava stands in the first-floor hallway at her locker when her phone vibrates. She hesitates for a few seconds, thinking maybe Wells has decided to check in again. After working up the courage to speak with her boss, Ava locates the phone inside of her bag and clicks the home button.

(1) New Text Message from Unknown Number

Bringing her bottom lip into her mouth, Ava protectively brings the phone closer to her body.

This has *to be Daniel.*

She looks both ways down the hall for any sign of Chloe and, not finding her, presses the messaging app.

—— **Monday, March 12** ——

– Unknown Number | 11:23 –

Good day and happiness, dear Rosalind.

Ava laughs loudly, attracting the attention of two underclassmen walking by. They give her a strange look before resuming their conversation. Ava covers her mouth a moment too late, a wide smile hidden under her palm. With one hand, she saves the number as *Orlando* before responding with another quote.

– Rosalind | 11:24 –

What would you say to me now, an I were your very very Rosalind?

Her phone immediately shows that he is typing. Seconds later, Daniel's message pops up.

– Orlando | 11:24 –

I would kiss before I spoke.

Ava reads the message over three times, her body feeling light as a feather. It takes every ounce of her self-control not to jump up and down with delight. He could have used any line in the play and *that* is what he chose.

I feel like an actual teenager.

I've... never felt like this before.

The warning bell sounds, alerting Ava to the start of sixth period. She shuts her locker and sends out her response.

– *Rosalind | 11:27 –*

Put your money where your mouth is, Orlando.

***

The next few days seem to inch by. Chloe and Ava spend every afternoon together planning out what they'll do at Disney and how they can fit all the clothes they'll need into carry-on luggage. Daniel texts Ava after class each day, and she forces herself to take her time responding. Wells doesn't call again, but Chris does.

Ava is dancing through her packing list when her phone lights up with his name. She drops the crop top onto her bed and pauses the music to answer the call. "Hey, stranger."

"Hey, bub. It's good to hear your voice."

"You too. It's been what? Two weeks?"

"Something like that."

"How've you been?" Ava asks, starting to pace around the room.

"Really good. That's actually why I'm calling. Or part of the reason. I also called to say I'm sorry for being such a crappy friend these past few months."

Ava nods to herself but tries to keep her voice cool. "How do you mean?"

"I was really hard on you about work, and kind of a dick to that teacher—,"

"Daniel, his name is Daniel," she interjects.

Chris' deep chuckle fills her ear. "Yeah, I was a dick to *Daniel* when I went to the school for you. Honestly, I was feeling kind of jealous."

Calling yourself my boyfriend made that pretty obvious.

"Why were you jealous?"

"I don't know... For a while there, I was the only guy in your life other than Nate. And he's your brother, so he would never vie for your affections. I wouldn't either, but something... changed for me, right after you took this assignment. Not seeing you around the office every day made me miss you. Then we're out for drinks one night and *Daniel* comes along and it's so obvious that you're into him... Something inside me just snapped," Chris breathes out deeply into the phone. "It made me think *I* was into you."

Ava chews on her lower lip while he speaks.

"I should have just talked to you, but I bottled it up and pushed you away as a result. That was really stupid of me, and I'm sorry."

"Hey, it's alright, Chris. I should have been upfront with you, too. I've known that I have feelings for Daniel for a while now, but I was in denial until recently."

"We kind of suck at talking about our feelings."

"Truer words never have been spoken," she agrees with a soft laugh. "I'm sorry too."

"Apology accepted. Can we go back to being best friends again? I need my bub."

"Yes, please! Now tell me why you're doing so well!"

"Okay. Don't freak out, but I met someone."

"Katherine?"

"I-how'd you know?"

Ava nearly snorts. *"I plead the Fifth.* The last thing you texted me two weeks ago. Ring any bells?"

"Oh."

"*Oh*, is right! So when did that start?"

"It all sort of just happened. You weren't at the office to talk to and Wells always deferred the background work to Katherine. We started monitoring your feed together until Wells took over. I didn't have the slightest notion that she was into me until about a month ago, the week after you were sick. By this point, the whole office was watching the footage once Wells was done with it. So we were watching Daniel apologize to you in the hallway about how unprofessional your relationship had been and Katherine just turns to me and gushes, *'Isn't it so romantic?'*. And I muttered something grouchy that I don't care to repeat."

Laughing softly, Ava urges, "Go on!"

"For some reason that I still can't fathom, she took pity on me. Katherine said she could tell I needed a drink and someone to talk to, and asked me out that same night."

"This is amazing, *Katherine Porter* asked you out?"

"I know. I'm slow on the uptake."

Smiling into the phone, Ava asks, "So you really like her?"

"Yeah, Ava. I truly do."

"Well, not that you need it, but you guys have my blessing."

"Maybe after you get back next week we can all hang out together? I'd invite you rock-climbing with us, but I know that's not your scene."

"Sure!" Only now does Ava realize she's failed to keep her friend in the loop with something major. "There's something I actually need to tell you, too."

"Hmm?"

"As I said, I have real feelings for Daniel and—,"

"You're not writing the story that Wells wants," Chris supplies.

142

"Yeah. I know this is a huge letdown for you, but I promise I'll make sure Wells knows this is one hundred percent on me. I just can't betray Daniel and his family."

"I don't blame you, bub. Like I've said before, a huge part of journalism is trusting your instincts. But what *are* you going to write?"

"I'm going to write about me."

Eighteen

March 16

Most of the students and chaperones on *American Airlines* flight 2691 fall asleep shortly after boarding.

ElRo had arranged shuttles from the school to the airport, just a short twenty-minute ride into Queens. Their flight departed LaGuardia Airport at 6:10 in the morning, meaning they'd all woken up in the middle of the night.

Ava, Chloe, and Quinn sit together in a row of three towards the back of the plane. The two teenage girls are among the passengers that chose to extend their slumber. Ava, on the other hand, is wide awake.

It's only a third of the way into the three-hour flight and Ava can't stop fidgeting in her seat. The small foil packet of peanuts and ginger ale she received after the airplane reached altitude have already been finished. Ava brought a book along in hopes of catching up on her reading, but she's read the same paragraph six times now and still can't remember what it says.

Leaning against her armrest, Ava looks down the aisle in both directions. Familiar faces of her classmates mix in with those of their family members and other people that just so happen to be on the same flight.

The one face I wish to see most is nowhere to be found.

Daniel had waved to her earlier from the window of a shuttle, but that one had been full, so Ava couldn't join him or even say hello. The airport security line moved extra slowly that morning and, choosing to err on the side of caution, Ava was among the last people to go through it. She couldn't risk someone seeing the birthday — or name — on her driver's license. Once they made it to their gate, Ava went to get coffee, resulting in her and Chloe being among the last passengers to board the plane. Wherever Daniel found a seat has been deemed a mystery to Ava.

A sudden jolt makes Ava gasp and face forward in her seat again.

It's just a little turbulence.

A little rough patch of air.

She closes her eyes and tries to focus on her breathing.

Inhale deeply and hold.

Count to seven. Slowly breathe out.

Repeat.

The plane bumps every couple of minutes, keeping Ava firmly planted in her seat. She tightly grips both armrests and risks opening her eyes to look at the girls next to her.

How are they sleeping through this?

After a few more minutes, the plane seems to find clear air. Ava stares at the illuminated seatbelt sign until it blinks off. She unfastens the buckle and stands up quickly, only to find her legs wobbly. Gripping the seat in front of her, Ava turns her head towards the back of the plane. The lavatory door has a red light on it, indicating that it's occupied.

Lacking the patience to wait, Ava carefully walks along the aisle until she reaches the end of the cabin. Abruptly, the plane drops. The descension is short, something that a seasoned flyer wouldn't bat an eye at. But this is Ava's first time on an airplane since she was a child coming to the States. She hasn't flown since the plane crash that caused her parents' death.

Ava reaches out wildly to brace herself against the small expanse of wall, fingers grasping for purchase. A ragged breath escapes her, along with a single tear.

Pull yourself together.

The plane isn't going to crash.

Carefully, she slides down the wall and sits on the floor outside of the bathroom. A man slides the door open and looks taken aback when he notices her on the ground. With a slight scowl, he walks around her and back towards his seat. Drawing her knees to her chest, Ava wraps her arms around herself and closes her eyes.

Don't think about them.

Do not go down that path.

Ava rocks her body gently, tiny whimpers escaping her.

"Ava?"

Daniel.

Lifting her head, Ava takes in the sight of him, and a new set of tears well up in her eyes. "D-Daniel," her voice comes out small and unsteady.

"Oh, sweetheart," Daniel murmurs, crouching down in front of her. He ghosts a hand across Ava's hair and onto her shoulder. "I looked for you when they started boarding." Daniel's thumb absentmindedly kneads into her clavicle. "I knew I couldn't sit next to you, but I hoped to at least be close by."

Wiping at her cheeks, Ava peers at his hand. "I'm so embarrassed that you f-found me like this."

"Is this your first flight since the accident?" Daniel's hand moves down her shoulder and he begins slowly stroking her arm.

"Mhm," she hums.

His hand is so large. How have I never noticed this before?

"Kriff," he curses softly. Daniel lifts her chin with his free hand. "I should have been there for you. It hurts me to think of what's going through your head right now, but I *promise* you we're going to be okay."

Staring up into his eyes, Ava nods once. "The logical part of me knows that. I just…" She sighs.

Daniel presses his lips together and mirrors her nod. On his knees, he moves next to her and sits down. The quiet of the airplane and Ava's emotional status leave Daniel no room to hesitate before wrapping an arm around her. If she weren't so upset, Ava may have balked at this first minor act of intimacy. Instead, she drops her head against his shoulder gratefully.

146

"I'm so sorry, Ava," he whispers, lips pressed against her hair. "I wish I could take your pain away, replace all that hurt with the happiness you deserve."

Her eyes flutter shut. "Do the memories ever haunt you too?" Ava unwraps her arms from her knees and hesitantly reaches out for Daniel's leg, settling a hand just above his knee. She can feel the muscles in his thigh tense up at the initial contact, but relax against her touch.

"Every time I get behind the wheel of a car. Which fortunately isn't that often, since I live in the city," Daniel laughs once, self-deprecating. "When I make a yearly visit upstate to see my mother, it's honestly worse. I'm a terrible son, but keeping her at arm's length makes it easier to keep the demons at bay."

Ava gives his thigh a firm squeeze. "Did she ever remarry?"

"No. Falling in love with my father was never part of her plan. She was married to her job before she met him and buried herself in work after... the accident."

"You were just a kid, Daniel," Ava says softly.

She can feel him shaking his head and his body goes stiff.

"We don't have to talk about this anymore. I'm just glad you're here."

He places a kiss gently atop her head. "Me too."

***

Once the passengers start to wake up and move around, Ava and Daniel return to their respective seats. Ava spends the rest of the flight sharing Chloe's earbuds, listening to her acoustic folk playlist.

A pleasant chime sounds and an announcement comes through the speakers: *"Good morning folks, we have just been cleared to land at the* Orlando International Airport. *As we start our descent, please make sure your seat backs and tray tables are in their full upright position. Make sure your seat belt is securely fastened and all carry-on luggage is stowed underneath the seat in front of you or in the overhead bins. Thank you."*

Squirming in the middle seat, Chloe repeatedly taps both armrests and makes an excited humming noise. "You *guys!* We're almost there!"

Quinn opens the window cover halfway, morning light shining across their row. "Finally, some real sunshine! I hope it's warm when we get there."

"Same here. I only brought one pair of jeans and I'm wearing them," Ava says, gesturing to her lap.

"I'm sure no one would let you go cold," Chloe says in an undertone, looking down her nose at Ava.

"We should buy matching pink Minnie Mouse hoodies to watch the fireworks show in. We'll be the new Pink Ladies." Quinn suggests.

"What a good idea," Ava agrees. She covertly sticks the tip of her tongue out at Chloe.

"Don't forget Jane! She's our fourth roomie… wherever she is." Chloe leans over the armrest between her and Ava, attempting to see down the aisle.

Ava sits back in her seat, trying to make herself as small as possible so that Chloe can look. "She was ahead of me in line for Starbucks, so she probably got a good seat up front."

"Oh," Chloe breathes, moving back into her own space.

Out the window, tiny buildings come into view as the plane angles forward, descending toward its destination. Ava stares through the window, both mesmerized and temporarily paralyzed by the view.

"My least favorite part is coming up," Chloe murmurs, also captivated.

"What's that?"

"The landing."

"What's wrong with the landing?" Ava asks, tearing her eyes away from the small panel to look at her friend.

"I hate the way the plane bumps when the wheels hit the ground."

"Great," she says with a groan.

She looks back to the window, cars below them getting more lifelike in size. A mechanical groaning sounds, the wheels of the plane being freed from their chamber. The plane continues on its downward path and just as it looks like they're going to land on top of the airport, they fly over it and land on the tarmac with a heavy *thud*. Ava breathes out loudly with relief. "I hate flying. Can we drive home?"

Chloe laughs and just shakes her head.

As the airplane speeds down the concrete, the speakers sound with the voice of one of the flight attendants. *"Ladies and gentlemen, welcome to* Orlando International Airport. *Local time is 9:03am, and the temperature is 78 degrees. For your safety and comfort, please remain seated with your seat belt fastened until the Captain turns off the fasten seat belt sign. On behalf of* American Airlines *and the entire crew, I'd like to thank you for joining us on this trip and we are looking forward to seeing you onboard again soon. Have a nice day!"*

Despite the direction they've just been given, the sound of seat belts clicking open fills the cabin. The plane has slowed substantially and through the small window, Ava can see the terminal a short distance away. She unfastens her seat belt and leans down to reach under the seat for her satchel.

Textbooks and laptop have been replaced with sunglasses, portable phone charger and other personal items. Ava shuffles things around until she locates the MagicBand the school has issued to everyone on the trip. It's a thick wristband that acts as the key to their hotel room, entry to theme parks, and even a way to pay for food on Disney property. Ava put preference aside at the pleading of her roommates, who insist the theme of the trip be all things Minnie Mouse. The MagicBand they chose is pink and covered in tiny hearts and the aforementioned mouse. Ava slips it over her wrist and snaps it snuggly in place.

Chloe holds out her left arm, and Quinn is soon to follow. They must have put their MagicBands on during the flight. "They look so cute!" Quinn decides.

"I'm so excited! Can we get a picture with Peter Pan?" Chloe asks. "I hope they have a cute, funny one like Disneyland had."

***

In the passenger pickup area, two large white buses with *Disney Transport* printed on the side in familiar writing await them. Ava hands her small wheeled suitcase to a woman who offers to stow it underneath one of the buses. She looks out at the crowd of people and easily locations Daniel, towering over most of them. It only takes a moment for him to sense her gaze and turn his head with a smile. Ava feels her skin warming from both the Florida heat and his attention.

"Did you have a pleasant flight, Mr. Adams?" she asks over the noise of so many competing voices.

"I usually dislike flying, but this one wasn't so bad," his voice carries.

Ava matches his smile with one of her own and waves her fingers at him before stepping onto the bus.

It's a relatively short drive to *Disney's Pop Century Resort*, one of the lower-priced properties. The rooms the school booked are in the 1980s section of the resort. A 40 foot Rubik's Cube is erected like a monument on one side of their building, with Roger Rabbit on the other. Across the courtyard, a giant Sony Walkman and accompanying headphone set anchors another building. In the middle of the courtyard is a computer-shaped pool, complete with a spongy keyboard that offers guests an alphabet-filled pool deck area.

Ava's room with the girls is on the third floor. They walk inside and immediately start to claim which side of each of the queen beds is their own, who gets to take the first shower, and how much dresser space each girl will be allotted. Lingering near the doorway seems like the safest course of action until the commotion dies down. Ava slips off her shoes and is setting her bag down on top of her suitcase when it vibrates.

She pulls her cellphone out and opens the door, stepping into the open-air hallway with socked feet. Ava clicks the screen on and types in her passcode while shutting the door.

(1) New Text Message from Orlando

—— **Friday, March 16** ——
– **Orlando | 9:57** –
Do you want to watch the fireworks tonight?

Nineteen

March 16, continued

⚜

After giving everyone an hour to settle into their rooms, group texts alert them that the bus to *Magic Kingdom* will arrive at 11 am. Ava changes out of her jeans into more weather-appropriate shorts, bleached denim with a raw hem. She keeps on the shirt she'd chosen for the flight and wears her shoulder-length hair loose for the time being.

In favor of traveling light, she places her sunglasses atop her head, wraps an elastic hair tie around her wrist, and pockets a small wad of cash. "You guys about ready to head down?" Ava asks, perched on the edge of the bed she'll be sharing with Chloe.

Jane is sitting at the small desk next to the television, between the two queen beds. She looks up from her phone and smiles. "I just got us FastPasses for Space Mountain, the Jungle Cruise, and the Magic Tea Party. So yes, I've been ready."

From the bathroom where the other two are curling their hair, Quinn calls out, "How the heck did you do that?"

"Our whole class trip is linked on the app. I can see what everyone else picked too."

Curious, Ava stands up and walks over to the desk. "Can I see that?"

"Sure," Jane says, handing over her phone.

Ava scrolls through the list of names and the character avatars her classmates and their chaperones had picked. "Aww, Chloe! Victoria's avatar is Marie from Aristocats."

"She's such a dork!" Chloe says with a laugh, walking out of the bathroom. Her glossy black hair is curled in loose waves around her face, nearly touching her shoulders.

Looking up at the sound of her voice, an awed expression comes over Ava. "You look like a princess."

Chloe beams, her cheeks coloring at the compliment. "Thanks," she says meekly. "We have to add Victoria to those reservations, Jane. She's already mad at me for talking her into coming and then deserting her to room with Ms. Richardson."

Ava scrolls quickly, looking in earnest for Daniel's name. She forgets to be looking for his chosen name and almost passes over *Nico Adams*. He hasn't selected an avatar and no FassPass+ entries show up next to his name. Holding back a frown, she hands the phone back to Jane.

"One sec," Jane says to Chloe. Her fingers dance over the screen and a few seconds later, she looks up with a grin. "Done. Anyone else?"

"Can you guys keep a secret?" Chloe asks, waving the girls toward her conspiratorially.

"Who would I even spill a secret to?" Jane deadpans, staying seated.

Quinn emerges from the bathroom, blonde hair pulled back into a high ponytail, with little pieces pulled out and curled into ringlets. "What are guys gossiping about?"

"Whatever, don't circle around me so I can whisper. Take all my fun away." Chloe breathes out a little sigh and shakes her head. "Okay so, you can't let on that you know this *at all*, but Victoria has the hots for Mr. Adams. If you mention this to her, she would flat out deny it, but it's the truth."

Ava's eyes narrow at Chloe, but Chloe doesn't acknowledge this.

"Having two chaperones for our group of four wouldn't raise any red flags," Jane says, already locating Mr. Adams and adding him to their plans. "Victoria owes me, big time."

Grinning, Chloe's eyes briefly meet Ava's. "Oh, I'm sure she'll be grateful."

***

Despite it being a Friday in March, a school day no less, *Magic Kingdom* is buzzing with people.

Emerging from the tunnel under the railroad, the New York tourists step out onto *Main Street, U.S.A.* Twentieth-century style buildings in pleasing pastels greet them, while in-character cast members work kiosks selling souvenirs. It looks like a small town, circled around a flagpole where Pluto is currently doing a meet-and-greet. Past that, buildings line either side of the street leading up to Cinderella's Castle in the distance.

"Oh my gosh, look!" Chloe squeals, pointing to four men dressed in straw hats, striped vests, bow-ties, spats, and taps of varying vivid colors. "It's *The Dapper Dans!*" She waves them on and speed-walks toward a building on the left-hand side called *The Emporium.*

Ava, Quinn, Jane, and Victoria all follow. They join in a small crowd as the four men pick up organ chimes and play *Zip-a-Dee-Doo-Dah.* Halfway through, they start to sing in harmony. Chloe is grinning and dancing along, and when they fade into *It's A Small World*, she lightly taps the arms of Victoria and Ava. "C'mon, they said to whistle," she whispers loudly. All four girls oblige, though to call it whistling would be a kindness in some of their cases.

The Dapper Dans end the setlist with *The Mickey Mouse Club March* and they all chant along, "M-I-C-K-E-Y M-O-U-S-E!" Applause erupts when the men walk off, Chloe by far the loudest. She turns to her friends with an elated smile, "That was so fun. I feel like I'm six years old!"

"You're embarrassing like a six-year-old," Quinn mutters.

Victoria shoots the younger girl a scowl before addressing the group, "Alright ladies, when's our first FastPass?"

Jane pulls her phone out from her back pocket and clicks on the app. "The Magic Tea Party at noon. We've got about twenty minutes to kill."

"I haven't eaten anything today except peanuts on the plane," Quinn says, rubbing her stomach. "And that was five hours ago."

"There's only one real quick-service restaurant in this part of *Magic Kingdom.* Unless you want ice cream or baked goods," Jane supplies.

"Raincheck on the ice cream!" Ava quips.

"I second that notion," Quinn agrees. "What's the quick-service place?"

"*Casey's Corner,*" Jane says. "It's hot dogs and all the fixings."

"Mama never buys hot dogs, that actually sounds delicious," Chloe nods eagerly.

"Hot dogs it is. Lead the way, Jane."

While the five girls walk down Main Street, Ava hangs towards the back of the group. She produces her cellphone from her shorts' pocket and composes a quick text message to Daniel.

—— **Friday, March 16** ——
– Rosalind | 11:42 –
Casey's Corner for lunch?

She hasn't seen him since the buses let out, so Ava can only assume he's mixed in with another group for the time being. Clicking the screen off, Ava looks back up, taking in the picturesque surroundings. They walk past a sweets shop, an art gallery, a jewelry store, and multiple apparel shops. Each one gives the illusion that they've stepped back in time.

A woman with a large bundle of balloons walks by. She's offering everything from foiled character face balloons to colorful mouse silhouetted ones.

"Ooooh, guys!"

"Later, Chloe," Victoria chides gently.

Chloe pushes her lower lip out sadly and nods.

Casey's Corner is the last building on the left-hand side of Main Street, U.S.A. It's painted yellow and white and embellished with the large *C* of the Cincinnati Reds logo. Victoria holds the door open so the girls can file inside.

The smell of fresh french fries mingles in with the red and white pinstriped walls and Coca-Cola chandeliers, giving off a very distinctive 1950s vibe. Joining the queue, Ava looks up at the menu board and reads her options. "Teriyaki hot dog? That sounds… Weird."

Someone a few people ahead of her in line turns his head around. "Don't knock it 'til you try it."

Ava lets out a soft laugh and gives the man half a smile. "I'll take your word for it."

He shoots her a quick thumbs-up before returning to his prior conversation.

A string of vibrations in Ava's back pocket alerts her to new messages. Her smile turns into a real one as she covertly brings the phone out and holds it just below her chest, angled so only she can see the screen.

(3) New Text Messages from Orlando

– Orlando | 11:45 –

Already beat you to it!

These boys can eat.

Hot dogs are not very romantic first date food.

Ava's mouth opens when she reads the last message. Walking forward to keep the line moving, she quickly types out a response.

– Rosalind | 11:46 –

This is NOT a first date either.

Where ever did your patience go, Daniel Woodard?

Three flashing dots let her know he is actively replying. Chewing on her bottom lip, Ava stands up tip-toed to try and peer into the adjoining dining room for a glimpse of him. Her phone buzzes and she nearly lets it slip from her hands.

– Orlando | 11:46 –

I've been very patient.

Some might say too patient.

She has time to type one last message, only one customer ahead of her now.

– Rosalind | 11:48 –

Your reward will outweigh the effort, I promise you.

Ava slides the phone back into her pocket for safe-keeping and steps up to the register, where a smiling man wearing an umpire's uniform greets her. His name tag identifies him as Rick from Des Moines. "Hello there! Welcome to Casey's Corner! Thank you for your patience," another happiest-place-on-earth smile, "Do you know what you'd like to order?"

"Yes, erm, Rick," she starts, glancing down at his name tag again. "I think I'll have the corn dog nuggets meal with a Coke. Are the nuggets any good?"

"Oh, yes!" Will agrees, already punching in her order. "Would you like to add a side of cheese sauce?"

"No, thank you." Ava scans her MagicBand and steps aside so the next customer can order.

Once all five of them have their meals on red plastic trays, Jane leads them outside to the terrace. "Guys! Over here!" Hallie calls from her table a few meters away. She's already sitting with Krista and Shawn, filling all but one seat of their small circular table.

Ava spots Daniel sitting with Logan, Isaac, and another adult she doesn't recognize. She smiles without meaning to and Logan seems to take this personally. "Hey, Ava. I didn't know you liked beef." He wiggles his eyebrows, ensuring she doesn't miss the message.

Unable to help herself, Ava rolls her eyes and walks right past his table. Shawn stands up and starts pulling tables together for the girls. They put their trays down and grab chairs to carry over. "Great minds think alike," Krista says, gesturing with her hot dog.

"Woman cannot live on airline snacks alone," Jane agrees.

Ava and her roommates, plus Victoria, take their seats. They discuss plans for the day and the weekend over a greasy and satisfying lunch. As they are finishing up, Daniel approaches the table with his left hand buried in the front pocket of his shorts. They're a navy color so dark it's almost black. Along with the yellow snapback and white t-shirt, this is the most casual Ava has ever seen him dress. He gives a half-wave to the table with his right hand. "Good afternoon, everyone."

Jane turns her head halfway, looks back at her tray, and then does a double-take. "Nico Adams? I didn't know you *owned* a pair of shorts… "

Daniel's brow furrows slightly, and he breathes out with a laugh. "Well, looks can be deceiving, Jane."

Half of the girls ogle him wordlessly. Seconds go by and the tips of his ears peeking through his hair turn pink. Finally, he clears his throat. "So, I'm told that I was added as a chaperone to your plans today."

Chloe, part of the non-ogling half, speaks up, "Yes! We were told one adult to every two students, and you were the last one available."

Jane opens her mouth in protest, only to be kicked under the table. She and Chloe share a meaningful look that ends in Chloe dragging her eyes over to Victoria. "Oh!" Jane whispers and then raises her voice to address the table. "That's right, Nico. I hope you're up for the teacups!"

"Somehow, I'm not surprised," he chuckles. "Lead the way, girls."

✳✳✳

Sometimes, things work in Ava's favor so that she can sit near Daniel, and other times they do not. For the Magic Tea Party, they ride with Victoria in a big purple teacup and Daniel spins the center disk until they nearly puke. He's far away from Ava on the Jungle Cruise and on an entirely different spaceship for Space Mountain. But she doesn't let it keep her from having fun. On the contrary, Ava thinks of this trip as her last hoorah with Chloe and the gang. She wants to make every moment count.

Inside *Mickey's Star Traders*, Ava pulls Chloe over to a wall of mouse-ear hats. "Let's get something matching."

"Yes!" Chloe agrees excitedly.

The pair model different hats, everything from classic Mickey, *Epcot*'s Figment, and even characters from *Cars*. Seeing the mini fashion show, the other girls soon join in.

Ava keeps coming back to the golden mouse ears with a rose in the middle, designed to look like Belle's dress from the ballroom scene. "What do you think about these?"

"I think they look perfect on you," Chloe says, looking at Ava's reflection in the mirror. "How about we each pick a different princess?"

"Yeah!"

Chloe chooses a turquoise and green Ariel hat, Victoria a red and blue Snow White hat, Quinn a pink and light blue Aurora hat, and Jane picks a purple and pink Rapunzel hat. After purchasing their items, the girls wear them out of the store. "Mr. Adams, can you please take our picture?" Chloe asks, leading the group in front of the Tomorrowland Indy Speedway.

"Of course."

Handing over her phone, Chloe puts herself in the middle of the group next to Ava. "Smile and say *Disney!*" she instructs.

"One, two, three," Daniel counts down, snapping candid shots in the meantime. "Disney."

"Disney!" Five voices echo before striking a final pose.

Chuckling to himself, Daniel nods. "Alright, perfect." He steps forward to hand the phone to Chloe and, to his surprise, she pulls him forward.

"We need one with you in it," Chloe insists. She smiles sweetly, the picture of innocence.

"I don't really do photographs," Daniel says carefully.

"Well, this isn't a *photograph.* It's for my Instagram story." Chloe continues to smile, unwavering.

With a small sigh, Daniel hands her the phone and moves to take Chloe's place. "Just one picture, Ms. Cuong."

"Yes, sir!" she says with a grin, motioning for the girls to squeeze in closer to their teacher.

Ava's lips curve upwards as Daniel moves between her and Jane, his hip bone brushing against hers. "Say *Disney*," Chloe orders.

***

The rest of the day is spent alternating between eating and waiting in line for rides. Mostly they agree on what to do, but Jane has to convince them to give The Carousel of Progress a chance. She and Daniel are the only ones who seem to really enjoy it.

They cross paths with other ElRo students throughout the day, but ultimately stay a group of six. As it gets darker, Ava and Daniel become more comfortable walking together and making conversation. They stay within earshot of everyone else, so the talks are about light topics like favorite movies and authors.

Around 8:45, the group squeezes into the Hub in front of Cinderella's Castle. The area is already packed with people, some of whom have held their spots for the better part of an hour. "We should have planned this out better," Victoria says, taking a seat on the ground in the middle of the five others.

"I hate to say I told you so, but..." Jane grumbles.

"It's fine. We have a good view of the castle and the sky, being front and center won't make the experience that much better," Daniel says calmly. "In fact, why don't I grab some Mickey bars for everyone to make the time go by?"

A chorus of yeses reply ardently.

"Alright, six Mickey bars, coming up," Daniel turns to excuse himself through the crowd.

"Wait," Victoria says, fingers moving rapidly over her phone as she composes a text. "Take one of the girls. You don't have six hands."

Cautiously, Daniel says, "Ava?"

"Yeah, great." Victoria is already elsewhere mentally, texting Nate about the day's events.

Daniel leads the way through the sea of people, trying not to step on any toes or unintentionally shoulder anyone. When they step out onto the clear sidewalk, both of them exhale in unison, relieved. Laughing softly, Ava asks, "Was this all part of your plan to get me alone?"

"Perhaps," Daniel says, his lips betraying just a hint of a smile.

Humming in response, Ava pulls her hair up into a bun and secures it with the band around her wrist.

Snack and souvenir carts are lining the pathway and Daniel points to one advertising frozen desserts. Joining the short line of people, Ava brushes her shoulder against his. "I think it's safe to say you had your derriere handed to you at Space Rangers."

Daniel's jaw twitches. "My laser was malfunctioning."

"Uh huh," Ava purses her lips. "I'm a better shot, and you know it."

"Blasphemy."

"Lies will get you nowhere, Daniel," she turns her head towards him. "It's been a struggle not to slip up and call you that."

He turns and smiles at her audaciously. "A lot of things have presented a special challenge to avoid today."

The customer in front of them pays, and Daniel steps up and places his order.

"I'm sorry sir, I'm afraid I only have one left. Someone is bringing more now, but it'll be a few minutes," the woman behind the cart informs him.

Checking his watch for the time, Daniel looks to Ava. "The show's about to start. What do you think?"

"Just get the one, I suppose. The girls can wait until after."

Daniel agrees and pays the woman, who then hands him a chocolate ice cream bar in the shape of Mickey Mouse. After thanking her, the pair approaches the edge of the crowd. He holds the bar out to Ava. "First bite?"

"Thank you." With a bashful smile, Ava takes the popsicle stick and takes a small bite off one ear, Daniel watching her intently the whole time. She licks some residual chocolate off her lower lip and hands it back to him.

"You're going to absolutely *end* me this weekend if you keep doing that," he says, his voice strained.

"Doing what?"

Daniel's eyes flit towards the castle, the colors starting to change. "Everything."

"And they all lived happily ever after ."

A booming voice fills the speakers around them, the show already starting. People stand closely together, blocking latecomers from weaseling their way in. More bodies fill in behind Daniel and Ava. "Guess we're stuck here," Ava notes, eyes drawn forward.

Sidestepping closer to her, Daniel says, "I'm not complaining."

A song begins once the narrator finishes his first speech. For the next seventeen minutes, Daniel and Ava's attention is held by the beautiful display of fireworks, lights, and projections onto the castle. Faces of familiar characters are imprinted onto the castle-like stained glass as the narrator declares, *"And so our journey comes to an end. But yours continues on. Grad hold of your dreams and make them come true."*

Daniel reaches out and brushes the back of his hand against Ava's. Unbeknownst to the other, each of them has tears in their eyes from the moving display.

"For you are the key to unlocking your own magic."

Ava takes hold of his hand and squeezes it tightly, as if her life depends upon this one small touch.

"Now go, let your dreams guide you. Reach out and find your happily ever after."

Daniel grips her hand with equal intensity and leans down, his breath hot against her skin. Shivers spark through her body as Daniel presses his lips against her ear. "I'm never letting go."

Twenty

March 17

⁂

"Everything is under construction," Chloe says dismally, as they walk through *Disney's Hollywood Studios* on Saturday morning.

It's a balmy 81 degrees, March offering the best of Florida weather. They've only been in the park for a short while, wandering through a few gift shops along Hollywood Boulevard. Their attention soon is directed to the large replica of Grauman's Chinese Theater at the end of the way.

"This used to be The Great Movie Ride," Jane informs everyone while they walk towards it. "It was actually going to be the main attraction in a show business-themed pavilion at Epcot called 'Great Moments at the Movies'. But, the CEO back then decided the idea was strong enough to lead an entirely new theme park. The idea for the ride was expanded and Disney-MGM Studios opened May 1, 1989. Now, they're going to put a silly mouse ride in there." She sighs dramatically. "Creativity is dead."

"That's so morbid," Quinn scolds, hitting Jane's shoulder lightly with her map.

"I think it's cool. *The more you know*, and all," Ava says, giving the girl a smile.

"Thank you, *Ava*."

"Anytime, Jane."

"Guys, we should go to the *Frozen* sing-along," Chloe suggests, pointing to the big screen on the Hyperion Theater advertising it across the walkway.

Rocking back on his heels, Daniel gestures to the watch on his left wrist. "That sounds like my cue to leave."

"You don't like musicals, Mr. Adams?" Quinn asks, smirking.

"Not that one, no," he chuckles to himself. "Some of the other students said they would be watching the Jedi Training trials. I'll just catch up with you lot afterward." Daniel raises a hand to wave, taking a step away from them.

Ava nods in agreement, although he is addressing the entire group of them. "Say hello to Darth Vader for me."

"Can do," he agrees and turns to walk down the pathway leading to Commissary Lane.

The girls join in the line outside for the *Frozen* show behind several of their classmates and costumed children. "Who would like Darth Vader? He's the villain," Victoria finally joins in the conversation, leaning back gently against the building's wall.

"He's got a pretty interesting back story," Jane shrugs. "Though most people relate more to Luke Skywalker, as he's the hero."

"Do you guys remember that onetime last semester? Mr. Adams told the class he'd bought an actual movie prop of Darth Vader's helmet," Chloe says with a laugh. "He was so excited, it was kind of weird to see him like that."

"Oh, I remember that! Logan asked him to bring it in and suddenly Mr. Adams got all protective of the stupid thing and changed the subject." Quinn shakes her head. "Boys and men, I see no difference."

People in front of them shuffle forward, the doors to the building having finally opened. The score to Frozen plays loudly from somewhere inside. Children bounce up and down while they walk, eager to see their favorite characters. Coming in behind the four girls, Victoria speaks louder than usual, "Sometimes guys will surprise you, Quinn. A little youthful vigor is a good thing."

"That's easy for you to say. Your dating pool is a lot bigger than ours is."

"You graduate next month! The world will be your oyster."

Chloe wriggles her nose, falling in step with her sister. "If you don't stop talking like Mama, I'm going to die of embarrassment."

"You're lucky I'm here with you *instead* of Mama."

Pursing her lips like she's just sucked a lemon, Chloe nods silently, eyes to the ground. Pleased, Victoria crosses her arms below her chest. "That's what I thought."

A large room opens up before them, with a stage as its focal point. Shades of blue, pink, and purple light up the curtain lined with faux icicles, while images of snowflakes dance around the room. On either side of the stage, props are set up to look like evergreen trees covered in snow. There are also large monitors set up to display lyrics once the show begins.

They file into the next available row and take their seats on the right side of the stage. While they wait for the show to begin, FastPasses are acquired for this park and a few things in Epcot later, thanks to Jane. After a few minutes, the curtains part, revealing the castle on a huge screen. *"Ladies and gentlemen! Boys and girls! All people of the kingdom of Hollywood Land, please welcome her majesty, the Queen of Arendelle!"* a man's voice fills the speakers.

"I thought the parents died in the—," Quinn starts, barely whispering.

"*Shhh!*" the other four girls silence her.

Princess Anna comes running out, stumbling onto the center of the stage. "You're here already… I mean, it's great that you're here! Welcome!" She hums to herself, looking out into the audience. After a few moments, she stage whispers, "*Elsa!* Elsa, where are you?" Running to the other side of the stage, she looks out past the set. "Elsa, this isn't funny!" Seeming to get an idea, Anna returns to center stage. "Oooh, I know!" Looking around the room, she sings, "Do you want to build a snowman?" With a dejected shrug, she says, "Yeah, that never works. Have any of you seen my sister? The Queen of Arendelle. She's about so tall," Anna gestures slightly above her. "Blonde. Kinda keeps to herself. Oh! And she has *weird,* icy snow powers." She pretends to shoot snow out of her fingers, making *pssh pssh* sound effects.

The audience bursts into laughter, Chloe joining in as loudly as some of the kids.

"No? Alright, just gotta do this by myself," Anna decides, putting her back to the audience to pump herself up. "I'm ready. I was *born* ready," she whispers to herself. When Anna turns back around, she wears a wide smile and gestures broadly to the crowd with one arm and then the other. "*Hello,* citizens of the kingdom of Hollywood Land! My name is Princess Anna of Arendelle." Trumpets sound when she says her name. "Please help me welcome the newly appointed royal historians of Arendelle!"

The rest of the thirty minutes pass by quickly. The two "historians" retell the story of *Frozen* and lead into the song clips. It's basically a glorified way to watch the movie in under an hour, but everyone joins in the fun. At the end, Anna, Kristoff, and Elsa take the stage and declare the audience honorary citizens of Arendelle.

"We should get pins to commemorate this moment!" Ava suggests jokingly.

To her surprise, nods and small noises of agreement sound on either side of her. The show ends with yet *another* round of *Let It Go* and the audience is set loose. When they walk back out into the daylight, Ava is surprised to see Daniel already waiting for them. He's sitting on the steps in the front of the building, doing a crossword puzzle in pen.

He looks so peaceful. I love seeing this side of him.

"How were the Padawans, Mr. Adams?" Chloe asks.

He looks up from his paper and grimaces. "Unstructured at best. I wrongly assumed it was going to be a show, not a group of random younglings." Daniel takes hold of the railing and boosts himself up, pocketing his phone. "Did you all enjoy your karaoke?"

"It wasn't karaoke," Quinn says, averting her eyes bashfully. "But yes."

Jane already has her cellphone in hand again and she points to the left. "We've gotta go down Sunset Boulevard for our FastPasses."

"Yes, time for some action!" Quinn pumps her fist into the air. "What's first?"

The six of them start off in that direction. A mock two-lane road is lined with palm trees, street lamps, and art déco buildings, most of which are facades. Big band jazz and swing music play throughout this section of the park. Marquees on top of the stores advertise products in twinkling lights.

Topiaries line the entrances. All in all, it truly feels like Disney manufactured 1930-1940s Hollywood. "The Rock 'n' Roller Coaster at ten-fifteen and then the Twilight Zone Tower of Terror at eleven."

Daniel and Ava exchange looks when Jane mentions the first attraction, both of them knowing there's no way Daniel can ride. It puts passengers in a "stretch limousine" speeding through Southern California for a fictional *Aerosmith* concert and is the second-fastest ride on Disney World property.

"I vehemently dislike *Aerosmith*," Daniel declares loudly enough for all of them to hear. "Count me out of the first one."

"Yeah, and I can't do rides that go upside down or I'll hurl," Ava adds.

"Alright," Victoria says, as they pass the Theater of the Stars. It advertises showtimes for *Beauty and the Beast*.

The six of them stop as the boulevard nears its end. Eerie music cuts through the air from the Tower just ahead, dueling with the rock music coming from the rollercoaster on their left. "Everyone else good to ride?"

Chloe, Quinn, and Jane all nod. Looking at Daniel, Victoria states, "I'll take them. Meet us in the FastPass line for the Tower of Terror at five till eleven."

"Sounds good," he agrees, his expression stoic as the four girls march off.

Ava and Daniel stand near the two stone gates that provide a transition from cheerful and lively Sunset Boulevard to the creepy, abandoned hotel. Despite being two extra faces in the crowd, they know that they're far from alone — students and chaperones from ElRo could be anywhere in the small theme park.

"We could just walk around," Daniel suggests. "Act like we're searching for the rest of our party."

"Can walking around include a snack? We passed a sweets shop a little while back."

Half of Daniel's mouth pulls back in a smile that displays one deeply set dimple. "How could I say no?"

They keep a good foot of distance between them as they walk back up the pathway. *Sweet Spells* opens to a pastry case with freshly baked goods in front of a partial kitchen. Cast members in gingham and light stripes scurry back and forth behind the counter, while one gentleman is dipping oversized marshmallows into melted chocolate in front of a large display window.

Ava makes a beeline for the window, her eyes widening as she watches the man shake off excess chocolate before placing the stick down on a parchment-lined tray. Coming up behind her, Daniel's rich voice is low, "You're a chocolate girl, huh?"

She nods, her attention still held by the exhibition in front of her. "It was always a special treat when I was little. Dad would bring home chocolates from his business trips, different kinds from all over the world." Ava looks over her shoulder at Daniel. "And then I didn't have it for a long time. Eventually, Nate figured out that it was my weakness and he'd scrounge up coins to buy chocolates to bribe me with. Just for little things, like doing his chores at the home or helping with his math homework," she smiles wistfully. "I'm so lucky to have been in the system with Nate. I don't know what I'd have done without him."

Raking a large hand through his hair, Daniel holds her gaze. "I'm glad you've had someone to watch out for you. Nate's a good guy."

"Yeah, he is."

"And if it's chocolate you desire, I'm more than happy to oblige." Daniel steps up to the register and offers a dazzling smile to the young girl there. "Do you have any of those—," he points to the cooling tray, "available?"

The girl tells him they do, and Daniel requests one. After he pays, Daniel hands it to Ava. "No bribery required."

"At some point, I'll have to stop accepting food from you," Ava says with a smile. "But today is *not* that day." She takes a large bite out of the chocolate marshmallow and closes her eyes while she chews. "Thank you."

Daniel mumbles a soft *"you're welcome"* and opens the door for her.

"Oh Daniel, look," Ava points to the assorted prop luggage just past the closest lamp post. "It's old Route 66." She nearly grabs his hand, but thinks better of it and just leads the way.

Five pieces of old-timey luggage surround a small sign for 'California US 66'. "This is so cool, I've always wanted to take a road trip down Route 66."

Ava reaches for the phone in her back pocket and pulls it out, gesturing Daniel closer with the marshmallow. "We have to take a selfie!"

"A *selfie?*" Daniel asks, shaking his head with mock disgust.

"Yes, a selfie!" Ava double taps the home button, bringing up the camera. She swipes the screen to switch to the front camera and holds her right arm out in front of her. "Please?"

With an exaggerated sigh, Daniel moves to the left of Ava. She swivels her arm a bit, trying to get as much of the sign and the props in the picture as possible. Smiling widely, Ava says, "Say *cheese.*"

"Cheese," Daniel repeats, ducking down awkwardly next to her. His mouth curves into a close-lipped smile.

"A real smile, please?" Ava asks, pressing her shoulder against his arm.

Looking down at her fondly, Daniel's mouth widens, showing off his teeth. Ava clicks the shutter button repeatedly until they're both looking at the camera. Moving away from him, she selects the gallery. Her smile only grows as she swipes through the pictures. "Perfect."

***

After spending half the day at *Hollywood Studios,* the ElRo group takes buses over to *Epcot.* Unbeknownst at the time of planning, they've come during the International Flower and Garden Festival. Entering the park, they are greeted with a large topiary display of Mickey, Minnie, Donald, and Daisy right in front of the Spaceship Earth geosphere.

"Do we have a FastPass for that?" Chloe asks, pointing to the giant golf ball-looking structure.

"Nah, but no one ever needs them," Jane replies. "We'll probably be able to walk right on."

They walk with the rest of their group past the monoliths where patrons had left their legacy in the form of tiny pictures and around the circular stone fountain. Joining in the railed queue, Ava finds herself at the front of her group and, unfortunately, right behind Logan Trite.

Standing with his arms crossed, a grin spreads across the boy's face when he sees Ava approaching. "Fancy meeting you here."

"Two buses just dropped the whole senior class off and this is the first attraction in the park," Ava says in a monotone. "What a surprise."

Logan slides along the railing to keep with the moving line. "Whatever you say. I choose to believe you've been dying to get me alone ever since we got here."

Ava's face tightens as if she's just taken a punch to the gut. "In no universe would that ever be the case, Logan. Besides, we're not alone," she gestures to the crowd behind them. "Like I just said, the whole senior class is here."

He shakes his head, undeterred. "Sure."

She huffs with a disgusted sound and turns to Chloe, who is walking behind her in front of Daniel. "Can we sit together?"

"Yeah, of—,"

As they enter the interior of the ride, Disney employees usher them into moving cars. "Two by two, watch your step," a young man prompts Ava and Logan into the back two seats of a four-person car.

With a frown, Ava gives a half-wave to Chloe, who is being shown into the front row of the next car, alongside Daniel. Chloe mouths a quick *'I'm sorry'*.

"This all part of your little plan, Eliot?" Logan asks, sliding into the car after Ava.

Ava chooses to ignore him, looking at the screen attached to the seats in front of them. The cars tilt up as they move steadily along into the dark.

"Like a grand and miraculous spaceship, our planet has sailed through the universe of time; and for a brief moment, we have been among its passengers. But where are we going? And what kind of future will we discover there? Surprisingly, the answers lie in our past," Dame Judi Dench's voice fills the car.

For the first few minutes of the ride, they sit in silence, focused on the animatronic scenes.

"By now, we're all communicating from anywhere on Earth and in 1969 from somewhere else." The car moves them past a scene of a family watching the moon landing.

Logan scoots over and the feeling of his body pressing up against hers makes Ava's stomach drop. She clears her throat loudly and moves as far to the right side of the car as she can.

"Where do you think you're going?" Logan asks, sliding an arm over her shoulder.

Ava clenches her teeth and elbows him gently in the stomach. "Get off me, Logan."

"Come on, Ava. We're basically alone. You don't have to act shy," he says, practically in her ear.

Her body tenses and Ava raises her voice as she says, "I am not *shy.* I'm simply not interested." Turning her head to him, Ava's face is lit up as the car moves past a model of an early computer. "Are you daft?"

Logan groans, but withdraws his arm.

When the ride gets dark once again, Ava feels a hand take hold of her knee. "*Dude,*" she growls, grabbing his wrist in an effort to peel his hand off.

"Ooh, frisky!" Logan chortles. Resisting her efforts, he slides his hand up her leg.

At this point, Ava's frustration is turning to alarm.

How much longer is this ride?

"Stop it, Logan," Ava says firmly, her voice sounding much more confident than she's feeling.

"I like it when girls play hard to get," he murmurs. Logan's hand halts its ministrations, having reached the top of her thigh.

Ava can feel sharp prickles of sweat beading all over her body and her breath is coming out shallow. She's frozen inside her own body and the feeling makes her want to scream, kick, bite, throw up — possibly all at the same time.

Her eyes are glued to the screen ahead of them, prompting them to answer multiple-choice questions about the kind of future they'd want.

Blessedly, this is enough to distract Logan. He leans forward and starts touching answers on the screen, Ava wrapping her arms around herself in the meantime.

What just happened?

The screen shows a loading message, Logan having finished working through all the options. He leans back and watches it play out an imaginary scenario for the future, the car moving them along the track.

When it ends, he wraps an arm around Ava once more. *"Logan!* Get your hands off me!" Ava shouts.

There is actual light at the end of the tunnel, the unloading bay coming into view. "Ava?" Daniel and Chloe's voices sound from the car a few feet behind.

The small door slides open, and Ava stumbles to get out and get away from this chauvinistic teenager. Fingers reach out to grab her waist, and instead, find purchase in the fabric of her t-shirt. "Wait up, we haven't gotten to the best part yet," Logan snarls, pulling her to the side of the entrance to Project Tomorrow.

Ava turns around and shoves him away from her.

"Hey!"

Both of their heads turn at the deeply menacing sound.

"What the kriff do you think you're doing to her?" Daniel shouts, bounding over to Logan in one long stride. He doesn't touch the teenager, but stands close enough to appear threatening.

Logan looks up at the teacher, scowling. "What I do is *none of your business,* teach!"

Looking down his nose, Daniel shakes his head once. "Don't feed me that crap, Mr. Trite." He breaks eye contact only briefly to check on Ava, standing a few feet away with Chloe now at her side. "Are you alright?"

Her shoulders slump, releasing their tension, and she looks over at Daniel with what can only be construed as relief. "Y-yes, I'm fine," Ava speaks softly.

A loud, snarky laugh pours from Logan's lips as he watches this exchange. "Oh, I get it. Everybody's favorite teacher has the hots for one of his students."

The scene has attracted a crowd of curious faces, most of which are part of the ElRo group. Logan seems to gain confidence from this, and he gazes around the room at their faces. "And it looks like she wants to screw him, too. If she's not already."

Looks of alarm spread through the sea of people, murmuring back and forth rapidly. "No!" Ava protests, stepping towards her harasser.

"Did you think you were slick, leaving all those notes on his desk?"

Her eyes widen. Logan puts up a finger to silence her, now that he has the room's full attention. "I saw him with his arm around you on the airplane, Ava. I've seen how you two look at each other when you think no one's paying attention. Like at the fireworks display last night."

"I can explain everything," Ava says, her heart heavy with the knowledge of what she needs to do.

For Daniel.

"Is that why you didn't want to do anything, Ava?" Logan goads, his voice spiteful.

Ms. Richardson pushes to the front of the crowd and places both hands on her hips. "What do you have to say for yourself, Nico? Is there any truth to Mr. Trite's accusation?"

Daniel's eyes drift over Ava's before he addresses his fellow faculty member. "No, that's absurd."

Logan's friends come forward, circling closely around the two teachers. They talk over one another, but it's clear that they're just backing up Logan's story with things they've also supposedly witnessed. "I've heard enough!" Mr. Richardson states loudly. She fishes around the purse slung over her shoulder and produces her cellphone. "To be honest, I don't know what to do right now. I'm going to call Principal Steele."

Shaking her head nervously, Ava puts a hand on Ms. Richardson's arm. "No! I can explain!"

She withdrawals the touch and turns to the crowd of students and chaperones. Everyone is staring at her, silently waiting for an explanation. "Let me tell you something. Listen very carefully. *Nothing* untoward has ever gone on between Mr. Adams and I." Ava straightens her shoulders and starts to pace.

Rip it off, like a band-aid.

"You know what? Right now, I don't even care that you're choosing not to interrogate the actual predator," she juts a finger over towards Logan. "I don't care about your social politics and all the blatant lies. For god's sake, I'm twenty-four years old! I'm an undercover reporter for *The New York Times* and I have spent long enough trying to hold my tongue around you people!"

Twenty-One

March 17 - 22

The crowd of students, family members, and teachers looks at Ava with a mixture of surprise and disgust. A spy in *their* midst? How dare she! Some people shuffle a few steps back as if Ava is a contagious pariah. For once, even Ms. Richardson appears to be speechless. She looks between where Ava touched her skin and Ava herself, mouth agape.

Pursing her lips, the weight of her words finally settles over Ava.

I did it.

I exposed myself to them.

Her gaze scans the crowd, trying to pick out faces that still appear friendly. Girls she has gotten to know this semester, has partied and even roomed with, refuse to meet Ava's eyes. Logan and his cronies whisper back and forth, sharing secrets. When he does look at her, Logan almost seems embarrassed.

Good. He very well should.

Still standing the closest to her, Daniel offers Ava a small but reassuring smile. He clearly wants to come to her, but given the truth bomb she just dropped, it could likely put his job on the line. People might even assume he's been in on it this whole time.

Ava gives him a barely discernible nod.

We'll talk later.

Her heart is pumping hard in her chest, not used to all this attention. Looking through the doors to Project Tomorrow, where unassociated people are playing game-like exhibits, Ava parts her lips to speak again. Before she can get a word in, Chloe's soft voice cuts through the mechanical sounds of the ride. "You-you lied to me?" She peeks out from behind Daniel, dark brown eyes wide as saucers.

Frowning, Ava nods once.

Chloe is the last person I ever wanted to hurt.

The least I can do is give her some... semblance of truth now.

"I did and I'm sorry. I never meant to get this close to you," her eyebrows lower, and she sweeps her gaze around the room. "To any of you."

Quinn acknowledges Ava at last with a grimace. "You don't belong here, Ava. If that *is* your real name."

"You're right, I don't," Ava clears her throat and takes a step closer to the next room. "I got the story I came for, so my job is completed." She catches Ms. Richardson's eyes. "I'll get an Uber to the hotel and be gone before you all get back tonight."

Ms. Richardson stares at her silently for long enough to make it uncomfortable. Eventually, she speaks, "See that you are." Gesturing to the large group, she heads toward the double doors. "Let's go, Eleanor Roosevelt students."

As they walk through, Ava can hear her name muttered along with several expletives. She drops her hazel eyes to the floor, heat rising in her body.

This whole thing has possibly been the worst twenty minutes of my adult life.

An exaggerated cough draws Ava's attention back up. The only one left standing there, Chloe still wears the same wounded baby animal expression. "Chloe," Ava breathes the girl's name out softly.

Only a few feet are between them, but the situation makes it feel like a vast ocean. "I always thought you were mature for your age... I guess now it makes sense," Chloe says, her voice small.

"I'm sorry I had to lie about certain things, but I promise you that all the details and... emotions, that was me." Déjà vu overcomes Ava, this feeling eerily similar to when Daniel found out her true identity. "You can ask Daniel. He knows how badly I wanted to tell you, too. How much I value our friendship."

The younger girl's eyes narrow. "Who's Daniel?"

"Oh, um, Mr. Adams."

Chloe's jaw sets, the look of betrayal replaced with one Ava has never seen on her. "All this time, you *did* like him. But you lied about that as well." Her nostrils flare. "My family welcomed you into our home, but you returned trust for deception." Shaking her head, Chloe walks towards the doors to join everyone else.

"Please, if you would just let me—,"

"I don't want to hear anymore, Ava."

***

Text alerts and phone calls light Ava's phone up like yesterday's fireworks display. Imagining who they might be from and what those people may have to say is more than enough to keep her from investigating. Ava's only solace is that she hasn't worn a camera in weeks, so the likelihood of Mr. Wells trying to reach her right now is slim.

She tears her eyes away from where her cellphone sits on top of her bag and looks over to the driver's seat. Listening to the Uber driver talk about her busy week is a welcome break from Ava's thoughts.

"… And you'd better believe I gave his crazy self one star! He should think twice before ever trying to get in *this* car again."

"You don't have to accept his ride, Jess. You deserve to be treated with respect," Ava remarks.

"Thank you! That's exactly what I'm saying!" Jess gestures widely with her right hand, left hand on the wheel.

The car pulls up to the *American Airlines* drop off at Terminal A and Jess pops the trunk. She puts the car in park and unbuckles her seat belt when Ava shakes her head and lightly touches the woman's arm. "That's alright, I can take it from here."

Shifting in her seat, Jess nods. "You take care of yourself. I hope you can change your ticket for an earlier flight."

"Thank you," Ava smiles, picking up her satchel off the floor before opening the passenger side door. "I'm crossing my fingers that you get only normal riders this afternoon."

Ava steps out of the car and walks around to the back, lifting the trunk up. She retrieves her small suitcase and places it on the curb. Shutting the trunk, she steps out of the road and gives a little wave to Jess.

A baggage handler wearing an *American Airlines* polo approaches Ava, offering to check her suitcase curbside. Shaking her head, Ava explains she needs to change her ticket. The man directs her to the check-in desk inside and she thanks him with a smile. Pulling her suitcase behind her, Ava reaches into the bag on her shoulder. Her fingers wrap around her wallet and she extracts it, stepping through the automatic doors. She locates her boarding pass for Monday along with her license and joins in the small queue.

She parks the suitcase in front of her and places the documents on top. With nothing else to occupy her mind, Ava finally withdrawals her cellphone. A sharp intake of breath allows her to summon the courage to unlock it and face the music.

(6) Missed Calls

(2) New Voicemails

(3) New Text Messages from Nate

(8) New Text Messages from Orlando

Scrunching up her nose, Ava clears the notifications away and clicks Nate's name first.

—— **Saturday, March 17** ——

– Nate | 4:14 –

Are you okay? Victoria just sent me this.

FWD from The Babe: *Chloe is freaking out. Her best friend Ava turned out to be some kind of undercover reporter. The happiest place on earth has a metaphorical rain cloud over it right now. I don't know what to do. Why can't you be here?? What happened, Ace?*

Ava uses her foot to push the suitcase forward in line and types back.

– Ava | 6:17 –

BLARGH.

I'll explain tonight. I'm trying to get a flight home now.

She clicks back to the inbox and lets her finger hover over Orlando's name. A small victory in all of this, Ava edits his contact information to 'Daniel Woodard' and adds a picture of them in front of the Route 66 sign. The sight of Daniel smiling down at a grinning Ava makes her smile, and she touches the screen affectionately.

Another text comes through from Daniel, opening the thread automatically.

—— Saturday, March 17 ——

– Daniel Woodard | 4:12 –

I'm sorry, Ava. I couldn't stop myself.

I almost punched the little kriffer.

Maybe I should have. Then you wouldn't have had to come out to everyone.

– Daniel Woodard | 4:31 –

I wish I could have left with you. You're the whole reason I volunteered for this trip.

– Daniel Woodard | 5:17 –

Where are you now? I had to bring Isaac back to the hotel, he thinks he got food poisoning.

– Daniel Woodard | 5:23 –

Either you're not in your room or you won't come to the door. I'm worried about you. Please answer your phone.

– Daniel Woodard | 5:47 –

Are you at the airport?

– Daniel Woodard | 5:53 –
You're killing me, woman.

– Daniel Woodard | 6:17 –
I'm coming to the airport.

Someone behind her clears their throat and Ava looks up to find that she's next in line, holding everyone else up. Her cheeks flush and she mumbles an apology, dropping her phone into the bag. The clerk behind the counter smiles, not altogether impatient. "Ma'am? How may I help you?"

Ava bends down to pick up her documents and takes the handle of her suitcase. She walks up to the counter, offering the woman a radiant smile.

Please be nice to me.

"Hello, how are you doing today?"

"Well, thank you, ma'am. How may I assist you?"

Handing over her boarding pass and identification, Ava says, "I'm hoping you have a flight to *LaGuardia* tonight. My ticket is for Monday, but I can't stay here."

"Not enjoying the weather, ma'am?"

"Oh, it's been lovely. I just… need to get home."

The woman nods, perfected smile still in place. "Let me see here," she directs her attention to the computer monitor in front of her.

"Thank you." Ava tries to look casual, as if she's not completely desperate. She tucks an unruly section of wavy hair behind an ear and pretends to study the illuminated *American Airlines* sign.

"Ahh. We have a seat on the 7:55, but it's in business class."

Snapping to focus, Ava speaks, "I'll take—,"

"But there will be a fee to change the flight on top of the upgrade."

"I see," Ava nods solemnly. "How much is this going to cost me?"

"$400, plus tax."

Without meaning to, Ava flinches. Her eyes squeeze together like she's expecting a punch to the gut.

"Would you like to just take your previously scheduled flight on Monday?"

Opening her eyes, Ava shakes her head with determination. "No, I'll take it."

It pains her to hand over the slate-colored emergency credit card, and she has to tell herself it'll be worth it.

Wells is going to have *to promote me.*

Then this will just be a drop in the bucket.

The woman takes the payment, hands Ava her license and new boarding pass, and wishes her a happy flight. Thanking her, Ava grabs the handle of her suitcase and walks towards the security checkpoint.

For being late afternoon on a Saturday, the line isn't very long. Ava is nearly to the security officer when a deep, familiar voice calls out her name.

"Ava! Wait!"

She turns around, scanning the large room for the owner of the voice. Daniel Woodard stands near the queue's entrance, bent over with his hands on his thighs, chest heaving.

"Daniel!" Relief at seeing him floods her body. It's as though an invisible corset has been loosened, and suddenly she can breathe deeply again. "Excuse me, I'm so sorry," she mumbles, rushing back through the line.

Stopping a few feet away from him, Ava drops the handle of her suitcase. Daniel crosses the space between them, meeting her in the middle.

He doesn't hesitate to wrap both arms around her waist, encompassing her with his broad frame. Her hands snake around his neck in response. Their faces draw close, eyes locking briefly. Daniel wastes no time, the months of build-up ending when he presses his lips against hers.

Ava hums a small sound of surprise that subsides into satisfaction halfway through. Despite his eagerness, Daniel's full lips are gentle. They caress her lips patiently, as if he's afraid he'll break her by pressing too firmly. By showing her what he wants.

Not satisfied with this, Ava parts her lips, capturing his lower lip between them. Suddenly, Daniel's hands slide down her lower back and Ava's right hand cradles his head, fingertips stroking along his jaw. Her thumb brushes against his hair and when she sucks softly on his lip, he responds in kind; her kiss heightening every one of his senses.

Daniel bends her backward slightly. His hands drift farther down until they're cupping her bottom, squeezing the ample flesh. This elicits a barely audible moan. Tentatively, Daniel runs his tongue along her lips and Ava breathes out a soft laugh. She places another kiss on his mouth before pulling back, burying her face against his neck.

"Hi," Ava murmurs, her breath shallow.

"Hi," he repeats. Daniel brings an arm around her waist again, his right hand coming up to stroke her hair. "Sorry, I just—,"

"Don't you dare apologize for that," Ava lifts her head abruptly.

Daniel's deep brown eyes are glazed over, which only makes her grin.

"I've wanted to kiss you since…" he trails off, shrugging after a moment.

"Me too."

Ava lets one hand slide down his chest, the pads of her fingers lingering over his ribcage.

"Are you going home?" Daniel asks. He raises and lowers his eyebrows before shaking his head. "Of course you are. Sorry."

"There's nothing left for me to do now but finish what I started," Ava says. "I don't know how long it'll take. I have quite a few things to sort out…" She sucks in her bottom lip and looks up at him like he's the man with all the answers. And maybe, for her, he is.

Daniel nods, eyes traveling over her features as he smiles absentmindedly. "When can I see you again?"

Tomorrow.

Every day for the rest of my life.

"I'll let you know when I've finished."

"And the second that you do, I'm taking you out."

They share a quiet laugh, his finger wrapping around a lock of her hair.

"Is that a promise?"

"It's an oath. A pledge of my allegiance." Daniel leans closer, his lips brushing airily against hers. "To you."

***

Ava leans back against the firm wooden chair, stretching her arms in front of her to pop her elbows. "It's done," she murmurs to no one but herself.

Five whole days she has spent cooped up in the tiny apartment. After her flight home Saturday night, Ava slept more soundly than she had in months. She'd woken early on Sunday, called a family meeting to explain things to Nate, and sent a long warning email to Chris. She would not tell Wells anything in advance, he'd be reading it along with everyone else. For the rest of the week, Ava wrote, revised, and wrote some more.

She eyes the time in the corner of the computer screen, *8:32 pm.* If he doesn't see it tonight, no doubt it will be the first thing Cillian Wells sees tomorrow morning.

Earlier today, Chris had supplied her with an administrator's login for *The New York Times Online.* Thanks to him, the seven-million-plus subscribers would see the front-page editorial with Ava Thompson's byline on tomorrow's email.

The article is one of the most personal things Ava has ever written, and by far the most intimate thing she's chosen to share with the world. She wrote about her personal tragedy, how it affected the rest of her upbringing, the vast difference between her high school experiences, and what this says about society. Ava also wrote about Logan, without including his name, and a call to arms for proper education to identify such predators as early as possible. Interwoven amongst all this, she told stories of forged families and friendships and about finally, at the ripe age of twenty-four, falling in love for the very first time.

It is nothing like the piece Wells wanted her to write, but it's the story Ava was *meant* to write. Without this experience, she would never have learned so much about herself.

On her phone, Ava sends a link to the article out to all her contacts, albeit a small group.

One hundred percent honesty from now on.

When the phone rings a few minutes later, she answers it without even looking at the name. Assuming it simply must be Daniel. "Thoughts of hearing your voice are among the only things that kept me going these past few days," she purrs.

And thoughts of other things.

"Really?" The surprised voice on the other end of the phone call is most definitely not Daniel's.

"... Chloe?"

"I read the article you sent me, Ava," her voice is thick and full of sadness. "I had *no idea* what you have been through. I'm so sorry for being such a brat."

A sob is caught in Ava's throat that comes out mixed with a laugh. "*Chloe.*" Ava smiles so wide it nearly makes her cheeks ache. "You have nothing to be sorry for!"

"Yes, I do. I jumped to false conclusions that I had no right to."

"I should have told you sooner, or at least when Daniel accidentally found out."

"Ava, I wish you could have seen him this week!" Chloe laughs melodically. "He keeps looking over at the empty seat next to me, all wistful and starry-eyed. The man's got it *bad.*"

Another laugh pours out of her. "I-think-I'm-in-love-with-him," Ava says, the words rushed together. The first time she's ever uttered them.

"I know, silly. I said I read the article."

"Oh." Despite being alone in her bedroom, Ava's body warms up.

Everyone will read that.

Daniel *will read it, too.*

"I think it's wonderful!" Chloe coos.

Ava can just imagine the younger girl, laying on her stomach and fidgeting with her fringe. For not the first time, waves of missing her crash over Ava. "I hope he thinks so, too. I'm pretty sure the guy is supposed to say it first, but what do I know?"

"He'll definitely say it," Chloe says firmly. "Mr. Adams has probably been in love with you for months."

"I miss you," Ava blurts out. "I don't want to sound weird, but can we still be friends?"

The few seconds it takes Chloe to answer make Ava's heart beat mercilessly. "I certainly hope so. I've been secretly calling you my best friend ever since you came over for dinner."

Knowing what she has with Chloe differs greatly from her friendship with Chris, Ava can confidently say, "You're my best friend, too."

***

After planning a lunch date with Chloe, Ava spends the rest of the evening watching Spring Training with Nate. It's nearly midnight when she fumbles for the light switch in her room. The notification light on her cellphone is blinking blue.

Ava walks over and picks it up, taking a seat on the edge of her bed as she turns on the screen.

(1) New Text Message from Daniel Woodard

Her ears burn and her heart skips a beat, eyes reading the message over once. Twice. A third time.

—— Thursday, March 22 ——
– Daniel Woodard | 9:01 –

This is probably breaking all sorts of first date rules, but I want to take you out before eight o'clock. Let's do something a bit different before dinner. Have you ever been to the Hayden Planetarium? I want to show you the stars. And then wine and dine you. My only request is that you wear that blue excuse for a dress I saw you in at The William.

Twenty-Two

March 23

The sound of her phone ringing jolts Ava awake.

What time is it?

Squinting in the early morning darkness, she rolls over to the edge of her bed and runs a hand blindly along the floor until she touches the device. She drowsily brings it up, holding the phone close to her face.

Cillian "The General" Wells is Calling...

Her heart speeds up, adrenaline coursing through her veins. Sitting upright, Ava leans against her headboard and swipes to accept the call. "Good morning, Mr. Wells."

"You honestly have the audacity to say *good morning* to me?" he booms.

"... Yes, sir."

"How dare you go behind my back? I know one measly journalist couldn't have done this by herself," Wells growls. "You must have had help. I demand you tell me who else is involved!"

Ava gulps audibly.

It's too early for this.

"Miss Thompson!"

"I didn't have any help. I'm perfectly capable of getting an administrator login myself," she says carefully.

"Preposterous. I knew you were daft, but this is a new level of stupidity. Not only did you *not* write the story you were assigned, you wrote — what? A personal discovery piece?" He sounds disgusted.

Furrowing her brows, anger bubbles in Ava's stomach. "I'm sorry, sir, but you have no right to talk to me like that. I have always treated you with respect and I don't think it's too much to expect the same from you."

For once in all the time she's known him, Cillian Wells does not come back with a retort. Taking this as encouragement to keep talking, Ava continues, "I realize I didn't give you the story you wanted, but I'm a decent human being. I can't just *use* someone to find out all their dirty secrets and then betray them. These are real people, Mr. Wells. Their personal lives and issues are not something to put on display without express consent. So if my story does terribly, I'll accept that. If no one reads it, I'll tender my resignation. But *please*, just give me a chance." Words are tumbling from her lips so quickly that Ava can barely comprehend the weight behind them. "I was born to be a writer. I've never been more sure of anything. In fact, I should be thanking you. If you didn't give me this assignment, I wouldn't have met all these amazing people and… Yeah." Ava laughs softly. "Thank you, Mr. Wells."

Seconds stretch uncomfortably until he says, "I suppose I could give you a few days. See how the story resonates with our readers."

Ava rubs the sleep from her eyes, making sure she's actually awake. "Oh my goodness, thank you, sir!"

"To be clear, your job depends entirely on the outcome. I won't be made a fool in front of my colleagues."

She claps a hand over her mouth to hold back a happy squeal. Nodding rapidly, Ava says, "Absolutely. I understand completely."

"… Good. I expect to see you Monday morning in my office."

"Yes, sir," Ava agrees, smiling to herself. "Oh, and Mr. Wells? Please, read the article."

***

Placing the curling iron down on the bathroom counter, Ava admires the reflection in the mirror. Her brunette tresses have been curled loosely into glossy beach waves. She's also located a makeup palette she'd long forgotten about and attempted a smokey eye with the help of a YouTube tutorial. A fuchsia pink emboldens full lips, complementing the vivid teal blue dress Daniel has requested. For all her lack of cosmetic experience, the completed look isn't half bad.

After tucking her hair behind her ears, Ava opens the small box Nate gave her when she graduated. A pair of gold ball stud earrings shine in the fluorescent lighting. Humming along to the song playing from her cellphone's speakers, she pierces them through her ears and attaches the backs, one by one.

It's nearly half-past four in the afternoon, meaning Daniel is probably home from the high school. Not for the first time, Ava feels slight relief that their first date is earlier in the day.

Otherwise, Nate would be home from work and more than likely teasing me about how I rarely wear lipstick.

She's been to the American Museum of Natural History, but never to the planetarium. Already, Daniel is introducing Ava to new things. It only adds to the excitement she feels over finally being able to get to know him as a normal adult.

Ava gives a generous two spritzes of perfume, flips down the light switch and picks up her phone, the music blaring as she walks into her bedroom. She bounds across to room to the back corner and places the cellphone on her desk. Crouching down in front of her closet, she sorts through her minimal shoe collection with one hand. It's mostly pairs of practical kitten heels and wedge sandals, along with some running shoes in need of TLC. Undisturbed towards the back is a pair of strappy nude heels. Ava pulls them free and takes a seat in her desk chair, fastening the thin straps around her ankles.

The text notification sound cuts through the song and Ava eyes the screen. *(1) New Text Message from Daniel Woodard*

Once she finishes adjusting her shoes, Ava unlocks the device and taps on the message.

186

—— **Friday, March 23** ——
  – Daniel Woodard | 4:34 –
  I just got off the subway. ETA according to Google Maps is seven minutes.

A smile spreads across her brightly painted lips. It's been nearly a week since she last saw Daniel at the Orlando Airport. Six long days without hearing the resonance of his voice. One hundred and forty-four hours and twelve minutes, approximately, since they shared a room-spinning, life-altering first kiss.

Ava's fingers glide over the screen, typing out a response.

– Ava Thompson | 4:34 –
  Can you make it in six?

Three little dots tell her that Daniel is writing back. Ava nearly bites into her lower lip but remembers her lipstick in the nick of time. Instead, she opts for twirling a freshly curled strand of hair around her right index finger.

– Daniel Woodard | 4:34 –
  Impatient, sweetheart?

Taking a small silver clutch with her, Ava types as she walks out of her bedroom and down the hallway.

– Ava Thompson | 4:35 –
  You have no idea. Are you?

She's just walked into the living room when Daniel's reply pops up.

– Daniel Woodard | 4:35 –
  In vain I have struggled. It will not do. My feelings will not be repressed.

A soft laugh pours from Ava's lips. She places the clutch on the coffee table and reaches into her satchel. Locating her wallet, Ava takes out her license and bank card. She opens the clutch and slides those inside before replacing the wallet into her larger bag. Tucking the clutch under her arm, Ava heads towards the front door, typing.

– Ava Thompson | 4:35 –

Are you honestly quoting Austen to me right now?

Ava's keychain dangles from a hook in the flat's entryway. She takes her keys and opens the deadbolts on the door, keeping one eye on the phone screen until he's replied.

– Daniel Woodard | 4:35 –

... Possibly.

After unlocking the last one, Ava opens the door to the shared apartment building hallway. She walks out and locks up behind her. Placing her keys in the clutch for safekeeping, Ava walks through the hallway, down the stairs, and out the front door of the building.

She looks both ways down the street as she steps into the early evening glow.

No sign of Daniel.

Ava leans against the building's paneling and composes another message.

– Ava Thompson | 4:37 –

Alright, I'll allow it. Who am I to question Fitzwilliam Darcy?

His response pings seconds later.

– Daniel Woodard | 4:37 –

Actually, that would be very Elizabeth Bennet of you.

Vibrant lips part and spread into a devilish grin.

– Ava Thompson | 4:37 –

This whole "English teacher" thing you've got going on really does it for me.

"Your coquettish text persona does it for me, too." Daniel's voice catches her by surprise.

Straightening up, Ava turns in the sound's direction. Her grin morphs into something softer as she takes in the welcome sight of him walking towards her.

Bloody hell, it's all over for me.

Dressed in all black, Daniel looks as handsome as Ava's ever seen him. The silky texture of his tie stands out nicely against the matte black of the suit. The only color to be seen on Daniel is a hint of red at the bottom of his shoes, visible briefly when he takes large strides.

"You're perfect," Daniel says, awed by the sight of her.

At the same moment, Ava coyly asks, "Don't you clean up nicely?"

They share a soft laugh and then, all at once, Daniel comes to a stop right in front of her. No longer whispering in private or dramatically rushing towards each other as in the past, first-date jitters seem to fall over them. Ava opens her arms for a hug while Daniel leans down to kiss her, resulting in a one-sided embrace and a kiss placed atop her head. "Oh, er, sorry," she says softly, releasing him.

"My apologies," Daniel agrees.

Ava's cheeks redden, but she tries to hide it by leaning forward on her toes to press a soft kiss on Daniel's cheek. "Here."

"You… smell wonderful," Daniel whispers as she pulls back slightly.

"Thank you." Her eyes widen when she realizes she's left a pink imprint on his cheek. "Oops, I left a little… "

She reaches out to wipe the pout off and Daniel gently stops her, wrapping his fingers around her wrist. "Maybe I enjoy being marked."

His words cause Ava's breath to catch in the back of her throat. Nodding, she lowers her hand. Daniel lets go only to lace their fingers together. He stares at their hands, wide-eyed, for a few moments. When he looks into Ava's eyes again, there's a slight smile on his lips. "This feels surreal."

"Yes, it does." Ava gives his hand a squeeze. "I feel like we know so much about each other, and yet, nothing at all. Does that make sense?"

Raising his eyebrows a few millimeters, Daniel agrees, "Nothing about this has been conventional." He gestures forward with his head, and they walk towards the 125th Street subway station. "But it'll make a great story one day."

One day?

"Speaking of great stories," he whistles. "Ava, I thought I knew your writing but, wow."

"You liked it?" Ava's stomach feels like it's doing cartwheels.

He read it.

He read the whole thing.

"It's the most powerful thing I've read of yours." Daniel catches her eyes meaningfully. "You should be proud."

"I actually am, so thank you." She fidgets with the clasp on the clutch as they walk. "Mr. Wells called me about it this morning. He's royally peeved."

"Did he read it?"

"No. He wanted to know how I posted it online by myself and what I was thinking," Ava laughs once, nervously. "For the first time, I stood up to him. It felt reckless but so empowering."

"How did that go over?"

"Surprisingly well. He's letting the article run through the weekend, to see how our subscribers respond." She releases his hand to walk into the subway entrance. Behind her, Daniel ducks as he walks through. "I'm going back to the office on Monday to discuss it with him. Hopefully, I'll still have a job."

Each of them produces a MetroCard and they swipe it, entering through the turnstile. "Wells would have to be inept not to appreciate what you've written. If he doesn't want it, I bet the *Tribune* or the *Post* would."

"I hadn't considered that, but you've got a point."

It's dimly lit inside as they make their way down the steps to the subway platform. Stopping a few feet back from the painted yellow line, they regard each other with shy smiles. Daniel places a hand on Ava's lower back and

190

warmth spreads through her. His hand nearly spans her entire back. At 5'7, she's never considered herself petite. But next to Daniel's colossal stature, she feels almost dainty.

Ava steps into his touch, brushing her bare shoulder against his arm. "How was your week back at ElRo?"

He groans, long and drawn out, mildly playful. "Miserable."

Laughing, she nudges him with her arm before winding it around his waist. "You're full of crap."

Daniel rubs his thumb against her thoughtfully. "It was fine, I suppose. Every time I saw Logan Trite, I wanted to physically shake him. Ms. Richardson can't meet my eye. I think part of her still believes the little punk. But classes were normal. We started the last book of the year, *Death of a Salesman*."

"No more Byronic heroism?"

"Not for this senior class."

"Okay, so *next year* you'll meet another mysterious seventeen-year-old and—,"

"Let me stop you right there. First, that's not funny." Daniel narrows his eyes, which only makes Ava laugh at him. "Second, you are a very special circumstance. And finally, I never quite believed you were seventeen!" A loud rumbling fills the station, the subway speeding down the tracks. "Can we agree never to bring this up again?"

When it comes to a screeching halt, Ava steps forward with him. "Oh, but Daniel, how will we tell our children the tale of how we met?" The words have only just met the air when Ava realizes the mistake she's made.

"Our children?" Daniel repeats.

Crap.

When the doors open, he takes his arm back, allowing Ava to board first. Grateful that he can't currently see her inflamed face, Ava walks on and to the left. She heads to the back of the car, spotting open seating. Despite the noisiness of the station, the subway car itself is fairly quiet. Ava slides in and takes a seat, Daniel only a step behind her. Directing her face towards the darkened window, Ava quietly says, "Forget I said anything, please."

"Ava, I…" Daniel starts, his lips agape with thoughtful intention. Feeling the discomfort practically radiating from her, he leaves the subject alone for the time being.

They move through the tunnel, brief flashes of light rushing by the windows. "So, the planetarium," Ava says, clearing her throat. "Have you been before?" She turns her face to Daniel, brows raised.

"Yes, many times. My mother's side of the family has been donors since she was a little girl. We frequented AMNH throughout my elementary and junior high years." Daniel's face remains neutral, but Ava could swear she spots a little pride in his eyes. "Philanthropy is her true passion, one that running the company allows her the freedom to indulge."

"Your mother must be an extraordinary woman." Ava smiles encouragingly.

Daniel nods. "I'll have to introduce the two of you, she's sure to love you."

"I'd really like that."

For the next few minutes, they discuss the finer details of their week. When the subway comes to a stop at their station, they exit together, holding hands. It's such a minuscule detail, but it feels monumental to Ava. Holding hands, flirtatious banter, the way their eyes are drawn to each other's lips — it's something she never foresaw for herself.

But now that it's happening to me, I can't imagine anything feeling more natural, more right.

Walking down 79th Street, a large glass cube comes into view. "That's the Rose Center for Earth and Space," Daniel tells her, gesturing with his free hand. "Do you see the giant white ball inside?"

"Mhm."

"It's where we're headed, the Hayden Sphere." He picks up the pace and Ava stretches her legs out to keep up.

Entering through a revolving glass door, they join a security queue. With only a small clutch to have checked, the pair makes it inside shortly. Up close, the sphere is even larger. Ava overhears a man tell his companion that it's eighty-seven feet in diameter. Models of Jupiter and Saturn hang in front of it, looking tiny by comparison. Daniel checks his watch before leading her towards the walkway. "The last show starts in just a few minutes."

"Is that why we're having a day date?" she asks playfully.

He chuckles lightly. "*Yes.* But make no mistake, I plan to keep you out well through the night."

***

After the twenty-five-minute show narrated by Neil deGrasse Tyson, Daniel takes Ava to a tucked-away Italian restaurant in Brooklyn. There are only eight tables and a one-page menu, but what the restaurant lacks in space, it compensates with flavor.

They sit at a small wooden table, illuminated by candlelight, and drink cheap red wine. Ava asks Daniel to order her his favorites. As a result, her second "first" of the evening is trying steamed mussels. Roast chicken with fennel, gnocchi with burrata and Pomodoro sauce, and butterscotch goat's cheese panna cotta round out the meal.

"That was the best meal I've ever eaten," Ava declares emphatically, as they walk down the sidewalk. She presses a hand to her stomach, showing off the post-meal bloat.

"I'm glad you convinced me to order dessert," Daniel agrees with a nod.

He stops by the curb, gesturing swiftly at a cab that's just turned the corner. It makes a beeline for them and stops just a foot away from Daniel's shoes. Opening the back door for Ava, Daniel asks, "Did I wear you out or are you interested in seeing what else I planned?"

Ava mumbles a thanks and slides in. Once Daniel scoots in next to her, she says, "The night is young."

Leaning forward with his hands on the seat in front of him, Daniel asks the driver if he knows where Union Hall is. Upon confirmation, the cab rejoins the traffic.

When Daniel sits back, his left hand goes right to Ava's bare knee, as if magnets were connecting them. All evening long, they've given small, affectionate touches. A kiss placed softly on her cheek in the planetarium. Ava's foot grazing Daniel's leg under the dinner table. Hand holding like it's going out of style. But this touch feels more heated, possessive. Especially as Daniel's hand unhurriedly inches up her thigh.

Ava's body angles itself toward him automatically, their eyes meeting in the barely visible lighting. "Have I mentioned how beautiful you are?" he whispers, voice somehow still deep.

"Yes." Ava's fingers cross the space between them and meet his cheek.

Daniel moves closer to the touch, nuzzling her hand. "And how in that dress, you look—"

"Yes." Fingertips trail lightly down his face, over the hair gracing his chin, and, after a moment's hesitation, across his lips.

He parts them for her and Ava outlines his upper lip, then the lower. Their eyes are transfixed, both breathlessly watching this interaction. His tongue swipes against her fingertips, the feeling evoking a soft sound from the back of Ava's throat. "Kiss me," she whispers.

All at once, they lunge for each other. Their mouths collide hungrily, the shared taste of wine and butterscotch on their lips. Daniel cups each side of her face, holding her close, and parts her lips with his tongue, gentle but demanding. She grasps his hair, pulling him closer. Ava's kisses are all taking, a desire she never knew she had now awakened inside her.

Their kiss opens a bubble that spans eternities and galaxies, yet takes no time at all.

An alarming beep startles the pair, sending each back to their respective sides of the car. They hadn't even noticed the taxi coming to a stop. When Daniel leans forward to dig out his wallet and pay, Ava drops her gaze to her lap, running a finger over her bruised lips.

Did that really just happen?

Daniel comes around and opens her door, offering a hand to assist her onto the street. Together, they approach a brick building with large glass windows.

Inside, it looks like a combination of someone's living room and a classy library. Packed bodies crowd around the plush armchairs, Victorian-styled ornaments, and a lit fireplace. Loud rock music fills the air, and Ava has to press her lips to Daniel's ear to be heard. "This reminds me of The William!"

"I thought you'd say that!" he yells back with a smile.

Daniel leads her to a bar across from a set of floor-to-ceiling bookshelves and hands her a drink menu. "I'm a whiskey girl," Ava says, immediately setting the menu down on the bar. The words sound hilarious to her and she starts to laugh.

"And here I was thinking you were a red wine girl."

Collecting herself, Ava decides, "Whatever suits the situation." She shrugs coyly.

"I respect that."

A bartender comes over to them and Daniel orders two glasses of single malt whiskey, neat. "I've got these," Ava says, unclasping the button on her clutch.

"Ava… "

"*Daniel.*"

They share a pointed look. Undeterred, Ava lifts her eyebrows and frees the bank card from her clutch. "Can we start a tab?" she asks, handing it over to the bartender.

Not five minutes later, they have their drinks in hand and Daniel is guiding her through the crowded room. They pass two bocce courts, the sound of the music amplifying as they bound down a staircase. A four-piece band Ava doesn't recognize plays on a small stage, surrounded on three sides by dancing patrons.

Taking a sip from her glass as they join the crowd, Ava bobs her head in time with the drumbeat. Daniel stands close behind her. Their bodies lightly brush together, moving with the music.

Ava dances freely, the upbeat music sounding better than it probably is after all the drinks they've had. When he places his free hand around her hip, she backs up into him, closing any distance they'd left. "Hi," Ava yells, tilting her head up to see him.

"Hello." Daniel smiles down at Ava like she's the greatest thing he's ever beheld and kisses her.

III

No Sooner Loved

*"No sooner loved but they sighed; no sooner sighed but they asked
one another the reason; no sooner knew the reason but they
sought the remedy; and in these degrees have they made a pair of
stairs to marriage..."*
- William Shakespeare, As You Like It

OR

Little anecdotes about how they lived, happily ever after.

Twenty-Three

March 30, 2018

~~~~~~~~~~~~~~~

G entle knocks at the door cause Ava to look up from her laptop in confusion. "Who is it?"

Did Nate forget his keys?

More insistent knocking comes in answer.

"Be right there!" Ava shouts. She leaves her open laptop on the kitchen table and brushes the crumbs from her granola bar off her lap.

It's been just over a week since her article dropped and the reception has been more positive than in Ava's wildest dreams. *The Times* online engagement levels have gone off the charts with people writing in their thanks and, in some cases, their own similar stories. Mr. Wells practically had no choice but to keep Ava on — someone has to answer all those incoming responses!

While he has made himself very clear that she is never to go behind his back again, Wells already gave Ava a shortlist of topics to write next. People know her name now. *Written by Ava Thompson* will never again hide in the back of the paper. For the first time, Ava's personal and professional life both bring her immense satisfaction and happiness.

She walks to the front door with haste as the knocking continues. "I said I was coming," Ava says as she unlocks the door.

Her look of mild irritation morphs into delight. "Chloe! To what do I owe this surprise?" Taking a step back to let the younger girl in, Ava's gaze falls upon the plastic shopping bags in Chloe's hands. "And what's all this?"

"I'm here to cash in that rain check on a baking session!" Chloe declares as she walks in. Leaving the door open, she calls back, "C'mon, Vee!"

Ava laughs softly at the revelation of not one, but two Cuong women arriving unannounced. Victoria trails in behind her sister, aggressively tapping her phone screen. "Everything alright, Victoria?" Ava asks when they've all corralled in the kitchen.

With a huff, Victoria tosses her phone onto the counter. "It would be, if your brother was being reasonable for once."

Putting her hands up in mock defense, Ava says, "You're preaching to the choir. Nate tends to only listen to his inner voice."

"And what a frustrating voice that is," Victoria sighs.

"*Ladies!* This conversation does not pass the Bechdel Test," Chloe lectures as she unpacks the grocery bags. "We're here to celebrate Ava's incredibly successful article!"

"You are?" Ava implores.

"We are! With cupcakes!" Chloe states. "I dare you to name a better way to celebrate than by baking and then gorging ourselves on said cupcakes?"

"I never disagree when baked goods are involved," Ava says stoically.

Twenty-Four

May 4, 2018

"**N**ate Torres!" Victoria hisses under her breath. She gives his arm a playful, yet firm shove. "We're in the library, and you need to *focus.*"

"How am I supposed to focus when a total babe is quizzing me on physics? Hawking's got nothing on you." Nate grins.

Her countenance softens. It's only been a couple of months, but already she is in so deep. Both of them are hesitant to talk about feelings, but the implications are clear. They've discussed their collective futures far too often for this to be a casual fling.

By now, Victoria's influence has affected Nate's life monumentally. Her encouragement has motivated him to go after his dreams - dreams he's suppressed for so long. If things go according to plan, Nate will attend Northwestern University in Illinois this coming fall.

"You're retaking the SATs tomorrow, dude. This is important." Victoria juts out her lower lip and causes it to quiver. "Please?"

Nate lets out a deep sigh, his dark mahogany eyes zeroing in on her lips. He stares until they curve into a smile and turns back to the prep book in front of him. "Alright. Let's take it from the top."

Twenty-Five

June 26, 2018

⁓⟊⟊⟊⁓

Ava wears sunglasses and a baseball cap pulled low over her brows. The last bell rang roughly four minutes ago, so it won't be long until Chloe walks out the large doors of Eleanor Roosevelt High for the very last time. Eventually, Daniel Woodard will follow.

For the past three months, Ava has been spending most weeknights and nearly every weekend with Daniel. Sometimes they go out, but mostly they take turns hanging out at each other's apartments. He'll grade papers with her feet on his lap, Ava spread out on the couch, typing away on her laptop. They order takeaway food occasionally, but it doesn't take long for Ava to discover how skilled a cook Daniel is. He always submits to her special requests.

Together, they are healing. Instead of continuing to be paralyzed by each of their great losses, Daniel and Ava have fallen into a pattern of intimacy that goes far beyond the physical. But then there's that, too.

With summer break now arriving for Daniel, she knows their relationship will only speed up. Part of Ava realizes that this is all happening rather quickly. Her parents dated throughout their college years and didn't marry until they were nearly thirty. Chris has mentioned, on more than one occasion, that there's nothing wrong with taking things slow. Daniel is the first man she's ever actually *dated* and statistically, the first guy isn't the one you grow old with. But despite all this foreknowledge, Ava has decided to just let things happen. She's seen enough romantic comedies to know that Daniel isn't the run-of-the-mill man. He's special.

Newly minted adults pour out of the high school's front doors, eager for one last summer before they start the rest of their lives. Ava runs her fingers over the wrapping paper of the small gift she's brought for Chloe. The actual graduation ceremony isn't until Saturday, but patience in gift-giving is not a virtue Ava possesses.

Chloe walks out of the school more slowly than some of the others, with Hallie and Krista by her side. The three girls cling to one another, arms wrapped around each other's waists. Ava diverts her attention to the passing traffic, granting them their privacy.

A few minutes pass before a hand gently touches her shoulder. Turning her head, Ava takes in the sight of her friend. Puffy, bloodshot eyes and a case of the sniffles; on any other day, Chloe would appear sick. "Oh Chloe, please don't cry," Ava says softly. She lifts her sunglasses off and sets them atop the hat. Opening her arms, she whispers, "Come here."

That's all the encouragement Chloe needs. The girls envelop each other in a tight embrace. Chloe's breath catches in her throat. "I'm happy to be done with it, but it's all so *sad*."

Ava gives her another squeeze before releasing her. "You'll see them again. These people will be your friends for life." She nods her head towards Krista, Shawn, and Hallie. "You're lucky to have met each other."

"Y-yeah," Chloe agrees. "I just wish at least one of them was going to Columbia with me."

Pressing her lips together, Ava nods. "At least you've got Victoria there with you for your first year."

"She's going to be miserable company," Chloe says with a shallow laugh. "With Nate at Northwestern, all I'm going to hear is how much she misses him."

"Then I'll come over. I'm not going anywhere."

Chloe wipes her eyes and smiles toothily. "*Sure* you will."

"What? Nate will be in Illinois. I'll have the flat to myself."

"Do you honestly think Mr. Adams is going to be happy letting you live by yourself?"

Gesturing outwards with both hands, Ava shoots the girl a quizzical look. "Uh, Daniel knows perfectly well that I'm an adult?"

"That's *not* what I meant, but alright. I'll go along with your mock ignorance."

"Oh-kay," Ava enunciates carefully. With a soft sigh, she presses the small package into Chloe's hand. "Anyway, this is for you. It's silly, but… well, just open it."

"Ooooh!" Chloe squeals, already ripping into the navy wrapping paper.

"It's just a small little something," Ava continues, watching her friend.

"A velvet box, I love it!"

"The box is *not* the present!" Laughing, Ava urges, "Open it."

Chloe unlatches the box, her eyes widening as they fall upon a minuscule gold kite and matching chain. Immediately, she removes it and tucks the box and wrapping paper into her bag. "Help me put it on?"

"Sure." Ava moves behind Chloe and pushes her hair to the side. Taking the ends from her fingers, she clasps the necklace and lays it gently against Chloe's neck.

Looking down, Chloe takes the pendant between her thumb and index finger. "I love it," she says, awed. "A kite, for Benjamin Franklin, right?"

Ava smiles, uninhibited. "Yes! I wasn't sure you'd remember."

"I remember everything, silly," Chloe sticks her tongue out playfully. Linking her arm through Ava's, she nods forward. "Now let's go get ice cream. It's boiling out here!"

Twenty-Six

June 29, 2018

decorative flourish

"What's her dog's name, again?" Ava asks.

She and Daniel sit together on the Cannonball train to The Hamptons. A trip that Daniel pitched as a weekend getaway to celebrate the end of the school year, but is really just a thinly veiled excuse to introduce Ava to Thea.

"Archie," Daniel repeats. "Darling, you need to relax. If anyone should be nervous here, it's me. I haven't gone on the company retreat with her since I was in high school."

"No offense, but meeting your boyfriend's mother is definitely a bigger deal." Ava places the novel she's been reading onto her lap and reaches across the armrest for Daniel's hand. "I don't know how to act around people's parents, other than the Cuong's. I just want her to like me."

Lacing their fingers together, Daniel looks into her eyes. "She will. She already loves you for making me call her every Sunday."

Ava searches his gaze, finding nothing but the truth. Slowly, she nods. "Alright."

"*Good evening, ladies and gentlemen. Destination time to Montauk is estimated at five minutes. Please begin collecting your personal belongings. Thank you for traveling with us.*" A woman's voice comes through the train's speakers.

Daniel squeezes Ava's hand. "If anyone other than Mom asks, we met at—,"

"The American Museum of Natural History," Ava interjects. "Daniel, *I know.*" She brings their intertwined hands up and presses a soft kiss onto the back of his before letting go.

The last few minutes of the ride are spent reorganizing her backpack and taking in the beautiful countryside as it speeds by. Daniel and Ava linger on the train, in no rush to push past other patrons on their way out. He pulls their weekend bag down from the overhead storage and takes Ava's backpack, slipping it over one shoulder. When the train car has thinned out substantially, Daniel gestures for her to go ahead of him, and they walk out onto the open-air platform.

"You don't realize how much the city stinks until you can breathe fresh air," Ava says softly, after inhaling deeply.

With a soft laugh, Daniel agrees. "It's a welcome change."

They make their way out and into the parking lot. A black *Lewisson Cruiser* sits idling by the curb in the distance. "Oh, that's gotta be us," Ava murmurs.

As they approach the vehicle, the passenger door opens and a grey-headed man steps out. He's dressed immaculately in a navy suit with a black turtleneck underneath. Turning towards the couple, he places one hand on his hip and waves with the other. Ava can hear Daniel groan softly and she looks at him from the corner of her eye. "What?" she whispers.

"Uncle William," he replies through clenched teeth.

Her eyes widen, and she stops in her tracks, turning towards Daniel. "You have an *uncle* and you never told me?"

"He's my mother's twin brother. We don't exactly get along."

Ava opens her mouth and then shuts it, unsure of what to think. Instead of directly replying to Daniel, she bounds towards the car ahead of him. With a large smile, she greets the middle-aged man. "You must be Daniel's uncle."

The man laughs dryly, an amused smile on his lips as he studies her. "Told you all about me, has he?"

"Well…" Ava shrugs, pursing her lips.

Daniel stops at her side. "Uncle," he greets the man, voice clipped.

"Daniel Woodard," William says, stepping forward to wrap his much taller nephew into an embrace. "It's been too long."

"Mm," Daniel sounds, going stiff as he is hugged.

"*Daniel!*" Ava whispers loudly, surprised to see her kindly beau suddenly acting so cold.

Releasing Daniel, William directs his attention to Ava and shakes his head. "It's alright, there are a lot of misunderstandings between the two of us."

"Misunderstandings, right," Daniel snorts, shaking his head.

"Well, I, for one, am happy to meet a member of Daniel's family." Ava stretches out a hand. "I'm Ava Thompson."

William regards her hand for a moment before shaking it once. "Pleased to meet you, Ava. My name is William Lewis." He opens the back right door to the vehicle and motions for her to sit down.

"Thank you," Ava says as she passes by the two men and steps inside.

Shutting the door behind her, William looks pointedly at his nephew. "She's good for you. I can already see the brightness her company has brought you."

"I'm so *pleased* to have your approval, Uncle," Daniel speaks sharply.

Without another glance in the older man's direction, Daniel walks to the back and pops the trunk. Stowing their baggage inside, he goes around to the left side and takes his seat next to Ava.

The drive from Montauk to East Hampton could have gone by quickly if it were filled with lighthearted tales from Daniel's childhood and probing get-to-know-you questions. Instead, the twenty minutes dragged by in awkward silence. The fickle men left Ava with no option other than to stare out the window and hope that her introduction to Thea Lewis-Woodard went much better.

As a result, she is feeling rather irate and carsick when the *Lewisson Cruiser* pulls onto a gravel driveway. The bumpy ride ends in front of a prodigious wooden mansion tucked back amongst vibrant green foliage. Already, the driveway is filled with other models of *Lewisson Motors* vehicles. William and the driver, who hadn't introduced himself, both exit the car and start toward the house.

Shifting her body towards Daniel, Ava sucks in her bottom lip. Her hazel eyes look especially green in the evening glow as they search for his. When he turns to her, Daniel wears a look of tenderness that nearly erases the unease of the drive. His large hand glides gently across her shoulder and they both lean in. "She's going to love you," he whispers. His parted lips brush across her cheek before they capture her lips in an affectionate kiss. "But not as much as I do," Daniel says softly, their faces still close. "That would be impossible."

Ava's mouth pulls back in a faint smile. "One more for good luck," she requests, one hand winding around the back of his neck. Tugging him closer, Ava presses a quick kiss to his lips.

Begrudgingly separating, they turn to open their respective doors and meet at the back of the car. "I don't want to look helpless," Ava insists when both of their hands reach for her backpack.

A brief staring contest ensues, but, as always, Daniel concedes to her. Flashing her teeth in a smile, Ava pulls the backpack out of the trunk and slips her arms through each of the straps. "No one could ever accuse you of that," Daniel mutters, lifting the weekend bag.

He shuts the trunk and leads the way off the gravel driveway and up the brick-paved sidewalk. Hesitantly moving his hand between the doorknob and the bell, Daniel is caught off guard when the door flies open.

"There you are!" A petite woman stands under the door frame, smiling at the couple like the cat that ate the canary. "Daniel, it's so good to see you!" she says.

When she opens her arms to embrace him, Daniel actually meets her halfway. Even though she's wearing heels, Daniel towers over her, the woman's head pressing into his chest. Keeping an arm around her son, she turns her head towards Ava.

Seeing them side-by-side, the resemblance is uncanny. They share the same full lips and cheeks, similar deep brown eyes. Ava's imagination fills in the details of where his father would have fit in the picture next to them.

Tall like Daniel, no doubt.

She can picture that Jack Woodard gave Daniel his pronounced nose and sturdy chin.

"And you must be the beautiful Ava I've been hearing so much about," she releases Daniel and steps in towards Ava. "He didn't do you justice," she adds, almost to herself.

"Mrs. Lewis-Woodard, I'm so glad to finally meet you. Your son thinks the world of you," Ava says, smiling too widely. Timid.

The woman laughs kindly. "I'm sure he does," she says jokingly, waving Ava forward for a hug.

Ava wraps her arms around her, the warmth with which she's met almost taking her by surprise. *It's been a long time since someone has hugged with this kind of fervor.*

Giving another little squeeze, Daniel's mother releases Ava, saying, "And please, call me Thea."

Twenty-Seven

September 21, 2018

W ith classes in New York having begun two and a half weeks prior, Ava accompanies Nate to where he'll be spending the next four to eight years — Evanston, Illinois.

They leave on a Tuesday and take their time driving through New York, Pennsylvania, Ohio, and parts of Michigan before arriving at their destination. For the foster siblings, this new chapter in their lives will be the first where they're so greatly separated.

"It's only eight hundred miles, Ace," Nate insists, stretching a shirt over a hanger before adding it to his small closet.

"Eight hundred and *eight*, actually."

Chuckling, Nate shakes his head. "You sound so much like Victoria right now. It's insane."

"Yes, well, she did tell me to embody her spirit since she couldn't escort you herself." Sitting down on the mattress, Ava wiggles her nose. "But obviously I'm not going to be giving you the 'proper goodbye' she would have wanted."

"Thank god for that."

Casting her gaze out the window of his bedroom, Ava smiles to herself. "Who would have thought that in less than a year, our lives would be this different?"

"I thought I was going to spend my days at the shop, most of those hopefully with Watson out of the picture." Nate takes a seat next to her. "In a lot of ways, we have your stickler of a boss to thank for all this."

"You still could have met Victoria!"

"Yeah, but I would never have left you in the city by yourself if you didn't have Danny and the Cuong's."

Ava hums thoughtfully and draws her knees to her chest.

Nudging her shoulder, Nate says, "It's a good change, I promise. I'm sure living with your boyfriend will be a lot more interesting than living with me."

"I'm just really going to miss you," Ava whispers, laying her head down atop her knees and looking over at Nate.

"Me too."

They sit in comfortable silence for a few minutes, both of them deep in thought. Eventually, Ava stands up and walks to the bedroom door. "Let's go meet your suite-mates."

Twenty-Eight

March 24, 2019

"Sweetheart, I forgot to tell you. Something came in the mail for you yesterday," Daniel calls out from the living room.

It's mid-afternoon on a Sunday. Ava and Daniel spent the morning strolling through the Bushwick Farmer's Market before coming home with their haul of freshly picked fruits, vegetables, and a loaf of sourdough. After a late lunch, Ava has resigned herself to writing in their bedroom - trying to get a leg up on her current assignment for *The Times*. "Really? I don't remember ordering anything."

The sound of her laptop closing with a *snap* and the heavy footfall of her socked feet can easily be heard from where Daniel is sitting on the couch. "I put it on the kitchen table," Daniel says when Ava appears in the doorway.

She pats his shoulder affectionately as she walks by and makes a beeline for the next room. Just as he said it would be, a small cardboard box addressed to *Ava Charlotte Thompson* sits next to the fruit bowl on their round table. "Is this from Amazon?" Ava asks loudly. She picks it up and rips the tab, the cardboard unfolding around a book.

Placing the box onto the table, Ava takes the book in her hands. It's a crimson-colored hardback book with beautiful gold filigree and Ava can't resist running her fingers over the detailing. Turning it over, she reads the spine in an undertone, *"The Portrait of a Lady* by Henry James." Louder, she adds, "Daniel, did you buy me a book?"

Daniel doesn't respond right away, so Ava continues to study it. The edges of the pages are gilded in a matching gold foil. Though the book looks like it was printed long ago, it is in pristine condition. A red ribbon that's been sewn into the bookbinding sticks out at the bottom. Curiosity leads Ava to open the book there, and the pages flip open to chapter 35. Her breath catches when she notices a paragraph has been highlighted.

> *"It has made me better, loving you," he said on another occasion; "it has made me wiser, and easier, and brighter. I used to want a great many things before, and to be angry that I didn't have them. Theoretically, I was satisfied, as I once told you. I flattered myself that I had limited my wants. But I was subject to irritation; I used to have morbid, sterile, hateful fits of hunger, of desire. Now I am really satisfied because I can't think of anything better. It is just as when one has been trying to spell out a book in the twilight, and suddenly the lamp comes in. I had been putting out my eyes over the book of life, and finding nothing to reward me for my pains; but now that I can read it properly I see that it's a delightful story. My dear girl, I can't tell you how life seems to stretch there before us—,"*

She's so enthralled by the words that she doesn't hear Daniel walk into the kitchen. So captivated that she doesn't see him kneel before her. When Daniel gently clears his throat, Ava looks over the top of the page at him and gasps, nearly dropping the book.

"Ava Charlotte Thompson," he says, voice teeming with emotion.

Ava closes the book and presses it to her chest, her eyes widening as she takes in the man before her.

"I've known that you are the woman I want to marry ever since you challenged me on the character of Edward Rochester. Of course, that feeling was unwelcome at the time."

They both laugh, the sound strained and nervous.

"Even so, it was there to stay. You burrowed your way into my heart. You are, in every way, my equal. More than that, you're my better half. You balance me with your light, your *goodness.*" Daniel's voice catches and he takes a deep, shuddering breath before continuing. "We were two somewhat broken individuals, and together we created a family with the people we each love. Every day I thank whatever superior personage is out there that you found me. I never want to find out what life is like without you in it, sweetheart. I love you with my entire being."

Daniel produces a velvet box, the same shade of crimson as the book, and holds it out toward her. "That's why on this day, one year since your kiss inexplicably captured my lifelong devotion, I ask you to do me the greatest honor." He opens the box, revealing the most exquisite piece of jewelry Ava's ever seen. A thin gold ring with what resembles a flower made up of diamonds in the middle, and two diamonds going down the band on either side. "Ava, darling, will you marry me?"

She's so awestruck at first that she can only nod, rapidly. Tears pour freely from her eyes. "Yes, Daniel. *Yes,* I'd love to marry you," she says, her voice wobbly.

Daniel lets out a short, relieved laugh and reaches for her left hand. Gingerly, he takes the ring from the silk and slides it onto Ava's finger.

"It's perfect," Ava murmurs, lifting her hand to admire the way the light catches on the stones. "*You're* perfect." She bends down into where he's still kneeling on the kitchen floor and wraps her arms around his neck.

He peppers kisses along her face, starting with her tear-dampened cheeks, her eyelids, her forehead, the tip of her nose, and finally, her lips.

Twenty-Nine

May 22, 2019

~~~

"Victoria Cuong!" Mr. Bollinger, President of Columbia University, announces.

The audience has been instructed to hold their applause until the end, so the row of Victoria's guests silently wave their hands and mime stomping their feet. Victoria walks across the stage in her cap and gown, shakes Mr. Bollinger's hand, and accepts her diploma before he announces the next name.

"She looks gorgeous," Ava whispers to Nate.

Keeping his eyes on Victoria as she walks off the stage, Nate nods once. "I know."

When the ceremony ends and the new graduates disperse to find their friends and family, Ava and Daniel hang back. Mr. and Mrs. Cuong fawn over their eldest daughter while aunts and uncles give Victoria affectionate hugs and discreet little envelopes. "I'm so proud of you, Vee," Chloe says, wrapping her sibling up in a hug. "I'm going to miss you so much."

"I'm going to miss you too, Chloe."

The girls wipe away tears as they pull back from the embrace. Finally able to greet his girlfriend, Nate grins and goes right in for a kiss. His flight got in late the previous night, and this is the first he's seen of her since spring break.

Mr. Cuong groans at the display in front of all their family and friends but doesn't say anything.

"Babe, you're incredible," Nate murmurs, wrapping an arm around her waist. "You got your BA in Archaeology *and* a cushy internship at twenty-three. You're gonna be a curator before I get started on my Master's."

Victoria's cheeks redden, both from their physical proximity and his words. "Someone's gotta bring home the bacon."

"That's actually what I wanted to talk to you about," Nate says, walking them a few feet away from the rest of the group. He slips a hand into his back pocket and pulls out a little box.

Looking at the pair, Chloe grabs Ava's shoulder and nods fervently in their direction.

"Nate, what is that?" Victoria asks, lowering her voice.

Chuckling softly, Nate opens the box. "Relax, babe."

Inside is a shiny silver key threaded through a matching chain. Victoria reaches for it, running her fingertips over the key. "We've spent the past eight months living hundreds of miles apart. Now that you're moving to Chicago for your internship at The Field Museum, I wanted us to have a place of our own."

"You bought a house?"

"Just a rental. It's in Edgewater, about halfway between my campus and your job."

A smile lights up Victoria's face. "I don't know what to say, other than how happy I am. Things are going so well for us and I keep waiting for some fluke… but it never comes."

Taking her chin in his hand, Nate shakes his head. "Kismet, babe."

From a few yards away, Chloe exaggeratedly shakes her head. "False alarm," she announces to the onlooking family members. "It's just a key."

217

Thirty

September 28, 2019

⚜

djusting the veil over Ava's face, Thea nods, pleased with her work. "Daniel's going to lose his mind when he sees you."

Ava smiles at her soon-to-be mother-in-law's reflection in the large oval mirror. "I might lose mine first," she says with a soft laugh.

Deciding to have the wedding at Thea's home upstate was a no-brainer. Neither Daniel nor Ava were into the idea of a lavish affair, especially since they could count their closest friends on their fingers. An early autumn wedding sounded perfect to them, with the leaves turning vibrant shades of orange and red. There's a slight chill in the air, but other than that, the day is exactly how they envisioned.

A knock on the door announces Chloe's presence before she enters, looking beautiful in a cobalt blue one-shouldered dress. "You ladies almost ready?"

Smoothing the fabric of her dress down, Ava takes one last look at herself in the mirror. Her wedding gown is a floor-length tulle and lace dress, blush-colored and cap-sleeved with a plunging neckline. It was her mother's before some very specific alterations made it her own.

"Ready," Ava says, smiling over her shoulder.

Chloe and Thea lead the way out of the bedroom and down the hallway, throughout the colonial house. When they reach the back door, Thea steps outside to allow the girls a moment of privacy.

Taking both of Ava's hands in hers, Chloe beams. "You make a beautiful bride, Ava Thompson."

"You, too," Ava says immediately. "A beautiful maid-of-honor, I mean."

"Mr. Adams—I mean *Daniel*, wow, still weird for me to say that," Chloe begins, shaking her head. "Daniel is a lucky man. A lucky man that has been waiting for you in the garden for the past ten minutes. I'm getting sweaty just thinking about how nervous he was looking when I went to grab you."

Unable to fight the grin, Ava peers towards the door. "I guess I should get out there, then." Squeezing Chloe's palms, she directs her attention back to her friend. "Thank you for being here, for setting up the lights, for... everything. I love you like I imagine people love their siblings."

"I love you, too. I know that one day you'll do the same for me."

"I will," Ava promises.

"Alright, well, I'm gonna get out there and start the music for you," Chloe says, taking her hands back. She lifts a small bouquet of light pink peonies and honey bracelet stems from a vase by the door and hands it to Ava. "I'll see you up there, okay?"

"Okay."

Chloe slips out the door, leaving Ava one last chance to collect herself. Without a father on either of their sides, Ava made the decision to walk herself down the aisle months ago. And with such a small guest list, she and Daniel agreed to just have a best man and a maid-of-honor standing at the altar with them as their two witnesses. Chloe had been her choice from the beginning, but it took Daniel some time to decide upon his best man. Most of his male friends were colleagues, and he didn't spend time with them outside of school very often. Eventually, Daniel decided Nate would be a good fit, and Ava couldn't have agreed more.

It had taken some serious finagling to convince Daniel to ask William to officiate the wedding. The late teenage years Daniel spent with his uncle after the death of Jack had left him jaded, but Ava was working hard to convince both men to start their relationship anew.

219

The first few chords of *Heartbeats* by José González start to play outside, Ava's cue. She takes in a deep breath, holds it, and slowly breathes out. "It's just a walk. Daniel is waiting for you," she murmurs to herself, thumbing the ribbon around her bouquet.

Mum and Dad would be proud. I can feel it.

When she opens the door, the music gets louder and suddenly the heads of all her seated friends turn expectantly to Ava. Chris shoots her a covert thumbs up, his free arm wrapped around Katherine's shoulders. Mrs. Cuong mouths something Ava can't make out, but it looks encouraging. Thea is seated in the front row, her Shih Tzu-Pomeranian pup Archie on the chair next to her. Nate and Chloe stand grinning on either side of the wooden arbor wrapped in fairy lights. Ava's stomach knots and stretches as she steps down onto the grass.

Just focus on Daniel.

Ava's mouth pulls back in a smile and she takes slow, deliberate steps towards her fiancé. Freshly shaven for the ceremony, Daniel looks across the garden at Ava with childlike wonderment. His smile fills her with warmth, the nervous tension fleeing Ava's body.

I love this man.

Daniel wears a grey three-piece suit with a crisp white shirt and blush-colored bowtie, to match her dress. Ava has never felt more fortunate than she does when she stops her walk in front of him. "Hi," she whispers, the music already fading out.

"Hello," he replies, smiling smittenly.

"Welcome, family, friends, and loved ones. We gather here today to celebrate the wedding of Daniel and Ava," William announces, beginning the ceremony.

His words are mostly lost on the couple, having a deep conversation with their eyes, until William says, "In the spirit of the importance of strong friendships to a marriage, Daniel and Ava have asked two friends to read selections about love that especially resonate with them." He hands a small card to each Chloe and Nate.

Chloe turns towards the small audience and begins, "This is *Sonnet 116* by William Shakespeare: Let me not to the marriage of true minds, admit impediments. Love is not love which alters when it alteration finds, or bends with the remover to remove: O no; it is an ever-fixed mark, that looks on tempests, and is never shaken; It is the star to every wandering bark, whose worth's unknown, although his height be taken. Love's not Time's fool, though rosy lips and cheeks within his bending sickle's compass come; Love alters not with his brief hours and weeks, but bears it out even to the edge of doom. If this be error and upon me proved, I never writ, nor no man ever loved." She finishes with a soft nod before looking back to William.

Nate clears his throat and lifts his card. "And this is a section taken from *Les Misérables* by Victor Hugo: You can give without loving, but you can never love without giving. The great acts of love are done by those who are habitually performing small acts of kindness. We pardon to the extent that we love. Love is knowing that even when you are alone, you will never be lonely again. And great happiness of life is the conviction that we are loved. Loved for ourselves. And even loved in spite of ourselves."

"Excellent," William mutters, a smirk on his lips. "We've come to the point of your ceremony where you will recite your vows to one another. Daniel, please repeat after me. I, Daniel Woodard, take you, Ava Thompson, to be my beloved wife, to have and to hold you, to honor you, to treasure you, to be at your side in sorrow and in joy, in the good times, and in the bad, and to love and cherish you always. I promise you this from my heart, for all the days of my life."

Daniel repeats the words, his fingers brushing against Ava's forearm.

I'm so kriffing lucky.

"Thank you," William says. "Ava, please recite the same words back to him."

"I, Ava Thompson, take you, Daniel Woodard, to be my beloved husband," she pauses, her voice catching. Daniel gives her hand an encouraging squeeze, and Ava continues, "to have and to hold you, to honor you, to treasure you, to be at your side in sorrow and in joy, in the good times, and in the bad, and to love and cherish you always. I promise you this from my heart, for all the days of my life."

"Thank you, Ava," William smiles at his new niece and then looks back and forth between the two witnesses. "May I please have the rings?"

Nate reaches into the breast pocket of his jacket and pulls out two matched gold wedding bands. He hands them to William with a nod. Ava passes her bouquet to Chloe. After William's instruction, Daniel reaches for Ava's left hand and says, "This ring I give to you as a token of my love and devotion to you. I pledge to you all that I am and all that I will ever be as your husband. With this ring, I gladly marry you and join my life to yours." He slips the ring onto her finger behind the engagement ring.

With shaky hands, Ava grasps Daniel's left hand and repeats the words back to him. Once they are both wearing their rings, William loudly broadcasts, "By the power of your love and commitment, and the power vested in me by the state of New York, I now pronounce you husband and wife! Daniel, kiss your wife!"

Daniel lifts her veil over her face. His hands find her waist just as Ava places a hand on either side of his neck. He leans down, pressing their foreheads together. "Mrs. Ava Woodard has a nice ring to it," he whispers. Ava tilts her head up and captures his lips.

Thirty-One

November 5, 2019

Ava paces the cold tile of the bathroom floor, forcing herself not to look at the applicators lined up on the countertop.

It's just residual wedding stress, throwing my body off.

We're always so careful.

I am not the person who gets pregnant on their honeymoon. I can't be.

Her eyes move to the timer on her phone, counting down the three minutes she has to wait. Inhaling, Ava picks up the phone and presses the messaging app.

—— **Tuesday, November 5** ——

– Ava Woodard | 5:39 –

Hi.

– Daniel Woodard | 5:39 –

Hello, darling.

I just picked up Indian around the corner. I'll be home shortly.

The timer beeps, and Ava swipes the notification away.

– Ava Woodard | 5:40 –

Ok.

– Daniel Woodard | 5:40 –

Is everything alright?

Ava places the phone on the counter, looks up at the ceiling and mouths *'please'*. Drawing on all her inner strength, she dares a look at the three applicators. One of them displays two pink stripes, another one a plus symbol, and the last one simply reads *pregnant*. "For kriff's sake!" Ava growls, placing her hands on the countertop and lowering her head.

Her phone chirps with another notification.

– Daniel Woodard | 5:42 –

Ava?

Unable to find proper words, Ava double clicks the button on her phone, bringing up the camera. She swipes down for the front-facing camera, lifts her shirt, and takes an oddly angled picture of her stomach.

– Ava Woodard | 5:43 –

[image]

– Daniel Woodard | 5:43 –

Um.
Is this how sexting works?

Despite her current emotional state, Ava laughs out loud. Shaking her head, she angles the camera over the sink and snaps a picture of the three pregnancy tests — all confirming the same thing.

– Ava Woodard | 5:44 –

[image]

Three dots tell her Daniel is already typing. Ava chews on her lower lip, eyes transfixed on the screen.

– Daniel Woodard | 5:44 –
 Really???
 Ava, did you take that picture?
 Sweetheart, if you're playing coy, my old heart can't take it.

Only Daniel could distract her from getting into her head at a time like this.

– Ava Woodard | 5:45 –
 Yes.

– Daniel Woodard | 5:45 –
 Yes, what?

– Ava Woodard | 5:45 –
 Yes, I took the picture.

Five knocks reverberate from the front of the apartment.

Leaving her phone in the bathroom, Ava strides across the hallway, into the living room, and to the entrance of their home. "Daniel?" she asks cautiously, her hand hovering near the doorknob.

"Sweetheart, can you get the door?"

She unlocks the deadbolt and opens the door, taking a step back.

"Does this mean what I think it means?" Daniel rushes in, places the takeout bag on the table just inside, and wraps both hands around her, lifting her up.

Ava lets out a squeal, her hair falling forward and brushing across his forehead. He walks further into the living room, still holding her up like that. "Ava!"

Still unsure of her feelings on the subject, Ava nods, her lips parting in a smile. "Yes."

225

Daniel spins her around the room, his joy written all over his face. "You're having our children?"

Laughing, Ava corrects him. "Our *child*. Yes, it appears so."

Bringing her down from the air, Daniel keeps her close, his lips brushing against her hair.

"And you feel... ?"

Pulling his head back, Daniel grins. "Happy. So kriffing happy." He takes her face in his hands now and presses a lingering kiss to her lips. "But you're going to have to remind me. How could this have happened?"

Ava can't help but giggle. The smell and feel of Daniel here in front of her, so solid, so sure, is putting her at ease. She darts her tongue out, but not quick enough. Daniel sucks her tongue between his lips, eliciting a moan. When he releases it, he brings his mouth to her ear and traces her earlobe with his tongue. "I ask you a question and you laugh at me. How do you think that makes me feel?"

Shuddering, Ava takes his hand and pulls him towards the couch. "I'm sorry, sweetheart. Let me make it up to you."

Thirty-Two

June 8, 2020

⸿

T he question of when the baby was conceived is confirmed when Ava is given her due date, June 23.

Honeymoon baby, for sure.

The next seven months are chock full as they move into a bigger flat and prepare the nursery, both of them continuing to work. Pregnant Ava is an absolute behemoth. The smallest thing can make her nauseous and despite working in an office, her feet throb and ache at the end of each day.

Father-to-be Daniel responds to her every beck and call. He packs her lunches with cute notes inside, rubs her feet before bed, and generally worships the ground she walks upon.

Convincing him to wait and "be surprised" by the baby's gender is no easy feat. Coercing Thea to help fight her side of the argument finally wears Daniel down. But surprisingly, Daniel goes along with her desire to have a more natural birth.

When Ava's water breaks and contractions start two weeks ahead of schedule, it's a welcome relief. Ever the rock, Daniel grabs the hospital bag, orders an Uber, texts their doula, and calls the school to let them know he's not coming in. Twenty minutes later, Ava is being rushed into her birthing suite at *New York-Presbyterian.*

For the next few hours, family and friends filter into the room. Chloe, Chris, Katherine, and Thea help Daniel keep Ava's mind off her contractions as she bounces on an exercise ball. Nate texts to say that he and Victoria will catch the next flight out.

Six hours in, Ava's contractions are timed at two minutes apart. Everyone except for Thea and Daniel is asked to leave the room. Ava, having changed from her hospital gown into a bikini top, settles into the hydrotherapy tub. She rubs her bulbous stomach gently. "We're ready for you, baby. We love you and we want you," she murmurs, closing her eyes.

Daniel comes up behind her, kneeling next to the tub, and kisses her neck.

The doula, a kindly older woman named Beth, sits on a stool a few feet away, coaching Ava through the process. She suggests breathing patterns and positions for Ava to move into. After a few minutes, Beth asks Daniel if he would like to be in the water for the birth.

Ava protests he didn't pack swim trunks, but Daniel just climbs into the water fully clothed. He sits in front of her and rubs her shoulders silently, letting Beth direct Ava on how to breathe.

The midwife, Jennifer, comes by with a thermometer to check both the temperature of the water and Ava. She pulls Beth to the side to confer briefly, and then both women turn to address Daniel. "Daniel, your wife is about to bring life into the world. Would you like to assist her?" Beth asks.

"Yes," he nods, all looks of weariness from the day's events gone.

Beth tells Daniel to sit behind Ava in the tub and hold her so that her body can relax. "Ava, up until now I've told you just to breathe, but now I need you to push. These babies are ready to meet their parents."

"*Babies?*" Ava gasps.

Daniel's hands knead against her hips, thumbs stroking her skin. Thea, who has been patiently watching this from across the room, speaks up, "Daniel told you twins run on my side of the family, didn't he?"

"I'm sorry," Daniel whispers into her ear. "The chances were so low... I didn't want to needlessly worry you."

"Of course not," Ava mutters, squaring her shoulders.

"Breathe and push," Beth instructs from her spot next to Ava and Daniel.

228

Ava closes her eyes, leaning back against Daniel and she rubs her hands against her thighs. "That's a good girl," Jennifer coos, the time for her to shine having finally arrived.

She slides a new set of gloves onto her hands before reaching into the water between Ava's legs. A whimper that turns into a groan pours from Ava's open mouth. "You're doing great, darling," Daniel says steadily.

Ava's hands find Daniel's legs under the water and grip them as she pushes. The strangest feeling yet overcomes her, as her body takes over. "There's the head, keep going, Ava," Beth directs.

Doing as she's told, Ava opens her eyes and looks down between her legs. A baby -*her baby*- who was an abstract idea for months is finally *here*. Something like a gasp and a sob sounds from deep inside her chest as Jennifer lays the infant on her chest. "Oh my god, Daniel," Ava murmurs, one hand coming up to steady the child.

As their gazes meet over her shoulder, Ava realizes they're both crying. Thea stands not far away, with a hand against her mouth.

"That was incredible, Ava. Can you do it for me one more time?" Jennifer asks.

"I don't think I can," Ava shakes her head, still looking at her husband. "Daniel, I

"You're the strongest person I know, Ava," he says.

The calmness of his voice affects her and before she knows it, Ava's body is pushing again until the second child is nestled up against her.

Shortly thereafter, once Ava has been dried off and moved into the suite's bed with Daniel at her side, Jennifer and Beth bring over the babies. "Congratulations, mom and dad. You've got a little boy and a little girl," Jennifer announces, handing one to each parent.

The full weight of their newfound responsibilities falls over Daniel and Ava as they look at the perfect little faces of their twins. "Can you believe we… made them?" Daniel asks, his voice thick with awe as the baby girl in his arms wraps her tiny hand around his index finger.

"I'm still trying to wrap my mind around there being two of them," Ava answers in a whisper.

Cheerful knocking on the door goes unnoticed by the pair. It's not until their bed is surrounded by the smiling faces of William, Thea, the entire Cuong family, Nate, Chris, and Katherine that the couple really see them. Everyone seems to talk at once, their words a jumble of gushing and cooing noises.

"They look like mini Ava and Daniel babies," Chris says a moment later, his eyes wide.

Katherine's hand moves to playfully smack his shoulder, something sparkling in the light. "That's because they are, Christopher."

"Whoa," Ava says, straining her head forward. "Katherine, what's that on your left hand?"

"Oh, this?" she asks, proudly displaying a princess-cut diamond.

"Congrats to you guys. When did that happen?" Ava asks.

"Actually, in the waiting room. Sorry, I didn't mean to rain on your parade, bub," Chris says with a regretful smile. "All the new life and happiness made me feel sentimental, and I just couldn't wait any longer."

"No, I think it's wonderful!" Ava nods encouragingly.

"You hotties make adorable babies," Chloe says with a grin, stepping in next to Ava's side of the bed. "Can I hold... ?"

"Him, this one's the boy," Ava says. Gently, she lifts her son into Chloe's waiting arms.

A chorus of '*careful!*'s sound. Smiling down at the baby, Chloe asks, "What are you going to name them?"

Ava looks over at Daniel and the now-sleeping baby girl. "Well... we didn't know the gender, so we *did* have boy and girl names already picked out."

She mouths something, to which he nods. Ava reaches a finger out and lightly runs it across her daughter's face. "This is Gwen."

"For her mother." Daniel and Ava share a smile, and then he looks up, his eyes moving between his mother and uncle. "And we decided to name our son after Dad."

Thea inhales sharply and a new set of tears fills her eyes. Wrapping an arm around his sister, William smiles proudly at Daniel. "Jack." His head turns toward his grandnephew and William nods. "It suits him well."

About the Author

Merrin Taylor is a wife, mother, gourmand, and self-proclaimed nerd. *For Love and Bylines* is her first novel.

You can connect with me on:

🐦 https://twitter.com/MerrinTaylor

Printed in Great Britain
by Amazon

79832993R00140